LEGION

A HEROICS NOVEL

Alex Kost

ISBN 978-1-48356-966-6

Dedication

This book is dedicated to the books I've read and the stories I've heard.

Without them, these books would be impossible.

Table Of Contents

Dramatis Personae

Heroics

AJ Hamil: 56; black hair; brown eyes; team medic (Anthony Sadik)
Brooke Hamil: 22; black hair; hazel eyes; mission control; enhanced intelligence
Casey Carter: 57; auburn hair; blue eyes; tech coordinator/boss (Robin van der Aart)
Cassidy "Cass" Hamil: 55; red hair; gray eyes; mission control (Tess Wechsler)
Ciaran Sullivan: 20; dark-brown hair; green eyes; "Orion"; enhanced accuracy
Isaac Sampson: 17; brown hair; blue-green eyes; "Blitz"; electricity manipulation
Jacob Hamil: 15; red hair; brown eyes; tech coordinator; enhanced intelligence
Katherine "Kate" Sullivan: 41; light-brown hair; green eyes; "Targeter"; enhanced accuracy
Logan Carter: 16; strawberry-blonde hair; hazel eyes; "Eisen"; metal manipulation
Niall Sullivan: 42; black hair; blue eyes; mission control
Ray Sampson: 39; black hair; blue eyes; "Blackout"; electricity manipulation
Riley Oliver: 14; blonde hair; brown eyes; "Sniper"; enhanced accuracy

Security Legion

Andrew Sullivan: 46; brown hair; blue eyes; "Flare"; fire manipulation
Maxwell "Max" Oakley: 34; brown hair; brown eyes; "Wraith"; phasing
Rowan van Houten: 22; black hair; dark blue eyes; "Fuse"; volatile constructs

Zachary "Zach" Carter: 58; blonde hair; hazel eyes; "Kov"; metal manipulation

Wechsler Industries

Alix Tolvaj: 34; brown hair with blonde highlights; gray eyes
Aubrey Hamil: 21; brown hair; light green eyes; enhanced intelligence
Justin Oliver: 40; dark blond hair; brown eyes; enhanced accuracy
Kara Hall: 38; blonde hair; hazel eyes; enhanced strength
Whitney "Finn" Finnegan: 30; white-blonde hair; brown eyes; enhanced reflexes

Military

General Henry Reznik: 64; black hair; brown eyes
Lieutenant Colonel Sarah Amirmoez: 47; dark-brown hair; brown eyes

Other

Kaita Dragovic: 46; brown hair; one blue eye/one brown eye
Matthias Clark Hobbes: 23; sandy-brown hair; green eyes
Richard "Rick" Sullivan: 17; black hair; green eyes
Thomas Carter: 11; auburn hair; blue eyes; metal manipulation

1

Wechsler Industries Warehouse #13 in Fuego Village was normally a quiet place, with little activity on a Saturday afternoon, but the twelve armed individuals in the middle of a standoff with police had guaranteed that wouldn't be the case this week.

The police sergeant on the scene was in the second hour of negotiation with the leader of the armed individuals, who had given himself the incredibly original pseudonym "John Smith," but he was getting nowhere. Smith was trying to leave with a tractor-trailer full of electronics that he had gotten out of the warehouse, and he was willing to kill his warehouse employee hostages if the police didn't let the truck out within the next half-hour.

As the sergeant hung up his call with Smith, one of his officers approached him. "Sir, Casey Carter is here."

"Who?" the sergeant asked, pinching the bridge of his nose as if he was getting a headache.

"Casey Carter. She owns half of Wechsler Industries."

"Oh, right. What does she want?"

"To talk to you."

"Bring her over."

The officer nodded and left, returning a few minutes later with a middle-aged woman with auburn hair and blue eyes.

"Sergeant," Casey Carter greeted. "I heard that these people have a few of my employees hostage."

"They do, and I'd appreciate it if you could tell me who would be here on a Saturday morning. I thought your warehouses were closed on weekends."

"They are. My sister and I had three floor workers, one manager, and one security guard here for overtime inventory. It needs to be done before the end of the month, and we figured this would be a good weekend for it."

"Apparently not," the sergeant replied dryly.

Casey smiled thinly. "Apparently not."

"Can you give me a list of everyone inside of that building?"

"Of course."

As Casey took out her cell phone, the sergeant squinted at her. "Out of curiosity, Ms. Carter, what's the CEO of the company doing at something like this? You could've easily sent a lower-level manager to talk to us, or one of your lawyers."

"First of all, it's *Mrs.* Carter. Second of all, I'm the owner of the company, but I'm not the CEO. That's Justin Oliver. Third of all, my sister and I respect our employees far too much to pawn something like this off on some underling." Casey held her phone out to the sergeant. "This is your list, Sergeant. If you don't mind, please get my people out in one piece."

The sergeant took Casey's phone from her slowly. "We'll do our best, ma'am. The only thing these guys want is to leave, and I refuse to let them do that. Whether you care about the products in that warehouse or not, I'm not letting armed thieves loose in my jurisdiction."

"Of course." Casey turned away as the sergeant handed her phone to another officer to copy the list of names. She pushed her glasses up on her nose, in the process tapping the communications button on the side of the frames. "Control?"

Cass Hamil's voice answered in her ear. *"What do you need?"*

"I don't think these guys are going to be able to defuse this any time soon," Casey said, mumbling so that nobody would notice her apparently talking to herself.

"Were you expecting anything else?"

"The cops in Caotico and Fuego aren't *that* bad."

Her sister scoffed. *"Keep telling yourself that. What do you want to do?"*

Casey glanced around briefly. "Send in the team."

"They're already there. We were just waiting for your report."

"Show off."

"I need to upstage you whenever I can."

"We're too old for this."

"Now you're just lying to yourself. I'll tell the team to go for it. Try to stay out of the line of fire, got it?"

Casey gave a short laugh that she stifled quickly. "You're the reckless one, sis."

"I know. Still. Don't get shot."

"I'll try."

Cass, laughing, disconnected their line of communication. Casey turned back towards the sergeant, who was walking over to her with her phone in his hand.

"Thank you for the information, Mrs. Carter," the sergeant said.

"You're quite welcome, Sergeant," Casey replied as she took her phone back from him.

"If you don't mind, could you get back behind the barricades? I don't want to risk your safety."

"Of course, sir. I'll do that right away. I—"

Casey was interrupted by an outbreak of screaming and gunfire that erupted from inside the warehouse. The police sergeant grabbed his radio. "Timmons, what is happening up there?" he demanded.

A voice over the radio replied, "*Uh, well, sir, I think this negotiation is going to be over soon.*"

"Why's that?"

"*Heroics is here. Looks like they've brought a few friends, too.*"

The sergeant frowned. "Friends? What kind of friends?"

The officer on the other end of the radio sounded like he was trying not to laugh. "*These guys aren't going to know what hit them.*"

"What friends, Timmons?" the sergeant asked again, sounding irritated.

"*Sorry, sir. They brought some people from the Legion.*"

2

Kate "Targeter" Sullivan crouched down as she balanced on one of the beams that ran across the roof of Wechsler Industries Warehouse #13. She was gripping the beam tightly with a gloved hand, but the teenager next to her was standing straight up and didn't seem the least bit concerned about the precarious position.

"You're going to get yourself killed, Eisen," Kate hissed.

Logan "Eisen" Carter smirked. "The metal's formed to my boots. I wouldn't be able to fall if I jumped."

"You'd fall if I pushed you, smart-ass."

"*Somebody's not in a good mood,*" Ciaran "Orion" Sullivan's voice said through the communications system in their sunglasses.

"I just haven't been in charge of a field operation in a while," Kate replied. "It feels weird being with you small children all by myself without any assistance from Blackout."

"*I'm not a small child, Targeter,*" Ciaran protested. "*I'm twenty.*"

"Pretty sure you'll be a small child to me until the day one of us dies, Orion." Kate took her bow off of her shoulder and pulled an arrow out of the quiver on her back. She squinted down at the circle of armed and masked individuals surrounding the small group of hostages. "Blitz, you were going on about your strategic skills the other day. What are your ideas?"

Isaac "Blitz" Sampson's voice joined the mix. "*Oh, uh... well, there's four of us and twelve of them. That's an even three people per person. Unless of course, we do a simultaneous surprise attack on four of them. Then we're each only responsible for two of them."*

Kate smiled slightly. "So your plan boils down to 'hit them until unconsciousness' then?"

"Basically, yes."

"Sounds like the typical Heroics plan. There's just one problem with it."

"What's that?"

"There's more than four of us."

"Yeah, Blitz, did you really think I'd miss this opportunity?" Zach "Kov" Carter said through the communications system.

"D-Kov!" Logan was grinning. "What are you here for?"

"I'll explain later. In the meantime, why don't you guys give me and Wraith something to do?"

"Six of us, twelve of them," Isaac said. *"Makes this even easier, if you ask me."*

"I agree." Kate aimed her arrow at the leader of the group, Smith, who was pacing back and forth with the phone he was using to talk to the police in his hand. "What do you say we clean this place up a bit, then? On three?"

"Make it on two. Keeps them on their toes," Zach said.

"On three," Kate repeated. "One... two... three!"

She fired a Taser arrow directly into Smith's chest, dropping him instantly. Then she slid down one of the nearby support beams, landing in front of one of the other thieves.

Five other thieves were felled at almost the exact same instant, with Logan and Zach each hitting one with a chunk of metal, Isaac hitting one with a short blast of electricity, and Max "Wraith" Oakley, whose phasing power didn't allow for long-distance strikes, simply stepping out of a support beam directly next to a thief and slamming the criminal's head into the metal object. One thief immediately tried to shoot Max, but the bullets passed through him without leaving a mark, allowing Zach plenty of time to mentally rip the thief's metal gun out of his hands.

As Zach used his powers to disable the gun and throw it across the room, Kate yelled to him, "Why didn't we just do that to all of them when we were hidden?"

Max was the one who answered. "Because Kov likes to make things difficult for everyone?"

"Fair enough."

Logan, who hadn't left the roof when Kate did, closed her eyes briefly. In half of a second, all of the guns were yanked away from the remaining thieves and piled on the opposite side of the room. "Huh," she said, opening her eyes again. "That *was* a lot easier."

"Lot less fun," Zach grumbled.

Isaac ducked out of the way as a thief tried to punch him in the face. "You and I have two very different definitions of 'fun,' Kov."

Ciaran cursed quietly as one of the thieves hit him in the back of one of his shoulders. He stabbed the thief with a Taser arrow and sent a second one flying into a thief that was about to take a swing at Kate while she was busy dealing with another one. The three criminals still standing were taken out by quick strikes from Isaac, Logan, and Zach.

"Not bad," one of the hostages, the warehouse security guard, said.

Kate laughed and helped her to her feet. "We try our best. Why don't you all go outside and tell the police that everything is clear in here?"

As the hostages hurried out of the building, Zach and Max walked over to Kate. "That was fun," Max said. "It's a lot less boring than what the Legion usually ends up having me do."

"It's not our fault that your power sucks, Wraith," Zach teased.

"You have absolutely no idea how wrong you are." Max looked at Logan as the girl slid down the nearby support beam to join them. "This one's yours, right, Kov?"

"Yep," Zach said with a wide grin, messing up Logan's strawberry-blonde hair with a gloved hand. "I'll introduce you properly when we're back at the Heroics base."

Logan ducked away from her father and irritably moved her hair back into place. "You're coming back with us?"

"Yeah, we have some things to discuss. That's why we ended up here with you today."

Kate hit a button on the side of her sunglasses. "Control, this is Targeter. The warehouse is clear. We're going to get out of here before the cops start trying to ask us questions."

"*You've got it, Targeter. See you when you're back at the base.*"

The Heroics base was in the basement of what was once known as the Phantom Mansion, a place that used to be disguised as a condemned building so as not to draw attention to it. The members of the first Heroics team had called it home when they were children, but it was now limited to the Heroics members who made up the base operations team.

AJ Hamil, the team's medic, met the group when they walked into the base. "All in one piece, I hope?"

"I don't think they managed to hit any of us except for Ciaran," Kate reported. "And he's okay." She squinted at her son, who was rubbing his shoulder. "You *are* okay, right?"

"You asked me that twenty times in the twenty minutes it took us to get back here, Mom," Ciaran said, an irritated edge to his voice. "I'm still okay."

"He's okay aside from the fact that he sucks at dodging," Isaac teased.

Ciaran took a light swing at the teen, but Kate caught his hand. "Boys, bicker later, please."

AJ, shaking his head slowly, looked at Zach. "We're meeting in the larger conference room. Casey should be getting back soon, and once she is, we'll get started."

"Good. We'll head over." Zach put an arm around Logan's shoulders and started leading her towards the conference room. "That was a lot of power you used today. Are you all right?"

"Yeah. Bit tired. I still need to work on focusing for that much metal at once."

"It took me a while to get that kind of accuracy down, so you're doing pretty good for your age. At sixteen I could move larger amounts of metal than you can, but not with your precision."

"Is that a bad thing?" Logan asked anxiously.

Zach chuckled softly and kissed her on the side of the head. "You're learning at your own pace in your own way. That's a good thing, kid."

Logan leaned into him. "Dad, what's going on? What do you and Wraith need to talk to us about?"

The smile on Zach's face vanished instantly. "Why don't we just wait until we're with the others, okay?" He rubbed Logan's arm gently. "It'll be simpler that way."

Several minutes later, the Heroics team was gathered in the larger conference room of their base. Casey Carter, who had built most of the tech and was generally considered to be in charge of the operations of the base, since she owned the building, was seated at one end of the table. The seat at the other end of the table was taken by Ray "Blackout" Sampson, Isaac's father and leader of the field team. Kate, his second-in-command, was seated to his right, followed by Ciaran and Isaac. Next to them was Riley "Sniper" Oliver, the team's youngest member at fourteen, along with her father, Justin Oliver. Justin was also Kate's younger brother; he had been forced to retire from active duty on the Heroics team due to an injury. Max had taken an extra seat between Justin and Zach, and Logan was in between Zach and her mother, Casey. The other side of the table was primarily members of the base team, with Cass Hamil seated next to Casey, her husband, AJ, seated next to her, and two of their children, Brooke and Jacob Hamil, seated next to him. Two other former Heroics members, Alix Tolvaj and Kara Hall, followed.

"You all obviously know Zach," Casey began, shooting the man an affectionate grin.

"Never seen him before in my life," Logan deadpanned.

"Who are you again?" Jacob asked, squinting curiously at Zach.

Casey gave a tired sigh but ignored them, continuing, "He's brought a friend with him, one we're going to be getting to know quite well."

"Why's that?" Jacob asked.

"I've been having more and more responsibilities in the Legion," Zach said. "It's making it harder and harder to be consistent in my responsibilities as the liaison between us and you guys." He clapped a hand on Max's shoulder. "That's where this guy comes in. He's been appointed to take over that position."

Max grinned and gave a small wave. "Max Oakley. The Security Legion calls me 'Wraith.'"

"You mean we won't need to see your stupid face as often anymore, Zach?" Ray asked, also grinning. "Fantastic."

"Fat chance. I live here, dumb-ass. I'm married to your boss. You'll never get away from me."

"Unless I divorce you," Casey joked.

Logan rolled her eyes. "Yeah, because that would make a difference. We still see Niall all the time even though Kate divorced him."

"Thank you for reassuring me that your mother would never leave me," Zach said dryly.

"No problem!"

"All right, all right, knock it off," Cass said. "There's no need to scare Max off with our insanity this quickly."

Max shrugged. "It's okay. I find it amusing, honestly."

AJ gave a small sigh and shook his head slowly. "You won't after a while."

"Where *is* Niall, anyway?" Zach asked.

"Dad's with Rick. They went with Claire and James to that college tour. They should be back tomorrow."

"Possibly later, if my son has his way," Kara muttered. "He said something about dragging Claire and the others to a soccer game."

"I'm sure Rick will *love* that," Ciaran said sarcastically. "He's about as into sports as my mother is to showing up to things."

Kate flinched slightly but kept her expression calm as she changed the subject. "You said that you had a few things to discuss with us, Zach. I'm assuming you aren't here just to introduce us to the new you."

Max looked concerned, but instead of commenting on Ciaran's jab, he said, "Please, I am *not* going to be *anything* like Zach."

"We'll see," Kate said in a mild voice. She raised an eyebrow at Zach. "What's the deal?"

Zach leaned forward. "We arrested a guy with powers a few days ago. He said that he was glad we had caught him, because he was afraid."

"Of what?"

"He didn't know."

19

Kate snorted. "Was this guy perhaps drunk, Zach?"

"No," Max replied. "He was terrified. He just wasn't sure of what. He said that someone's been watching the empowered criminals. It's been going on for a while. The thing is, some of the people who were the most certain that they were being watched... have started to go missing. Not even their closest friends or family know where they are."

An uneasy silence fell over the Heroics team. A few of them glanced at Alix, who hadn't looked up from her tablet. When she did, her metal-gray gaze was distant. "I know what you're thinking," she said, her voice soft. "It's not her. Alice is dead. I put those bullets in her myself."

Cass leaned forward slightly and lowered her voice. "If you could just—"

"I'll make sure," Alix replied, equally quiet.

"Thank you."

Brooke leaned back in her chair, her left leg bouncing uncontrollably and her fingers tapping against her arms. "Whataboutthecops?" she asked, her voice so fast that her words slurred together.

Max looked confused, but nobody else at the table seemed to have had any issues understanding her. "I already checked with my police contact," Zach said. "They don't have any of the missing people. The feds don't, either."

Casey raised an eyebrow at him. "You have contacts with the *feds*?"

"No, but the president does," Zach said casually.

"Wait a minute, *what*?"

Zach blinked at AJ. "… Tamara… Kingston?"

"I know who the president is," AJ retorted irritably.

"Logan doesn't," Jacob snickered.

Logan gave her cousin a tired look. "Yes I do."

"Then how did you fail the U.S. Presidents test in sixth grade?"

"They wanted to know *birth cities*. I can bend a car in half with my mind; I don't need to know that crap!"

Brooke, still bouncing in her chair, snorted. "Yeah, J, don't you know? Metal good; paper bad!"

A pen flew out of the jar in the center of the table, but it froze inches from Brooke's face. "Children," Zach said, his voice heavy with exasperation, "can it wait until *after* we're all done talking?"

"No fun," all three of them said simultaneously.

AJ shook his head. "Five kids with Wechsler DNA and only one of them isn't a bastard."

"Hey," Casey protested, "what about Thomas? Or do you actually think Aubrey's as bad as these three?"

"Good point. *Two* of them aren't bastards."

Alix leaned forward and made eye contact with Max. "Run away, Wraith. Run away and don't look back."

The pen flew backwards and smacked her in the forehead.

"*Ow!*"

"When you're done injuring Alix, Zach," AJ said calmly, "could you please explain how you *know the president*?"

"Oh, right. She used to be Redwood."

The silence in the room fell so quickly that Brooke even stopped moving around in her seat. "Isn't... that... the Legion hero with wood manipulation powers?"

"Yes, Brooke, it is," Casey replied. "She's the president now. Of course, she obviously retired from active hero duty so that she could do her current job more effectively."

"*You knew?*" Cass demanded of her sister, sounding offended. "You knew and you didn't tell me?"

Casey blinked. "I didn't tell you?"

"*No!*"

"Well, that explains this mess." Casey pushed her glasses up on her nose. "Zach told me when she was running. I guess I forgot."

Cass shook her head slowly. "You're a bastard."

Casey paused before shrugging. "Technically, you're not wrong."

Brooke, who was bouncing again, said, "Isn't there a UCONN soccer game tonight?"

The complete change of subject made everyone in the room pause, and AJ carefully said, "Honey, you're doing it again."

His daughter stared at him for a long moment before flinching. "Sorry. I-I just..."

"I know," AJ said, his voice soft. He gently squeezed Brooke's hand once before looking at Zach and saying, "So you have no ideas at all as to where those people may have been disappearing to?"

"None. We've been doing everything we can to look into it, but we have nothing."

"Okay." Casey leaned back in her chair, interlocking her fingers in front of her on the table. "Here's what we should do, then: Be careful. We all know that things that affect empowered criminals usually end up finding their way back to us. So watch your backs, all of you. Got it?"

After she got murmurs of agreement from around the table, Zach said, "That's really the only thing we can do if you don't have any other ideas on what might be happening."

"I don't think we do. But we'll let you know if we do."

"That would be great; thanks." Zach leaned past Logan to kiss Casey quickly.

Logan made an irritated noise. "Get a room."

"You already have *one* little sibling."

Logan groaned loudly and shoved her father back into his chair. "I'm starting to wish *I* was never born."

Zach ruffled his fingers through her hair. "But *then* who would I torment?"

"Anyone," Casey replied dryly.

Her husband laughed and turned to Max. "Come on, Wraith. We should get out of here before my family ruins your day any more than they already have."

Max shrugged. "I don't know. I think anyone who puts you through hell is good in my book."

Casey smirked. "I knew I liked him."

Outside of the conference room, Cass pulled Alix aside. "Are you okay? We didn't get a chance to talk before the meeting, but you seemed annoyed when I walked in."

Alix pulled her navy blue leather jacket tighter around her shoulders. "Ah, I'm just pissed about these idiots trying to rob you earlier. It makes me feel like I'm not doing my job."

Cass gave a soft laugh. "Al, security at the *headquarters* is your job. You aren't responsible for every single warehouse Casey and I own. That would be ridiculous."

"Doesn't mean I have to like it." Alix narrowed her eyes. "What about you? Are you okay?"

"I don't know what you mean."

It was Alix's turn to laugh. "Cass, I know when something's bothering you."

Cass shifted her weight from one foot to the other anxiously. "I just... wish Aubrey had come. This isn't the sort of meeting she should be missing."

Alix rested a hand on Cass's shoulder. "I'll talk to her, okay? She's probably back at the office."

"On a Saturday?" Cass asked with a scoff.

"It's *Aubrey*."

"You have a fair point." Cass sighed. "I should go find my *other* daughter, since she somehow disappeared from that meeting without any of us noticing."

"She's good at that."

"I just hope she's taking her meds," Cass muttered as she headed for the elevator.

Alix turned and noticed Max heading towards the back exit of the base. "Hey, Wraith!"

Max paused and faced her, looking confused. "You can call me Max, you know."

As she walked over to him, she said, "That's not as much fun. What kind of hero name is Wraith? Are you a superhero or a drag racer?"

"Don't you go by 'Thief'?" Max shot back. "How is that any better?"

Alix gave him an approving look and held out a hand. "Alix Tolvaj."

He shook her hand. "Max Oakley."

"I'm still calling you Wraith."

"Then I'm calling you Thief."

Alix laughed softly. "Fair enough. Before you leave, you should talk to Casey. She'll get you a Heroics communication device. It's the best way to keep in touch with us. I'm assuming you'll be taken out on a few patrols with us as well, so that you get a feel for how we do things. That's how Zach started out."

"Sounds good to me." Max unzipped his black leather Legion jacket so that the dark-gray t-shirt underneath was visible. "I heard you still go out into the field, despite, uh…"

"Not having powers anymore?" Alix finished mildly.

"Er… yeah."

"I don't go to things that will probably get me killed, like that warehouse this afternoon, but I help where I can." She shrugged. "Can't help myself, I guess."

"Too ingrained in your system to give up heroing completely," Max said lightly.

"I suppose so."

They stood there for a moment, a slightly awkward vibe in the air that didn't help ease the way Max's fingers had been tingling ever since they had shaken hands. Before one of them could figure out what to say, Casey walked up to them, a brown box in her hands. She took in Max's outfit—black combat boots, black pants, black leather jacket with dark-gray Legion symbols, dark-gray t-shirt—and sighed. "What is it with the Legion and black?"

Max shrugged. "Honestly? I asked for red."

Casey looked at his uniform again and gave a short nod. "Red would go." She opened the box she was carrying, dug around in it for a moment, and pulled out a pair of red communications sunglasses. As she handed them to him she said, "These can tap you into our general communications, and they can also be used to contact one specific member of the team. They also do a bunch of other things, like calculate distance, give directions, translate sign language to a text readout, switch to night vision..."

"Do they get box scores from Caotico Cavalry games?" Max asked with a grin.

"Yes," Casey said, sounding almost tired. "Kara played professional softball before she was paralyzed. There was no way she was going to let me not give her access to the baseball scores."

"The girl with super-strength played softball? Isn't that... cheating?"

Alix scoffed. "Only if you don't take into account the fact that she never hit more than the average good player and her strength didn't have anything to do with her talent for playing well in the field and having good enough accuracy to actually make contact with the ball when she was at the plate."

"Huh." Max gave a small nod. "Seems fair."

Casey closed the box and said, "Al, can you show him how to use those? I don't want him, like, blowing something up by accident."

Max, who had been in the process of trying the glasses on, slowly removed them. "They... can do that?"

"No, but an exaggeration is the best way to make sure you're careful."

"Got it."

Alix shook her head slowly. "I'll walk him through it, but he's going to have to get that walkthrough by catching a ride into the city with me. I need to take care of some things."

Max shrugged. "That's fine with me. I came here in Zach's car, so I can just leave with you. I think he'd prefer that anyway."

"It's likely." Alix smirked. "He's had a few night patrols recently, so he probably would appreciate some time alone with his wife."

Casey lightly hit her upside the head. "Get the hell out of here, you pain in the ass."

"Gladly. C'mon, Wraith."

3

It wasn't a far drive from the Heroics mansion to Caotico City, but on the way Max managed to learn quite a bit about the sunglasses he had just received. Alix gave him a clinical breakdown of the functions, sometimes using much more technical terms than Max could understand.

"You know a lot about these things," he commented.

"My eyes don't handle light very well, so I use them often. Casey figured out how to apply a tinted coating to contacts to help me out a bit, but the sunglasses are the best option for me. Over the years I've taken the time to learn how they work." Alix turned her sports car into the parking garage of the corporate headquarters of Wechsler Industries, pausing to swipe her security ID, which lifted the gate into the lot. "You're sure you want to walk from here? I can go back and drop you off somewhere."

"It's okay. I don't live too far from here. My apartment is over on Wedge Avenue." Max folded his sunglasses up and hung them from the collar of his t-shirt. "May I ask you something?"

Alix shrugged. "You can, but there's no guarantee you'll get a straight answer."

"Is it strange? Not having powers after having them for your whole life?"

She was silent as she pulled into her marked parking space. "It was very strange at first. It was uncomfortable. It took a while for me to figure out how to do certain things—including fighting—without my powers. I was so used to my shadow abilities that suddenly not having them was difficult to grasp. But now? It's normal for me. And besides, my powers were killing me. I'd rather not have them and still be around to help my friends than have kept them longer and be too dead to be of any use."

"Makes sense," Max said quietly. "I'm sorry if that's a question you're tired of answering. I know it's been a lot of years."

"And it's been a lot of years since I've been asked. The answer's a bit different now than it used to be. It's okay." Alix turned towards him and lowered her own sunglasses, which allowed him to see her metallic-gray eyes. "I'm sure Ray will be in contact with you at some point in the near future so you can accompany the team on a patrol. Try not to lose those glasses."

"I never lose anything."

Alix gave a scoffing laugh and pushed her glasses back up on her nose. "I'm sure that's completely true."

"It is." Max held out his hand. "Thanks for the ride, Thief. It's been a pleasure. I'm sure I'll be seeing you around."

"I live at the mansion, so you undoubtedly will." Alix shook his hand. "It's been... relatively pleasant, Wraith."

Max smiled slightly. "You're a smart-ass, you know that?"

Alix mirrored his smile. "I try."

"You do very well." Max turned and got out of the car without opening the door, simply stepping right through it.

Alix got out of her car the proper way and leaned on the roof, looking over at him. "Show-off."

Max shrugged, grinning. "Intangibility is too fun not to use when I can."

"Doesn't make you less of a show-off."

"I'll accept that."

Alix glanced at her watch. "I'd love to continue this conversation, Wraith, but I really do need to be going."

"Of course. I'll head out."

"Do you know how to *get* out?"

Max smirked. "Walk through the wall?"

Alix gave a long, slow sigh and turned towards the elevator, rubbing her hands together absentmindedly. "Like I said. Show-off."

Before heading down to the basement, Cass made a stop at her eldest daughter's bedroom. Brooke was tearing her room apart in the way one does before cleaning it, tossing things around without even paying attention to what they were or where they were ending up. She was muttering to herself and occasionally tapping her fist against the side of her head, and she apparently hadn't seen her mother yet. If she had, she probably would've tried to quickly hide the half-dozen vodka bottles scattered over her desk.

"Brooke," Cass said quietly, "are you all the way up to auditory hallucinations?"

Her daughter froze and slowly lowered her fist away from her head. "N-No."

"Please don't lie to me."

"They aren't that bad," Brooke insisted, continuing to dig around in a crate next to her closet.

"Brooke."

"I'm taking the meds. It's just a bad day. I'm fine."

Cass carefully sat down on Brooke's bed. "When was the last time you slept?"

"Eh..." Brooke pulled out a soccer ball and started absentmindedly kicking it into the air over and over again. "Two days ago."

"Honey, that's not 'a bad day.' That's more, and you know it."

Brooke suddenly stuck the soccer ball under her arm and grabbed an unopened bottle of vodka out of a desk drawer. "Do you know if Matthias is home? No. Why would you know if Matthias is home? I'm going to go see if he wants to goal-keep for me. I'm too good to need to practice, but he could use some work."

"What about your room?" Cass asked casually, raising an eyebrow.

There was a long pause as Brooke looked around her torn-apart bedroom. "What about it?" Without waiting for an answer, and almost bouncing on the balls of her feet, Brooke turned and walked out of the room.

Cass sighed and took out her cell phone. After only two rings, a male voice answered.

"Mrs. Hamil?"

"Hey, Mat. Brooke's coming over to see you."

A pause. *"Which one is it?"*

"Mania. It's fall. She always hits mania in the fall."

"Right, of course. Alcohol?"

"Vodka."

31

"Must be a bad day. I'll keep an eye out for her, and if she doesn't get here in an appropriate time I'll let you know."

"Great. Thanks, Matthias."

"Never a problem. You know that."

"I do."

Cass put her phone back in her pocket. She closed her eyes and pinched the bridge of her nose, sighing heavily. After a minute or so, she stood and headed downstairs.

On the fifteenth floor of the thirty-story Wechsler Industries building, Alix made her way to the only office with light coming from it. The door was open, making it easy for her to see the twenty-one-year-old woman behind the desk who was staring at her monitor as she absentmindedly pulled her brown hair into a ponytail.

"Should I have brought coffee?" Alix asked quietly, leaning against the door frame.

Aubrey Hamil jumped so badly that she slammed her knee into her desk. She mumbled a curse in a language that wasn't English before glaring at Alix and saying, "How about some warning next time, Al?"

"If I had warned you, you would've shut your door and turned your light off and pretended that you weren't in here working on a Saturday."

"True." Aubrey rubbed her eyes and leaned back in her chair. "It's not my fault this time. That *jackass*..." She cleared her throat. "I'm sorry. My *boss* hasn't done any of his own damn work, and it all needs to be done by the end of the month. Y'know, five days from now. And he's on vacation. So all of the stuff that he decided not to do has fallen to me, in addition to the work that's my own to do. Hence the Saturday workday."

"Did you tell your mom any of this? I highly doubt Cass would—"

Aubrey cut Alix off by laughing loudly. "These people already think that I nepotismed my way into this company, Al. They don't care that I graduated college with honors at nineteen. They see my surname and write me off as the company owner's daughter who talked her way into a job. If I report my boss's inadequacy, it'll only get worse."

"They're giving you a hard time?" Alix asked, anger seeping into her voice.

"Not directly. They aren't that stupid. But neither am I, and I know damn well what passive-aggression looks like."

Alix walked into the office and carefully took a seat on the edge of Aubrey's desk. "If I can do anything, you know you only have to ask."

Aubrey started slowly spinning her ring around her right ring finger in sets of three rotations. "I know. Thanks, Al."

"Never a problem, kid." Alix hesitated. "Y'know, since you know what passive-aggression looks like, perhaps you can recognize it in your own behavior."

There was a pause as Aubrey waited to finish one of the sets of three before lowering her hands to grip the arms of her desk chair. "I'm not being passive-aggressive," she said quietly.

"Mm. Avoiding your parents for fun, then?"

"Alix."

"We had a meeting called by Zach this morning, Aub. When the Security Legion calls us to a meeting, that's not a joke. That's something that could affect all of us."

"I'm not a member of Heroics," Aubrey snapped. "I don't want to be, remember?"

"*All of us.* That includes you, because you still live in the mansion no matter what that apartment here in the city claims. Things that could be really dangerous? Could be really big? Affect you, too, because whether you're a member of Heroics or not, by association you're at risk."

Aubrey stared at Alix for a long moment, a note of challenge in her light-green eyes that was extremely similar to one frequently found in her mother. "Did I miss anything vital to my survival?"

"... No," Alix admitted.

"Then why does it matter?"

"You're too smart for me to dignify that with a response." Alix pushed a loose strand of hair behind Aubrey's ear. "Are you okay? You aren't usually this snappy with me. I'm supposed to be the fun aunt."

"I'm sorry." Aubrey rubbed her eyes again. "I'm just tired of being in this office."

"What do you have left to do?"

"Well, today I've been logging invoices, and I still have a few of those left to do."

"Can you do them on Monday?"

Aubrey gave a small sigh. "Well, yeah, but—"

"Then *do them on Monday.*" Alix rested a hand on Aubrey's shoulder, the contact getting the younger woman to look at her. "You don't have anything to prove,

Aub. I know you think you do, but you don't. It's not your job to work way more than you need to so that you can make up for other people's failures."

"Easier said than followed," Aubrey said weakly.

Alix gave a soft laugh. "For not being a member of Heroics, you sure do have a lot of our faults."

"Familial hazard." Aubrey leaned further back in her chair and closed her eyes. "I *do* kind of want to just go get a drink."

"Then go. Everything else will work out." Alix stood up. "But do me a favor? When we have meetings called by the Legion, *show up.* Because one of these days, it'll be something that *could* get you killed, and the information might not filter to you fast enough to do you any good."

Kara wheeled into the mission control room of the Heroics base, where Cass was getting ready for the next patrol. "How did that hostage situation this morning go?"

Cass opened the line of communications with the field team and then turned to face Kara. "Pretty well. Turns out they were just thieves hoping to steal stuff, didn't realize our employees would be there, panicked when the cops showed up, and winged it from there."

"Did a pretty good job of winging it from what I heard."

"Yeah, well, this is Caotico. Our criminal underworld is basically 50% incompetence, 50% genius."

"Good point."

Cass leaned back in her chair. "How are the college visitations going with James?"

"Not bad. He's not too concerned with making up his mind since he's only a junior, though." Kara snorted. "I don't really help matters since my college decision was made entirely based on softball."

"I'm sure Claire *loves* that."

"The phrase 'Kara, I'm going to kill you' has been said in my house a few more times than I'd like, but she's managing." Kara ran a hand through her hair, laughing slightly. "Between me and James, I think Claire's starting to hit her patience limit."

Cass scoffed as she turned back toward the monitors. "I find that hard to believe. You were more of a pain in the ass when your spine was in one piece."

"True, but James wasn't a moody teenager at the time, so it's balanced out."

"Poor Claire."

"Her anxiety levels aren't helped much by the fact that he wants to be a cop."

Cass turned her chair back around, surprised. "James wants to be a cop?"

"Yeah."

"Why?"

Kara gave a long, slow sigh. "Because he watched me lose the function of one of my legs to the fight against crime in our city, and he decided that even if he doesn't have powers, he's not going to let that stop him from continuing what I can no longer do."

"A noble reason, although one that won't exactly keep your blood pressure low."

"Crime fighters in Caotico don't have a very high survival rate," Kara murmured.

Cass reached out and rested a hand on top of Kara's. "True, but this kid was raised by you and Claire. If he has even a fraction of the stubbornness and toughness that the two of you have, he'll be too damn stubborn to die."

Kara chuckled softly. "Bit cliché, but I'll take it."

"Good." Cass put an earpiece in. "You're welcome to stick around, but it seems that Ciaran is getting his ass kicked by a bank robber."

"Caotico is a haven for bank robbers, isn't it?" Kara asked with a laugh.

"You know, I'm really starting to think that it is."

"How many bank robbers are in this freaking city?" Ciaran's voice demanded in Riley's ear as two men ganged up on him in a fistfight.

"Enough to wipe the floor with you, apparently," Riley replied as she adjusted her position on the roof above him. She aimed her sniper rifle and fired a shock round into the robber that had been about to hit Ciaran in the face, dropping the man with a well-placed blow to the chest. "You're welcome. What happened to your bow?"

"No idea. You're all the way up there. Can't you see it?"

Riley squinted through her rifle's scope until she found Ciaran's pale-yellow bow. "It's about six feet to your four o'clock."

"Wow, just far enough away to be useless."

"You aren't very good at this, are you?" Riley commented as she tried to get a clear line of sight on the second robber her cousin was fighting. "Eisen said you were the only one to get hit this morning, too."

"Thanks for pointing out all of my flaws, Sniper."

"It's what I do best," she replied as she put another shock round into the chest of the second robber, sending him to the ground next to his accomplice. Riley watched as Ciaran adjusted his yellow vest and walked over to pick up his bow. "Where to next?" she asked.

"Why, so you can watch me get pummeled again?"

"It's enjoyable."

Ciaran gave a humorless laugh. *"Why can't you be more like your mom?"*

Riley stood up, slinging her rifle over her shoulder. "She asks that same question a lot."

The mansion's library was quiet as AJ read through a report on his tablet. He looked up quickly as the silence was disrupted by the door slamming open. Jacob walked in, a frustrated expression on his face.

"Do you know where Brooke is?"

"With Matthias. Why?"

"Because she's stupid."

"Jacob Carter Hamil," AJ said seriously.

The teen folded his arms across his chest in irritation. "She is! She spent all day yesterday telling me how to do my job, but she doesn't know anything! And I *know* I'm right, but now I can't find her to prove it!"

"What are you trying to do?"

Jacob took in a deep breath to calm himself. "I'm putting together a system that we can install throughout

Caotico City and Fuego Village so that we can get more precise and exact monitoring at all times. I know exactly how it would work, but *Brooke* thinks my math is wrong. The math isn't even the important thing at the moment. The important thing is that the system would *work!*" He proceeded to list a complicated series of plans that made absolutely no sense to his father.

"Do you have that whole thing memorized, or did you just come up with it now?" AJ asked, pinching the bridge of his nose and closing his eyes to try to ward off a headache.

"Dad, memorization is the one symptom of dyslexia I have never had to worry about," Jacob replied. "An issue with math problems might be, but I am absolutely never going to tell Brooke that."

AJ sighed. "Can you ask Aubrey? She's not currently running on a complicated 'I am the best in the universe' high, so she would probably be the safer bet for you."

"I'll ask, but she doesn't do anything with us anymore. I don't see why this would be any different," Jacob muttered.

"Give her a break, J."

Jacob stiffened. "Why, because she went and got herself a real job? No offense, Dad, but I don't see how working for Mom and Aunt Casey is any better than being a member of Heroics."

"That's not what I'm saying. I'm saying that what your sister is doing is just as good as what you and Brooke are doing, and you need to respect that whether you like it or not."

"Can I respect her by mocking her like I usually do?" Jacob asked rebelliously.

"I don't care *what* you do, so long as you're as nice to her as you would be if she was working here."

Jacob thought for a moment. "So... not nice at all?"

AJ shook his head slowly and looked back down at his tablet. "I really wish I could say that wasn't true."

Casey walked into the bar that she owned and headed over to the counter where her bartender and manager, Kaita Dragovic, was mixing a drink. "Slow night?"

Kaita shrugged. "It's early. Most people aren't in a bar drinking at five in the afternoon."

Casey gave a short laugh. "You've been working here *how* long?"

"True. Slow night." Kaita delivered the drink she had made to a woman at the far end of the bar, then walked back over to Casey and leaned on the counter. "Can I get you anything, boss?"

"Soda. Doesn't matter which one." Casey jumped over the counter, pushing her glasses back up on her nose when the landing jarred them loose. "Amazingly, I'm still tempted to say scotch."

"Even though you're twelve years sober?"

"Alcoholism is a bitch, Kaita."

"I noticed," Kaita said sympathetically. Her brown and blue eyes glanced past Casey to the door, and she smiled slightly. "Well, look who finally came out of her hole."

Casey turned and saw Aubrey walking into the bar. The young woman noticed her aunt, flushed a bit, and awkwardly made her way over to the counter. "You're not going to yell at me too, are you?" she asked.

As Kaita moved down the counter to take care of some customers, Casey said, "Let me guess. Cass sicced Alix on you?"

Aubrey sighed and took a seat on one of the barstools. "I don't know if it was that or if it was Alix's own irritation, but she sort of read me the riot act for not showing up at that meeting."

"I won't do a repeat showing, but seriously, Aubrey, I feel like I haven't seen you in days."

"I've been busy," Aubrey said, a note of protest in her voice. "I work for a living, remember? *For you.*"

Casey leaned forward. "Yeah, *for me*, which means I should see you more than once a month, shouldn't I?" She pulled Aubrey forward and kissed her on the top of the head. "Quit being such a stranger, kid. We live in the same house."

Aubrey pulled away from her, jokingly annoyed. "Yeah, yeah, all right. Are you going to get me a drink or are you going to just keep giving me a hard time?"

"I have to choose?" Casey smirked and got a glass out from under the counter. "What do you want?"

"Uh, anything that will help get rid of this work week."

Casey glanced at the bottles lined up behind her. "We have cinnamon whiskey?"

"Sounds horrible. I'll take it."

Her aunt laughed as she poured the liquor into the glass. "Rough week?"

"You could say that."

"I still have trouble accepting the fact that you're old enough to drink," Casey said as she slid the drink over to Aubrey.

"You're getting old, Aunt Casey," Aubrey teased.

"You're getting to be a jackass just like your mom."

Aubrey raised an eyebrow as she took a sip from her glass. "'Getting to be'?"

Casey paused. "Good point. You were always just as much of a jackass as your mother."

Aubrey swirled the liquid around in her glass three times. "Brooke keeps calling me. Her messages run so fast I barely know what she's saying. She's in one of her manic phases, isn't she?"

"Yes. I could see it in the meeting. But she's been taking her medication, and she's getting better at handling it. Sort of. She'll be okay." Casey rested her arms on the bar and leaned forward. "What about you? How are you handling your own thing?"

Aubrey spun her alcohol three times again. "It's fine," she said casually.

"Hey." Casey reached out and put her hand on top of the hand Aubrey was using to hold her drink. "Are you taking *your* meds?"

Her niece gave a noncommittal noise and wouldn't make eye contact with her.

"Aubrey," Casey said in a wary tone.

"They just make my head feel more messed-up, okay?" Aubrey swirled her glass thrice more and then set it down. "I don't need them. I can handle it."

"You should talk to your father," Casey murmured.

"Dad doesn't know everything, Aunt Casey," Aubrey whispered.

"No, but he's a place to start. You got put on medication for a reason, Aubrey. You know your dad wouldn't have let you take it if you didn't need it." Casey glanced at the door. "One of your friends is here. We'll talk about this more later."

"Yippee," Aubrey grumbled. She turned to see who was walking over to her.

Rowan van Houten was about an inch taller than her and a year older, with dark blue eyes and a faint, yet obvious, Czech accent. Thick, black, wavy hair fell just to her shoulders, where it blended in with her black leather Legion jacket.

"I figured I could find you moping in a glass of liquor," Rowan said with a grin as she took a seat on the barstool next to Aubrey's.

As she sat down, Rowan's elbow knocked a menu out of place, and Aubrey instantly put it back where it belonged. Rowan clearly noticed, but instead of commenting, she said, "What's got you drinking today, Hamil?"

"Nothing out of the ordinary. Are you supposed to be wearing that jacket if you're not out on patrol?"

Rowan shrugged. "I *was* out on patrol. I just haven't changed yet." She shrugged out of her jacket, turned it inside out so that all of the gold Legion insignias were no longer visible, and put it back on. "There. Problem solved."

Aubrey rolled her eyes. "One of these days you aren't going to have an easy solution to all of your problems, van Houten."

"Luckily, today is not that day," Rowan retorted with a grin. She turned to Casey. "Have you seen Kov recently, Mrs. Carter?"

"I saw him a few hours ago, but I don't know where he is at the moment. Is he in trouble?"

Rowan shook her head. "No, but the Galaxy Boys are."

Casey's brow furrowed. "What did Seamus Sullivan do now?"

"From what I can tell, he's been getting his friends to pickpocket people, and he might have gotten in over his head. Nobody's really heard from them in a few days. I don't think it's related to the other disappearances, but I was hoping to ask Kov if he thinks we should check it out."

"I can tell him the next time I talk to him, and he can get in touch with you."

"I'd appreciate that. Thanks, Mrs. Carter."

"Any time."

Rowan turned back to Aubrey. "Since we're off shift, a few of us were going to go to an underground bar in the Village. Care to join us? No offense, Mrs. Carter."

"None taken. It'd be nice to get some of you hooligans out of my bar for a bit."

Rowan looked offended. "*Hooligans?* Who do you think I am?"

"The kid who blew up the dart board in the corner."

Aubrey finished her drink. "She has a point, Ro."

"That was an accident."

"Oh, really."

"Thomas dared me to do it!"

44

"He was *nine!* You were *twenty!*"

Rowan folded her arms across her chest and said in an irritated tone, "At least I wasn't the one ordering drinks under a fake ID!"

Aubrey elbowed Rowan in the side as Casey gave her an incredulous look. "How the hell did *you* order alcohol before you were twenty-one? Everyone who works in this bar knows who you are and how old you are at any given time."

"Not the newest hires at any given time," Aubrey said innocently.

"See what I mean about hooligans? Now both of you, go, get out of my bar, shoo."

Once Rowan had gotten up and walked a few feet away, Aubrey leaned towards Casey. "Are you going to tell Mom and Dad that I'm not taking my meds?"

Casey sighed. "Aubrey, I don't know. I *should.* They can't make you do anything because you're an adult, but I should tell them anyway."

"I can handle it, Aunt Casey."

"And what if you can't, kiddo?" Casey asked softly. "I don't want anything to happen to you."

Aubrey spun her ring around her finger in a slow set of three. "I'll give it a day or two and then I'll talk to Dad, okay?"

Casey didn't look happy, but she nodded. "All right. But if you haven't talked to him by day three, I'm going to do it myself. Got it?"

"Got it."

Casey leaned back. "Rowan, have you met Kaita? I'm not sure you've both ever been in here at the same time."

Rowan, loitering a bit further down the bar, shook her head and held out a hand to the bartender. "Never had the pleasure. Rowan van Houten."

"Kaita Dragovic. That accent. Czech?"

"Yes."

"I promise not to shoot your next archduke."

Rowan snorted. "Serbian?"

Kaita gave her an approving look. "Thank god. Nobody's ever gotten that joke before. Yes. Both sets of grandparents were born there."

"Well, I won't hold it against you."

The bartender laughed. "I like this friend of yours, Aubrey. Bring her around more often. We can argue historical Balkan and Central European geopolitics."

"We're *Eastern* European, thanks."

"Not according to the Internet," Kaita said innocently.

"Okay, I might hold *that* against you."

Aubrey rolled her eyes. "All right, knock it off. Kaita has things to do, and we have places to be."

"Fair enough," Rowan said, tapping her hands against the bar counter. "We'll finish this later, Serb."

"And I'll win, Czech."

"In your dreams."

Rowan turned and noticed that Aubrey had already walked out. Frowning, she put her hands in her pockets and followed.

They met outside the bar. "Everything okay?" Rowan asked mildly as they started walking.

"Yeah. Aunt Casey's just worried."

"About what?"

"About the fact that I haven't been taking my OCD medication."

Rowan stopped in her tracks. "Aubrey, what the hell."

"My head hurts enough without pills making it worse, Rowan."

"Then get different pills. Don't be stupid." Rowan winced as Aubrey glared at her. "Sorry. I know you don't like to talk about it, but come on. When was the last time you took them?"

"Last week."

"*Miláček*, you've been getting worse since last week. When you were on your medication you weren't fixing menus, and you certainly weren't doing the tapping thing before."

"The—" Aubrey looked down and noticed that she was tapping her hand against her leg in sets of three. "Dammit. How did I not realize I was doing that?"

"You know why, Aub."

"I don't really need the lecture right now, Rowan." Aubrey started walking again, forcing Rowan to continue as well. "And don't bring up the other thing, either."

"I wasn't planning to, but since *you* did..." When Aubrey shot another glare at her, Rowan laughed. "I know, I know. Relax. Don't kill me."

"Don't worry. You're not my type."

They walked in silence for a long while until Rowan said, "You've got to stop doing this to yourself, *miláček*."

"Doing what?"

"Hiding everything from your family."

Aubrey shrugged. "They don't care."

"You *know* that's not true."

"Look, Ro, I'm happy with who I am. I just don't want my parents to get involved in any of it. I don't want them to distance themselves from me any more than they already have."

The two women turned down an alleyway that led to a hidden tunnel to Fuego Village. Rowan paused again, and Aubrey stopped next to her. "They love you, Aubrey. I know they've screwed up, probably more than they even realize. But they love you. You can tell them anything. I know that."

Aubrey put her hands in her pockets. "I wish I had your confidence."

"Are you kidding me? I thought *you* were the one with confidence."

"Well, then, either we both have it or neither of us does."

Rowan laughed. "I'm going to go ahead and hope for the first one, thanks." She adjusted her father's leather wrist cuff around her forearm. "In all seriousness, Aubrey, you're a lot braver than you think you are. And you're a lot more loved, too."

Aubrey shifted awkwardly. "I'm not so sure about the second one."

"Don't be an idiot. You know I'm right."

"Yeah, maybe," Aubrey muttered, not sounding convinced.

Rowan rolled her eyes. "I swear," she muttered. She leaned forward and kissed Aubrey on the mouth. When she pulled back, Aubrey punched her in the arm.

"You're not supposed to do that in public, Rowan!" she hissed.

"So sue me," Rowan retorted, amused.

Aubrey was flushed pink. "I'm not going to sue you. I'm going to kill you."

"Too cliché."

"Dammit, Rowan!"

Rowan kissed her again and then dodged out of the way of Aubrey's responding fist. "That was far too predictable, Aub. Next time try kicking me or something."

Aubrey, struggling to look angry while laughing, opened her mouth to reply when suddenly her expression went blank. She stared out at the street, pale and wide-eyed.

"What's wrong?" Rowan asked immediately.

"I-I-I think I saw Alix," Aubrey stammered.

"Tolvaj?"

"Yeah."

"You *think* you saw, or you *saw*?"

Aubrey swallowed. "I'm almost positive it was her."

Rowan bit her lip. "Aw, hell. Did she see—"

"I don't know," Aubrey interrupted.

"Well, you did say there would come a time when I wouldn't have an easy solution to my problems, *miláček*. That happened way too quickly."

"*Rowan!*"

"*What?*" Rowan noticed the anxiety on Aubrey's face, and she put her hands on the other woman's shoulders. "Relax. What do you want to do?"

Aubrey hesitated. "I'll have to go home and talk to her and see what exactly she saw and if she did see anything, see if she's going to tell my parents. Hopefully I can talk to her before she rats me out."

"Do you really think she'd do that?"

"No, but I'd rather make sure."

Rowan lowered her hands and put them in her pockets. "I'm sorry, Aubrey."

Aubrey blinked, surprised. "It's not your fault."

"Yes it is. This is the whole point of the 'not in public' rule, and I'm a stupid jackass."

"Well, I won't argue the second point, but it's really not your fault. I'm the coward who can't just tell her family the truth."

"You aren't a coward, Aubrey," Rowan said softly. "Never a coward."

"Yeah, well, let's see how true that is over the next few days." Aubrey checked her watch. "I'm just going to go home and wait for her there. It'll be better than trying to find her."

"Want me to walk with you?"

"Nah; I'll be fine."

"Okay." Rowan paused. "I really am sorry, Aubrey."

"I know. Next time try not to be a complete idiot, all right?"

"Am I a complete idiot or a stupid jackass? I can't keep up."

Aubrey laughed. "Honestly, I can't decide at the moment."

"Eh. Either will work."

"Glad you can admit it." Aubrey pulled Rowan forward by the collar of her jacket and kissed her. When Aubrey saw the surprise on the other woman's face, she said, "I figure that if we already blew the public rule today, doing it again won't make things any worse."

"Makes sense."

"All right." Aubrey released Rowan. "Time to face the music."

"It'll be okay, Aub," Rowan said quietly.

"I know it will." Aubrey's fingers started tapping against her leg again. "At least, I certainly hope so." She hesitated. "C-C-Can you keep your phone on? In case I need you?"

"Absolutely. Anything you need."

"A time machine would be great."

Rowan chuckled and gently pushed Aubrey towards the Fuego Village tunnel. "Trust me, if I had one of those, you'd know about it by now."

"It was worth a try," Aubrey muttered as she walked away.

4

Aubrey stepped through the front door of the Heroics mansion and almost ran directly into Matthias Clark Hobbes. The young man, his sandy-brown hair disheveled and his glasses crooked on his face, gave her an awkward grin and stepped back.

"Sorry, Aubrey."

"Brooke trying to get you to sleep with her again, Mat?"

Matthias shrugged. "It's progress from trying to sleep with every guy in our calculus class. She can do what she wants, but when you know that it's not actually what she would do if she was in a more stable mood, it starts to get uncomfortable." He pulled a half-empty bottle of vodka out of the front pocket of his sweatshirt. "I also confiscated this when she was distracted with trying to dismantle my television."

Aubrey gave him a sympathetic smile. "Brooke's mania is an interesting little monster."

"Indeed." A look of fear crossed Matthias's face and he shoved the bottle back into his pocket as Brooke bounded down the steps.

"Aubrey!" Brooke grabbed her sister's shoulders excitedly. "We have to help Jacob with a project. It involves math, Aubrey. And science. And engineering. And computers. And technology. And it's perfect, Aubrey. We should do it." Her gaze shifted past Aubrey to look at absolutely nothing. "Shut *up*, dammit!" she hissed, reaching up to rub at her temple. Mumbling curse words, she turned and walked away.

Worried, Aubrey moved to follow, but Matthias waved her off. "She's okay. She just mixed medication with vodka when I wasn't paying close enough attention, so she's going to pass out in a few minutes anyway. I've got her."

"Sounds like it."

Matthias fixed his glasses and gave her a weak smile. "I do my best?"

"At least you're doing something."

"Yeah." He started to head off after his friend, but he paused and turned back to Aubrey. "How are *you* doing? I feel like I haven't seen you in a while."

"I'm... okay."

Matthias frowned. "You don't sound sure."

"I'm okay, Mat."

"Well... all right..."

He disappeared after her sister, and Aubrey, taking in a deep breath, headed upstairs.

Alix opened the door of her bedroom and found Aubrey standing in the hallway.

"Are you busy?"

"Not at all," Alix said. "Come in."

Aubrey stepped into the room. "We need to talk."

"Go ahead and sit down," Alix said, gesturing at a chair as she shut the door behind her.

"I'm not sure I can."

"Then we'll stand," Alix said with a shrug. "What's on your mind?"

"I-I-I think we need to talk about what you might have seen today."

Alix hesitated. "What I may or may not have seen today need only be discussed if you're ready to talk about it."

"Honestly, Al... I think I really need to talk about it with somebody, and now's as good a time as any." After taking a moment to gather her thoughts, Aubrey said, "I'm presuming that you saw me... get kissed by a-a-another girl today."

"I did," Alix replied calmly.

"Her name is Rowan van Houten. She's a hero for the Legion."

"'Fuse,' right? Volatile constructs?"

"Yes." Aubrey took in a deep breath. "She's my girlfriend. I-I-I'm gay." When Alix didn't respond, Aubrey continued, "I've known for a while, but I didn't want to say anything, because I didn't want yet another thing about me to make me different from Brooke and Jacob. And while I know that it's not like anybody here would judge me for it, I didn't want to put myself through trying to explain that I'm not just trying to be even more different than them, and I'm already the least favorite child since I didn't want to be involved in Heroics, and-"

Her breathless rambling was cut off when Alix pulled her forward and hugged her tightly. "Shhh. There is *nothing wrong* with being different from your siblings, Aubrey," Alix murmured. "And I know that it's hard for you, with the position you're in, to believe that your family doesn't somehow like you the least. But I swear to you, kid, it's not the case. You're allowed to choose what you want to do with your life, and you're allowed to be happy." Alix gave a slight laugh. "And no matter what that brain of yours tells you, nobody is going to think that you're pretending to be gay for attention. If anybody *does*, I will gladly beat the hell out of them for you."

"I think I'd let you," Aubrey muttered, her voice muffled by Alix's shirt.

"That's the spirit."

Aubrey sighed, a long, ragged sigh that sounded like she was releasing years of pent-up anxiety. "Why do I always have to be the different one, Alix?" Her voice cracked, and she started to cry. "Why am I always the one who isn't anything like the other two?"

Alix tightened her grip on the younger woman. "It's just who you are, Aub," she replied softly. "It's not good or bad; it's just who you are. But you know, you really aren't all that different from Brooke and Jacob."

Aubrey pulled out of the hug, confused. "Of course I am. They're all science and computers and technology. I'm math and business and finance and language. I don't understand a thing either of them say unless Brooke happens to bring up the math portions of her expertise."

"Fields of interest aren't what I'm talking about, Aub. You're different from them in a lot of ways, yeah." Alix rested a hand on Aubrey's cheek and smiled slightly. "But all three of you are extremely smart kids with good hearts, a lot of talent, and more sheer willpower than most people twice any of your ages. You might go about that in different ways, but it's all there. It's all inside of you. *That* is who all three of you are, Aubrey. You're one of them whether you work with Heroics or not, whether you like the technical side of things or not, whether... well, whether you're *straight* or not. Don't get so preoccupied with how different you and your siblings are externally that you think you have nothing in common with them internally."

Aubrey sniffed, wiping tears off of her face. "When did you get so good at pep talks?"

Alix grinned. "I've been given more than a few of them in my life. I figured out how to give them so I could return the favor."

"I love you, you know that?"

"I love you too, kid." Alix straightened and shrugged her shoulders, glancing at the clock on the wall. "I have a meeting in ten minutes, but if you want me to stay and talk, I can blow it off. Cass can get over herself."

Aubrey laughed. "No, it's okay. Go meet with Mom. It's probably important. Can you just... keep all of this between us?"

"Of course." Alix rested a hand on Aubrey's shoulder. "But you know that you should—or, rather, *can*—tell your parents, right? It would be okay."

"I know it would. And maybe I should. I guess I'm just not entirely sure of how to even start that conversation."

Alix smirked. "I don't recommend the way you started it with me."

"Oh, you mean I *shouldn't* drag Rowan over here so that I can kiss her in front of my parents and then use that to force the conversation?" Aubrey asked dryly.

"I mean, it would certainly work, but I'm not sure that's really the way you'd want to go about it."

"No. Probably not. I'll think of something."

"I'm sure you will." Alix hugged her again. "It'll be okay, Aubrey. I promise. You'll figure this whole thing out, and if you need anything, anything at all, you know where to find me."

"Wherever the nearest trouble or otherwise deadly thing is?"

Alix grinned as she released Aubrey and headed for the door. "You know me so well."

Rowan was sitting alone at a table in the underground vigilante-only bar in the Village, staring at her bottle of beer instead of drinking it, when Zach Carter and Andrew Sullivan joined her.

"Mrs. Carter spoke with you?" she asked Zach.

"She did. She told me you wanted to talk to me about the Galaxy Boys, which is why I brought Flare here."

Rowan winced. "I'm not sure this is something he's going to want to be hearing, sir."

"I can handle it," Andrew growled. "What's my idiot son gotten himself into now?"

There was a pause as Rowan took a sip of her beer as if steeling herself. "The thing is, sir, I have no idea. The entire gang is missing."

Andrew's expression froze. "What do you mean by 'missing,' Fuse?"

"I mean that they always act in the section that I'm responsible for, and I haven't seen or heard from them in days. I was getting daily complaints that they were pickpocketing people in my area, but before I could get a chance to talk to them they completely disappeared. Nobody that I've talked to has seen them in any other part of the city, and I don't think they're hiding from me, because they've never given a damn before."

Zach drummed his fingers on the table. "What do you want to do?"

"I-I don't know. I was going to ask you if you think I should look into it."

"Of course you should," Andrew said irritably.

"Andrew," Zach said in a quiet voice.

"*What*, Zach? My son is missing, do you really think—"

"What I think," Zach interrupted calmly, "is that if it *wasn't* Seamus, you'd take a few more minutes to consider our options before you sent Rowan here off to chase somebody who might not be missing."

Andrew opened his mouth to argue, but instead he closed it again and bowed his head.

Zach looked at Rowan. "How many people are tentatively missing?"

"Five. Diego 'Pluto' de la Fuente, fire manipulation. Galen 'Mercury' Beitel, phasing. Joshua 'Jupiter' James, electricity manipulation. Rabi 'Neptune' Amjad, earth manipulation. And..." Rowan cleared her throat uncomfortably. "And Seamus 'Mars' Sullivan, fire manipulation."

There was a long moment as Zach frowned down at the table, thinking. "Okay. Give it a few days, say three, to see if they show up. We can't drop our responsibilities to look for people who are, let's face it, criminals, when they're most likely just hiding. I know we've been dealing with some disappearances, but these guys have been known to go off radar because they don't want to deal with Seamus's dad. If you don't hear anything on them by Wednesday, Rowan, you can start looking into this."

Rowan nodded. "Yes, sir."

"I want to be involved," Andrew said immediately.

"No. Flare, you aren't very reasonable when it comes to Seamus. You'd make things worse. We'll keep you up to date, I promise, but if you get involved you're only going to get someone killed. Okay?"

Andrew looked prepared to argue, but after a moment, he nodded. "Fine."

"Good. Now go home. Doesn't Emma have her first at-home senior year tennis match tomorrow?"

"Yeah."

"Then go home, get some sleep, watch your daughter play, and worry about your son later. I *promise you* that if something's happened to him, we'll find out." Zach put a hand on Andrew's shoulder. "All right?"

Andrew gave a long, slow sigh. "All right. I trust you, Kov, but I'm still going to worry."

"I don't blame you. But if I see you anywhere near the Legion base tomorrow, I'm going to punch you in the face."

The other man gave a weak laugh. "Thanks, Zach."

"Not a problem," Zach said brightly. "Now go on, get out of here."

Once Andrew had walked away, Rowan said, "Do you really think it's nothing, Kov?"

The smile on Zach's face was gone. "I don't know, Fuse. But I do know what happened the last time this many criminals started going missing." He stood up slowly. "And too many good people have ended up dead already."

"Yeah. I'm aware."

59

Zach paled, startled and embarrassed. "I-I'm sorry, Rowan, I forgot."

"Don't be sorry. It's okay." Rowan fidgeted with her wrist cuff, a distant look in her eyes. "I just hope we won't need to add to the list."

Sunday was extremely quiet, with almost no activity on the patrols. This made it extremely easy to convince the younger members of Heroics—Ciaran, Isaac, Logan, Riley, and Jacob—to go to their classes the following day with the family and friends who weren't involved with the group, due to either being too young, in the case of Logan's younger brother, Thomas, or not having powers, like Ciaran's cousin, Emma and younger brother, Rick.

During school hours, patrols were made up of Kate and Ray, with occasional assistance from Alix and, if necessary, Zach. With Zach no longer being the only liaison, Monday's patrol this week was made up of Kate, Ray, Alix, and Max.

"I never really took into consideration how school would affect the patrols you guys do," Max said as he jumped from one rooftop to another, following Ray.

"It's always been a factor for us. When I was a kid, we would go to school, come home, do a patrol, do homework, do another patrol, then go to bed and do the whole thing again the next day," Ray said. "Once it's routine, it's pretty easy to pull off."

Max gave a soft laugh. "I guess homeschooling wasn't an option?"

"For us, no, because our boss at the time, Stephanie, wasn't too big on the idea of vigilantism in the first place. She wanted us to be 'useful members of society,' or whatever the hell her actual reasoning was, so she made sure we went to a real school. As for the current group of kids, trust me, they tried to convince us that homeschooling was the best option. None of us bought it. Believe me when I say that the only reason Blitz and the others wanted to be taught at home was so they could do the bare minimum amount of work and not have to actually do anything. Nobody fell for that." Ray hopped over a small gap between roofs. "Do you have kids, Wraith?"

"No."

"Do you want kids?"

"Not really." Max paused. "I like them, but I don't really want any of my own."

Ray grinned at him. "Damn. I was hoping I could pawn mine off on you."

Max snorted. "Not a chance, Blackout."

They got to the next street and saw a small group of armed men running out of a pawn shop. "*Thank hell,*" Kate's voice said in their ears. "*They aren't robbing a bank.*"

"Are banks... worse?" Max asked hesitantly.

Ray laughed. "No, but we have a habit of ending up in fights with bank robbers, so we're convinced that 85 percent of criminals in Caotico are here just for that purpose."

Max shrugged. "Money is easier to handle than whatever *schlock* these guys are stealing, I'd bet."

"Unless they're stealing pawn shop money."

"True."

A purple arrow hit the bag one of the robbers was carrying, causing it to split open and spill jewelry and watches all over the sidewalk.

"Sorry to ruin your theory, Blackout."

"Well, that's just rude, Targeter." Ray grabbed a pipe that went down to the sidewalk and slid down it.

After following, Max said, "This should be fun."

"Isn't it always?" Ray hit a robber who had decided to run at him with a small burst of electricity in the chest. When the man dropped to the ground, unconscious, Ray said, "That was pretty dull, actually." He adjusted his sunglasses. "Targeter, get down to street level. We should do some one-on-one combat. You haven't really done that in a while, and it's no good for you to get out of practice."

"See you in a second."

Literally a second later, Kate was on the ground, courtesy of a pipe similar to the one Ray and Max had used. She immediately engaged the robber closest to her, while two more got into a fight with Max and Ray. The two remaining robbers ran, but they had barely gotten five feet away when they found themselves in front of Alix.

"Hi there," she greeted, a grin on her face. "You're missing all of the action."

Both robbers pulled guns out of the backs of their pants. One of them, the taller one, said, "And you're missing a gun, *hero.*"

"That problem will be resolved in a minute or so," Alix replied calmly.

Max knocked out the robber he had been fighting and moved to give her a hand, but Ray, who had also disabled his opponent, put a hand on his shoulder. "You want to know what you're dealing with, don't you?" Ray asked with a smirk. "Just watch."

Alix just stood there as the robbers pointed their guns at her. The taller robber seemed to be getting frustrated. He took a step forward, putting the barrel of his gun in her face. This seemed to be what Alix had been waiting for, as she immediately pushed the gun aside, grabbed the robber by the wrist, flipped him onto his back, kicked him once in the head to disorient him, and aimed the gun at his accomplice.

"There," she said, not even out of breath. "Now I'm not missing a gun."

As Kate, who had knocked out her own opponent, joined Ray and Max, the last remaining robber stared at the gun in Alix's hand. Then, very slowly, he set his gun on the ground and raised his hands.

"Nice decision," Ray said. He walked over to him and hit him in the back with a small sphere of electricity, knocking him out. "Unfortunately for you, I don't really feel like tying you up." He looked at Alix. "Little sloppy this time, don't you think?"

Alix shrugged. "I was just waiting for him to get in my space."

"They might've gotten into your space with a bullet."

"Aw, come on, Blackout, don't ruin it." Alix looked past Ray to Max, who was staring at her with a blank expression on his face. "You okay, Wraith?"

"Uh, yeah," Max said, his voice slightly hoarse. He cleared his throat. "I'm fine. Definitely. I g-guess I just wasn't really expecting that."

Alix laughed. "You really thought I was useless without my powers, didn't you?"

"N-Not at all," Max stammered. "I just d-didn't' know you were that... effective."

"I have my moments." Alix checked her watch. "Oh, hell, I was supposed to be at work fifteen minutes ago. I'll see you guys later." She turned and practically sprinted down the street to where she had parked her sport bike.

Kate shook her head slowly. "That woman was more organized when she was half-insane and dying."

"Don't tell her that," Ray said in a warning tone. "She might try it again."

"I doubt it." Kate looked at Max, who was watching Alix leave and had barely heard them talking. "Hey, Wraith, you still with us?"

"Yeah, absolutely," Max said, turning his gaze back to her.

"Good. Because we've still got work to do."

As Kate and Ray headed off down a nearby alley, Max glanced back at where Alix had gone once more. He then shook his head quickly, as if to clear it, and followed the other two vigilantes.

As Alix hurried through the front door of the Wechsler Industries corporate headquarters, the front desk secretary, Jung Choi, glanced up at her and smirked.

"Not exactly a good example for your employees, are you, Alix?"

"I don't know what you're talking about," Alix replied as she hit a button on the elevator.

The secretary scoffed. "I'm sure. Bet you don't know what a watch is, either."

Alix hid her left arm behind her back. "Nope. Never seen one before in my life." She stepped into the elevator, laughing quietly, and hit the button for the third floor.

The third floor housed the security offices of Wechsler Industries, which were staffed by several people and were run by Alix. When she stepped out of the elevator, she was immediately met by Whitney Finnegan, who looked completely unsurprised by her tardiness.

"I was listening in on this morning's call so I would know when you were going to show up. I gave Jones and Rodriquez their assignments while I waited."

"I knew I promoted you for a reason, Finn," Alix said with a grin.

The younger woman raised an eyebrow. "To do your job for you?"

Alix clapped a hand on Finn's shoulder. "Yeah, pretty much."

Finn smiled slightly. "As long as you show up on time next week, I'm okay with that."

"Right, going home for your mom's birthday."

"Mhm." Finn's brown eyes were bright, and she was almost bouncing on the balls of her feet. It was more genuine excitement than Alix had seen from her since the younger woman first found out that she still had a family. "I have to make sure to be there, since I missed so many of them when I was a kid."

"What are they going to do, ground you?" Alix asked with a smirk.

Finn flushed red. "No. I-I just want to be there. It's not like I'm obligated, but—"

"Relax. I'm teasing you, Finn. You still haven't quite gotten a grasp on that one, huh?"

"There are a lot of things I don't have much of a grasp on," Finn muttered, her brow furrowed in confusion.

Alix put an arm around the younger woman's shoulders. "That's okay. You're good at your job; that's all that matters."

Finn let out a slow, thin breath and started leading Alix to her office. "Speaking of jobs, you should probably get back to yours."

"You're my second-in-command, not my secretary, Finn."

"I'm not sure there's a difference, Alix."

Alix paused in her doorway. "Fair enough." She entered her office and sat down behind her desk, turning on the monitors that showed all of the security cameras in the building. "Has there been anything interesting today?"

Finn leaned against the door frame. "Nothing that's made it up to me. I know that Jones doesn't really like reporting things, though."

"Jones is an irresponsible jackass who only got this job because Cass and Casey like hiring people Heroics has beaten the crap out of to give them a second chance." Alix leaned back in her chair, staring at the stack of monitors in front of her. "It's a good goal, but not always one that works out. In the case of Jones, I don't think it's working out."

"I've never really thought putting those types of people in security jobs was a good idea," Finn agreed quietly.

Alix gave a small smirk. "You're right. Nobody that Heroics has fought could ever redeem themselves enough to be trusted with a badge."

Finn stared at her for a moment, not quite understanding, but after a moment she turned bright red. "Oh. Right. Me."

"Yeah, you." Alix shook her head slowly. "Actual emotional connections have changed you, Finnegan."

"For better or for worse?" Finn asked curiously.

"Well, you actually smile now, so I'm going to go with 'better.'" Alix squinted at one of the monitors and a grin formed on her face. She picked up her phone and hit the number for the front desk. "Jung, could you do me a favor? The woman who's at your desk right now. Send her up to me. But don't tell her it's me. Thanks." Once she hung up, Alix said, "Could you go to the elevator and bring me the woman Jung is sending up?"

Finn raised an eyebrow. "I'm *not* your secretary, though?"

"Oh, shut up."

With a short, scoffing laugh, Finn turned and headed back towards the elevator. A minute or so later, she returned with Rowan van Houten. The young woman looked unsure of what was going on, but as soon as she saw Alix, a mixture of embarrassment and fear spread across her face.

"Thank you, Finn. You can go back to your actual job now."

"I'm surprised she remembers what that is," Finn mumbled as she walked away.

For a moment, Alix and Rowan just stared at each other, with Rowan standing in the doorway, not moving. Then Alix gestured to the chair in front of her desk. "By all means. Have a seat."

Rowan bit her lip and sat down, setting the paper bag she was carrying on the floor. She ran a hand through her hair and pulled her black leather jacket tighter around herself. "I knew Aubrey didn't work on this floor. I was curious as to why I was redirected."

"I guess now you know," Alix said mildly.

"I guess now I know."

Alix leaned forward, resting her arms on her desk. She glanced at the paper bag. "Food delivery?"

"Uh, yeah. Aubrey is often the sort of person who forgets to leave for her lunch hour, but she also sometimes forgets to bring her lunch from home. She left this in her apartment this morning."

"So she made you go get it?"

Rowan hesitated. "Not... exactly. I stopped by the apartment to pick up something I'd left there, noticed it, knew she'd forgotten it, and figured I'd drop it off since I'd be in the area."

Alix gave a small smile. "So you have keys to her apartment."

There was a pause as Rowan seemed to struggle for words. "Y-Yeah. Is that a problem?"

"Absolutely not." Alix held out a hand. When Rowan took it, Alix pulled the younger woman forward so that she was closer to the desk. "I have no problems with you at all. But I'm also very fond of Aubrey Hamil. My only concern is her well-being."

"That's my only concern as well," Rowan replied, her voice calm.

"Then know that if you ever need anything, for any reason, you can call me. Aubrey doesn't get attached to people easily. If she's attached to you, you matter. Which means that her well-being is connected to whether you're safe just as much as it is connected to whether she's safe. I know what the field looks like, kid. I know what it can do to a person. I'm sure you do, too. So if you need something, ask me. I can help."

Rowan swallowed. She seemed to be trying- and failing-to keep her hand from shaking. "I'm not so great at asking for help," she admitted.

Alix laughed softly. "None of us are. Why do you think we spend so much time running towards people who are yelling for it?"

"I'll make you that promise on one condition," Rowan said, tightening her grip on Alix's hand.

"Which is?"

"You make the same promise back to me. Because Aubrey talks about you a lot. She loves you. And if I can do anything to make sure that she doesn't lose you anytime soon, I'd like the opportunity to do so."

They stared at each other for a few seconds until Alix loosened her grip on Rowan, allowing the younger woman to sit back more comfortably in her chair. "That's a promise, van Houten."

Rowan gave a small nod. "Then I promise."

"Good." Alix nodded at the bag at Rowan's feet. "Now, you'd better get that to Aubrey before she has a lunch of potato chips and whatever else she can get out of the vending machine."

"She only gets whatever is in vending machine option number thirty-three, so god knows what she'd end up having." Rowan stood up, but didn't leave Alix's office. "Did you have me brought here to size me up, or what?"

"I don't need to do that. I trust Aubrey's judgment. If she approves of you, then so do I; unless I see some serious evidence to the contrary. I brought you up here for two reasons: one, to make sure you understand that being a part of Aubrey's life means that I'm here for you if you need me. Two, to make sure you understand that being a part of Aubrey's life means that you're going to need to put up with crap like this pretty much all the time."

Rowan laughed sharply. "You're not all as uptight as she can be?"

"Ah, no. She's the most reasonable person in her entire family."

"Sounds like fun."

"Oh, trust me, van Houten," Alix said as she turned back to her monitors. "You have absolutely no idea."

Rowan stopped in front of the doorway to Aubrey's office and watched the woman hunched behind the desk for a moment. Aubrey looked tired already, despite having only been at work for a few hours. She was staring at her computer screen, her head resting on one hand while her other hand rested on the mouse. Before each click of the mouse, Aubrey would tap her desk three times with three fingers. It was something that Rowan had never seen her do before, which she was pretty sure was a bad sign.

Aubrey leaned back in her chair and rubbed at her eyes, sighing. As she lowered her hands she noticed Rowan, and a smile formed on her face. "What are you doing here?"

"You forgot this," Rowan said as she entered the office and handed the bag to Aubrey.

"Oh, hell. Thank you." Aubrey stuck the bag in a drawer of her desk while Rowan took a seat in the chair across from her. "You didn't have to bring this all the way over here."

"I have a shift in about an hour. It wasn't that far out of the way." Rowan looked down and started fiddling with the leather cuff around her wrist. "Plus, y'know, I haven't spoken to you since Saturday, so..."

"I'm sorry. I needed a quiet day yesterday."

"Understandable," Rowan said softly. "Doesn't look like you got much sleep for a quiet day, though. How did your talk with Alix go?"

"Fine. She was very... Alix... about the whole thing. And she promised not to tell anybody about us. She's leaving that up to me." Aubrey closed her eyes and massaged her temples for a brief moment. "I just needed to shut everybody out for a day, but it didn't help much. I couldn't sleep. I kept convincing myself that if I fell asleep, I'd oversleep and miss work."

"You do that every Sunday. At least, you do every Sunday you're off your medication."

Aubrey gave a dry laugh. "Your protest has been noted, Rowan."

71

"I'm not trying to talk you into doing something you don't want to do," Rowan said, her voice still gentle. "I'm just acknowledging that some of your worst issues go away when you're medicated."

"I can live with the worst issues. They aren't so bad."

"Really? You look exhausted, *miláček*."

"You're just mad that it's not your fault I'm tired."

"*Aubrey!*" Rowan said sharply.

"What do you want from me?" Aubrey asked, glaring at Rowan. "What do you want? The meds muddle my brain. They cause everything to slow down; they make me think like..." She paused, beginning to spin her ring around on her finger. "I can deal with being obsessive-compulsive. I can't deal with my brain working at the speed of everyone else's. I just..." Her voice cracked slightly and she lowered her head.

Rowan stood up, shutting the door to Aubrey's office. She then moved behind the desk and leaned against it just to Aubrey's left. In a low voice, she said, "You're pushing yourself too hard. You need sleep."

"I need to finish my work, no matter how long I need to stay here tonight and the next few days," Aubrey insisted.

"How good of a job will you do if you're half-asleep?"

Aubrey gave a long, slow sigh. "You have a point."

Rowan bent down and kissed her quickly. "I usually do."

"Arrogance doesn't suit you," Aubrey said with a scoff.

"That's a shame, because I'm so good at it."
Rowan grinned. "Go home as soon as you're done tonight, okay? Please?"

"Oh, all right." Aubrey rubbed the back of her neck. "It's an easy victory, since I'm too tired to really argue."

"This was easy? I'd hate to see what a difficult fight with you is like." Rowan pulled Aubrey forward and kissed her on the forehead before standing up and heading for the door. "I'll talk to you later?"

"Absolutely. Try not to die."

Rowan laughed. "Haven't managed to die yet."

"Great, now you've jinxed yourself." Aubrey leaned back in her chair and ran a hand through her hair. "I love you."

"Love you too." Rowan opened Aubrey's office door. "Seriously, *miláček*, actually go home at five today."

"I will."

Rowan grinned. "You'd better."

AJ walked into the control room, where Niall Sullivan was in the process of giving directions to Ray via the communications system. Once he was done, he turned around in his chair. "AJ. Need something?"

"Nah. It's almost eleven, so I figured I'd just come down and wait for my shift to start." AJ took a seat next to Niall. "How's everything going today?"

"Pretty fine. Alix got a chance to show off to the new guy before she ran off to work, so I'm sure she appreciated that." Niall ran a hand through his black hair and sighed. "I'm a little worried, though."

"What about?"

"Andrew told me that one of the Legion heroes reported to Zach that Seamus's crew has gone completely silent. Absolutely no contact. Now, Zach wants to give them until Wednesday in case they're just being, y'know... criminals... but I'm not sure I'm comfortable waiting that long. He's my nephew, AJ. I want to know he's okay."

AJ smiled slightly. "He's also twenty years old and known to be a problem. I'm not saying that nobody should look for Seamus and the others, but you can give it a few more days, Niall."

"What if they can't last a few more days?" Niall demanded. "What if something's happened to them?"

"Niall..."

"No, AJ, I'm serious. At the very least, let me mention this to Ciaran."

AJ folded his arms across his chest and studied Niall as the younger man drummed his fingers against his chair. "If you tell Ciaran, there's a very good chance he'll tell the other kids and they'll all run off and do something stupid."

Niall scoffed. "They wouldn't do anything *too* reckless."

"We're talking about the people who once held a competition in the backyard over who could destroy a wasp's nest more thoroughly without being murdered by all the wasps."

There was a pause as Niall just stared at AJ. "Okay, this is a fair point. We have very stupid children."

"They're aren't stupid. They're just too confident for their own good." AJ leaned back in his chair. "I can't stop you from telling Ciaran. It's your family. It's your call. But try to make sure he understands that he shouldn't run off half-cocked and get himself killed when it's entirely possible that nothing is wrong."

"I can do that. Or, at least, I can try. He *is* an Oliver."

AJ gave a dry laugh. "There's really not much hope for you, then."

Matthias was lying on the couch in the mansion library, just watching as Brooke paced back and forth in front of him. "I want to *do* something," she complained.

"You already bought every soccer ball in stock at three sporting goods stores."

"I needed to be prepared!"

He raised an eyebrow at her. "For what, the soccer recession?"

Brooke sat down on his legs. She was still bouncing a bit, though today it seemed more out of agitation than excited energy. "You're not funny."

"I'm a little funny."

"Not as funny as me."

Matthias started playing with her watch, which was hanging loosely on her wrist. "How are you feeling?"

"I'm starting to become aware of the things I'm not supposed to be doing, which is always a fun time." Brooke moved her arm so that she was holding his hand. "You and your patience. It's the one thing you do better than me."

"I wear glasses better than you do," he joked.

He immediately realized it was the wrong things to say, as she immediately stole his glasses off of his face and put them on. "Please," she said. "You never stood a chance. Look how good I look."

"I can't *see* you."

"I'm starting to get a headache."

"You deserve it."

"How do you see out of these things?"

Matthias sat up and took his glasses back. "It's really easy when your vision sucks."

Without warning, Brooke yanked him forward by the front of his polo shirt and kissed him. Matthias pulled back and quickly readjusted his glasses. He shook his head slowly, smirking. "You're a mess, Hamil."

"You keep coming over, though."

Matthias sighed. "Why do I get the feeling you'll be the death of me?"

"No idea. Though I've heard we Hamil girls cause that feeling a lot." Brooke stood up. "I need to *do* something. Maybe if I get rid of some of this energy I'll cool down a bit. I've gotten like twelve hours of sleep total the past four days and that's probably not a good thing."

"*Probably?*"

Brooke thought for a moment. "Hey, Mat..."

"I'm not sleeping with you, Brooke."

"Dammit. You will one of these days."

Matthias sighed again. "Ask me when you aren't buying out Soccer Xpress, downing vodka, and only sleeping three hours every night."

"Well, that's boring."

"Them's the rules, darling." Matthias stood up, stretching his legs to get the blood flow back into them. "Do you have any *other* ideas?"

Brooke chewed on her lip for a longer moment. "We could always see if the others have any good missions that our parents wouldn't approve of. I like that idea!"

As she bounded out of the room, Matthias sighed for a third time and started to follow her. "Death of me. *Death. Of. Me.*"

5

Rowan was sound asleep on the couch in Aubrey's apartment when Aubrey walked in a little over a half-hour after her workday ended. Aubrey gave a scoffing laugh and headed over to the sleeping woman. As she sat down on the table next to the couch, she murmured, "Wow, really, Ro? How am I supposed to prove that I actually did leave when I was supposed to if you aren't awake to see it?"

There was no indication that Rowan had heard her, as she simply shifted on the couch and continued to sleep. The movement pushed her shirt up, high enough that Aubrey could see the small tattoo just below the right-hand side of Rowan's rib cage, a red sixteen-spoke wheel. Aubrey smiled thinly and reached out, resting her fingers on the tattoo lightly.

Rowan snapped awake, grabbing Aubrey's wrist in one hand while a ball of orange light formed in the other. She recognized Aubrey immediately and the light faded. "Hell. Give a girl some warning, Hamil!"

"Sorry. I was looking at your tattoo."

"You look with your hands?" Rowan raised an eyebrow. "You're odd, you know that?"

"Oh, shut up."

Rowan glanced at her watch. "Well, what do you know. You actually managed to get home at a reasonable time."

"I did. I feel ill, but I did."

"Relax." Rowan rested a hand on Aubrey's knee. "You're fine. The world isn't going to implode because you didn't work overtime doing stuff that wasn't your job."

"Yeah, yeah." Aubrey set her hand down on top of Rowan's. "What are you doing here? You usually go home after your shifts."

"My mo—" A troubled look formed on Rowan's face. "My apartment building was getting some work done in it, so it was pretty loud. I didn't feel like staying there all afternoon."

"Reasonable enough." Aubrey shifted so that she was lying down on top of the table she had been sitting on. "Well, this is far less comfortable than I thought it was going to be."

Rowan still seemed bothered, but since Aubrey hadn't seemed to notice, she forced a smile. "Aren't you supposed to have an intelligence power?"

"It's more picking things up really quickly and being great at memorization," Aubrey said in a mechanical voice, as if she had answered the question several times before. She paused before turning her head towards Rowan, who was giving her a look. "Oh. Right. You already know that."

"I've known you for two years and dated you for almost just as long; I'm pretty sure it's come up before now," Rowan laughed.

"Yeah, well... shut up."

"Your retorts today are *fantastic*."

Aubrey groaned quietly. "Can we do something so that you can stop mocking me?"

"Do something out or... at home?" Rowan asked with a smirk.

"*Out,* you jackass," Aubrey said, lightly punching Rowan in the arm.

Rowan laughed quietly before saying, "We never did get to that bar."

"Alcohol. Perfect. Let's go."

Justin was in the process of packing up his bags to leave the office when his door opened and a man in a military uniform entered. "Justin Oliver?"

"I'm sorry, Justin Oliver already went home for the day, seeing as it's six o'clock and work lets out at five."

The man folded his arms across his chest and glared.

Justin sighed. "Yes, that's me. Who are you?"

"General Harry Reznik. You've probably seen me on television."

"Oh, of course. You're the guy telling everybody that the heroes are a danger to society and completely useless anyway because *you're* here to protect us."

Reznik smiled slightly. "Mr. Oliver, you were around a little over a decade ago when this city fell into utter chaos thanks to those vigilantes that you call heroes. They've done very little to repair the damage they caused this city. Crime rates are just as high as they've always been in Caotico, and the crimes are getting more and more absurd as criminals try to think of more ways to outsmart the vigilantes. Trust me, if this city wasn't still a mess, I wouldn't still be stationed here. But here I am, because Caotico City is an utter disaster."

Justin scoffed. "This is all very fascinating, General, but why don't you skip the campaign speech and get to the part where you tell me what you want from me?"

"Not very friendly, are you, Mr. Oliver?"

"I'm not very trusting of people who badmouth the ones who are out on the streets every day, fighting to keep me and my family safe," Justin retorted with a humorless smile.

"Of course." Reznik took a few steps towards Justin. "But I do wonder, Mr. Oliver, whether your passionate defense of the vigilantes doesn't have more personal motives."

Justin's expression didn't change. "Pardon?"

"Well, the other day, one of your warehouses was attacked. And Heroics personally came to diffuse the situation."

"Stopping criminals is what Heroics does, General. I can't control where or when they show up." Justin shook his head slowly, giving a small laugh. "If that's your evidence, sir, I have to say that it's not very good."

"It's just the latest in a stream of very suspicious activity surrounding Wechsler Industries," Reznik said. "For example, the company hires people that Heroics sent to prison. It also pays for damage done to vigilantes."

"If you're referring to our Second Chance programs and our Hero Insurance policies, I can certainly direct you to those departments, which I believe you will find to be completely legitimate business ventures. Mrs. Hamil and Mrs. Carter wholeheartedly believe in helping this city as best they can, and if that includes assisting in matters involving the heroes and the aftereffects of their activities, then that's what this company is going to do. None of that is illegal."

Reznik smirked. "Not yet."

Justin stiffened, his hands tightening into fists. "Are you threatening me, General?"

"Absolutely not, Mr. Oliver. I'm threatening the people who involve themselves with vigilantes." Reznik leaned forward slightly. "And that doesn't include you, right?"

Justin's jaw twitched. "I can quite confidently say that I have done nothing wrong," he said in a quiet, cold voice. "Now if you don't mind, I would like to get home to my family."

"Oh, of course."

They stood there for a moment, staring at each other, until Justin said, "That was a dismissal, General."

Reznik continued to smirk. "Naturally. Have a good night, Mr. Oliver."

"I'm not sure I wish you the same, General Reznik."

The general gave a soft laugh and walked out of the door. Justin swallowed and leaned against his desk, realizing that, for some reason, his hands were shaking. Something about the general had given him a bad feeling, one that told him that he and the others were in for a fight. And judging by Reznik's confidence, it was not going to be an easy one.

"What do you mean *missing?*" Brooke asked as she circled the table where Matthias, Ciaran, James,

Logan, Jacob, Thomas, and Rick were sitting in a corner of Casey's bar.

Ciaran's grip on his soda tightened as he shook his head slowly. "I don't know. Dad said that the Legion hasn't heard from Seamus or his crew in a little while."

"Well, that's completely unacceptable."

"I would've asked my mother whether they were doing anything, but she doesn't care about anybody, so…" Ciaran shrugged. "I didn't bother."

"Ciaran," Rick mumbled, giving his brother a disapproving look.

"What? Am I *wrong*? I—"

"What are we going to do about it?" Brooke interrupted, putting her hands on the table and leaning forward.

Thomas frowned at her. "We're not supposed to do something about it."

Logan laughed and ruffled her little brother's auburn hair. "Oh, Tommy. Sweet, sweet Tommy. You don't know us very well at all, do you?"

The boy groaned loudly. "We're going to get in so much trouble."

"Don't worry, buddy," Jacob said with a grin. "You're the baby. The baby never gets in as much trouble as everyone else. Trust me; I know. It was me until you were born."

"I'm younger than you, too," Riley protested.

"Yeah, but you're not a Wechsler. We got in a whole hell of a lot more trouble by ourselves than we ever got in with the rest of you."

"He has a point," James said. He rubbed the back of his neck. "I know you, Brooke. You've already thought up some crazy scheme all on your own. So what's the plan?"

"Why are we encouraging this?" Matthias asked with a moan as he put his face in his hands.

"Because it's fun." Brooke leaned against the bookcase and put her hands in her pockets. "We should go explore the old warehouses."

"Cool," James said.

"No," Rick said simultaneously.

"Oh, come on, bro. They aren't *that* dangerous."

Rick gave Ciaran a tired look. "Easy for you to say. You throw pointy objects at criminals every day. Nothing is dangerous from your perspective."

"Richard."

"Oh no," Rick muttered as Logan turned her chair towards him, put a hand on his leg, and moved in close to him. Rick swallowed and leaned back, flushing red. He cleared his throat and stammered, "W-What do you w-want, Logan?"

She pouted at him. "I want to know why you don't want to help your cousin. I'd do anything to help *my* cousins. Don't you love Seamus?"

Rick groaned and bowed his head. "I hate you. You're the worst."

Logan snickered. "I am not. You're just too easy."

A muffled noise of irritation came from Rick's throat, and he said, "Fine, okay, we'll go."

"Good!" Logan grinned and shifted her seat back into position. She handed a bowl of peanuts to Thomas, who was clearly trying not to laugh.

"This is probably a bad idea, but I won't let you go without me," James said. "I might not have powers, but I have a pretty good left hook." He smirked slightly. "At least, I do according to that jackass on my lacrosse team that I knocked out."

"Didn't you get a two-game suspension for that?" Thomas asked.

"It was worth it. He was being offensive towards my moms."

"I would say that I'm surprised, but I'm really not," Logan said. "I *am* damn proud, though."

"Ugh, don't congratulate him," Rick groaned. "We lost both games he missed."

James shrugged. "It's not my fault I'm the only good goalie we have."

"Sad but true."

"Well, I think this is a terrible idea, and you're going to get yourselves killed," Matthias said.

Brooke rolled her eyes. She rested her arms on Matthias's shoulders and her chin on the top of his head. She softly carded her fingers through his sandy-brown hair as she said, "Come on, Mat. *Please?*"

"You're going to lean on me until I agree, aren't you?"

She put more of her weight on him. "Yes."

"... Fine."

"Great!" Brooke stood straight up but kept her hands on Matthias's shoulders. "So, we need to—"

"Do I want to know what you all are doing?" Kaita asked as she walked over to the table to hand-deliver a soda to Thomas.

"Absolutely nothing," Thomas said. "Thank you."

"At least you're polite." Kaita put her hands in her pockets. "Seriously, do I need to call somebody, because I really don't want any of you doing something dangerous."

"Relax, Kaita, we're just going to see if we can find out where the Galaxy Boys are. It's nothing serious."

"That sounds like something serious, Logan," Kaita said slowly.

"It's not." Logan leaned back in her chair. "Have you heard anything through your connections about what might have happened to them, or any of the other missing people?"

Kaita shook her head. "I don't know anything."

Logan smirked. "Is this kind of like how we 'don't know' that you and Finn have been screwing off and on for the past year?"

The bartender paled and shot a quick glance at the blonde-haired woman who was seated at the bar, casually sipping a gin and tonic. "I-I don't know… what you mean…"

"Of course you don't." Logan slowly drank from her own glass. "What's she doing here, then?"

"It's a bar. People can be at bars."

"They can, but Finn's here an *awful lot* for someone who doesn't drink that much. Almost like she's actually here for the—"

"Logan."

"*View*," Logan finished with a smirk.

Kaita sighed. "I will kill you."

"And you're my godmother, too."

"That means I have permission to kill you."

"Is that really what that means? I personally think you're just mad that—"

"I. Will. Finish. You," Kaita interrupted with a growl.

Logan's smirk turned into a huge, mischievous grin. "Hopefully not the same way you 'finish' Finn."

Kaita just stared at her, completely lost for any response. After a long moment, she picked up a few empty soda bottles from the table, avoiding eye contact with the kids. "I hate you. Don't get killed. Try to stay out of trouble. I'll see you later," she said awkwardly.

The kids watched as Kaita walked over to Finn at the bar, absentmindedly ran her hand down the other woman's back, and whispered something to her. Finn immediately choked on her drink and gave the table of kids a terrified look. She flushed bright red, downed the rest of her gin, and disappeared into the back room that Casey had added on to the bar a few years earlier.

Brooke leaned down to whisper in Matthias's ear. "I wonder if she realizes that we know Kaita has a room back there."

"She's probably just trying to get away from all of us. You don't actually have proof of anything, you know," Matthias said patiently.

Brooke laughed and ran her fingers through his hair. "You're adorable." She patted his shoulders excitedly. "We should get going. We'll call Riley and Isaac on the way over. And... there's one other person we should bring into this."

"Who's that?" Jacob prompted.

"The person who actually knows her way around the warehouse district, and the only one of us who ever managed to figure out how to pick locks." Brooke looked at her brother expectantly.

"No. Absolutely not. If she doesn't want to be a part of this family, then I'm not going to bother trying to include her." Jacob folded his arms across his chest. "No way."

"She *did* help you with the math for your project."

Jacob gave a long, slow sigh. "Fine. Whatever. I'll call Aubrey."

"Don't bother!" Brooke took Matthias's jacket off the back of his chair and put it on. "Track her phone; we'll pick her up from wherever she is on our way out. It'll be harder for her to play the good child and rat us out then."

After playing with his phone for a moment, Jacob said, "Well, that's convenient. She's already in the warehouse district. The Kingsway Caterers building."

Ciaran gave a sharp laugh. "That's a front for an underground bar." He paused. "That I... know nothing about... because I'm not old enough to drink... and that would be wrong."

"We're at a bar right now, Ciaran. I'm not sure you need to make that pitch." Brooke pulled Matthias out of his chair, saying, "If we go right now, we'll be far enough away before my shift's supposed to start that I can just call my mom and talk her into staying late."

"That's not very nice of you," Jacob said.

"Do you want to go do it?"

"Absolutely not."

"Then shut your mouth and let's go see if we can find ourselves some answers."

6

"This is a bar?" Aubrey asked weakly as she sat down next to Rowan in a booth in the far back corner of a loud, crowded room.

"I suppose it's more a club," Rowan said as she took a sip of her beer. "Everyone refers to it as a bar, though, so the terminology gets a bit muddled."

A waitress brought a margarita over to Aubrey, who took it and handed over the requisite payment, as well as a small tip. The waitress proceeded to wink at her before turning away.

Aubrey flushed. "I'm very gay," she muttered.

"If only it was obvious enough that people actually realized it," Rowan said dryly.

"I take pride in how easily I've convinced everyone that I'm straight," Aubrey replied as she absentmindedly watched the waitress walk away.

Rowan lightly hit her in the back of the head. "Uh huh. I think everyone is just very, very blind."

Aubrey smirked and started to play with the collar of Rowan's jacket. "Oh, you're no fun." She pulled Rowan towards her slightly. "Live a little, van Houten."

"Are you already drunk? You didn't even take a sip of that margarita yet. And you're toeing the line of your not-in-public rule."

"I'm not drunk. I've just had a very long day, and I've decided to hell with it. I'm relaxing for five minutes. As for the public rule, this place is so busy that nobody's paying us any attention. I can risk a little bit of closeness."

"You're ridiculous, you know that?"

Aubrey laughed softly. "No, that's what's going to happen when you get me drunk."

"Oh, *I'm* getting you drunk?"

"Yes. I'm going to hand you a credit card, and you're going to keep ordering me drinks until any more would make it impossible for you to get me home." Aubrey yanked Rowan even closer to her. "Think you can handle that?"

Rowan swallowed. "I can't really tell if I'm scared or wishing that we could go back home now instead of drinking."

Aubrey laughed again. "Too bad, van Houten. We're drinking tonight."

The other woman gave a soft groan as Aubrey released her. "You're mean."

"I know. It's a character flaw."

"Yeah, well—" Rowan broke off as something in the crowd caught her attention and she paled. "Brooke."

"What?"

Rowan practically jumped away from Aubrey, putting a good foot of distance between them in the booth. "*Brooke.*"

Aubrey turned and saw her sister making her way over to the booth through the crowd. "Why does this keep happening to me?" she mumbled.

"I think it's a sign," Rowan muttered.

"Oh, don't you start."

Brooke stopped in front of the booth. She stood where she was, bouncing on the balls of her feet. "Aubrey! We need to talk. We—" She eyed Rowan cautiously. "Who's this?"

"It's okay. This is Rowan. She's in on the joke."

"I'm a friend," Rowan clarified.

"A rather good friend," Aubrey said, smirking slightly.

"Nice to meet you, Rowan. I'm Brooke."

As she and Brooke shook hands, Rowan said, "Aubrey's told me a lot about you."

"I'm sorry to say she hasn't told me anything about you." Brooke's gaze shifted back to Aubrey. "We need to talk about a missing friend of ours. Come on! Outside!"

"Oh, come on, I didn't even get a chance to drink anything!"

"Well, y'know, sis, that's tough." Brooke took Aubrey by the arm and pulled her to her feet. "We're on a *mission*."

"Crap. The goal-oriented symptoms of yours are always the most annoying."

"Don't be boring. Come on."

Aubrey shot Rowan a helpless look as Brooke dragged her out of the bar. Rowan immediately set her beer bottle down on the table in front of her and followed them.

Outside, in an alley behind the bar, Brooke, Aubrey, and Rowan joined the rest of the kids, who had been met along the way by Riley and Isaac.

"Oh boy," Aubrey said. "Whatever this is, it's probably a horrendous idea."

"That's what I said," Matthias mumbled.

"I told you we shouldn't have gotten her," Jacob grumbled at the same time.

"Shhh!" Brooke turned to face Aubrey. "Look, here's the deal. Seamus and his little gang are missing. We're going to go look for them. We need you in case we need to lock-pick our way into any buildings."

Rowan grinned and looked at Aubrey. "You know how to pick locks?"

"We had weird competitions when we were children, now hush." Aubrey met Brooke's gaze steadily. "The Legion is going to look for Seamus starting on Wednesday. Why not let them do that?"

Ciaran took a small step towards Aubrey, looking at her suspiciously. "How could you possibly know the Legion's timeline for this? My dad only told me, and I only told these guys a few minutes ago."

Aubrey glanced at Rowan, who extended a hand to Ciaran. "Rowan van Houten. The Legion calls me 'Fuse.'"

Ciaran just stared at her, and Rowan lowered her hand slowly. "You're a... Legion hero?"

"Yes."

"Then maybe you can tell me why the hell no one has been looking for my cousin," Ciaran demanded aggressively.

Rowan's calm expression didn't change. "I reported what I knew to Kov and Flare. It was agreed that due to the criminal nature of some of the activities the Galaxy Boys are involved in, they could quite possibly have disappeared of their own free will. Kov decided not to have me look into the matter until a decent amount of time had passed, so that we had a better handle on whether they were missing intentionally or unintentionally."

"So you're the one who knew they were missing?" Isaac asked incredulously. "And you didn't think it warranted some investigation?"

"I do my job as I'm instructed to do it," Rowan replied. "I'm not sure how Heroics handles things, but given this little mob demonstration, I think I can figure that out."

Aubrey stifled a laugh, which earned her a glare from Jacob. "Oh, yeah, go ahead and laugh, sis. You know, I find it *utterly hilarious* that you want nothing to do with the rest of us, yet you're spending your free time with a Legion hero. I knew you were a jackass, but I had no idea that you were a hypocrite, too."

"Jacob, don't," Thomas said softly.

"Shut up, Thomas," Jacob growled.

"No! Rowan's awesome! Don't give Aubrey a hard time for hanging out with her!"

Rowan laughed quietly and ruffled Thomas's hair. "Thanks for the backup, buddy."

"Tommy, you *know* her?" Logan asked, surprised.

"Of course. She comes into the bar. Mom and I have both known her for a while." Thomas looked around the group, a confused expression on his face. "Wait, none of you know her? How is that possible?"

"I don't really care, honestly," Jacob said. "I'm tired of Aubrey acting like she's so much better than the rest of us. And now she's going to bars with people who are just like us? Give me a break."

Aubrey's brow furrowed. "Better than... What the hell are you talking about?"

Before Jacob could reply, Brooke said, "Guys! Mission! Focus!"

Logan gave her a tired look. "The relationship between your siblings is completely falling apart, and you're—"

"Mission!"

"Right."

"Aubrey, will you please just help us out?" Rick pleaded. "I want to know if Seamus is okay."

There was a pause as Aubrey thought, spinning her ring around her finger. "Okay, fine. But we're doing this carefully, all right?"

"How else would we do things?" Logan asked with a smirk. She looked at Rowan. "What about you, Legion? Are you coming too?"

"Aubrey's going, so I'm going," Rowan replied. She shifted awkwardly as Aubrey shot a warning glance at her, but no one in the group seemed to notice anything odd about the response.

"Time to do some searching," Brooke said as she turned and led the others out of the alley.

Alix looked up and laughed when she noticed Max standing in the doorway of her office. "I guess I need to figure out how to improve security so that people like you can't just walk through the wall."

"Well, that's easy," Max said as he took a seat in the chair across from her. "It's all a matter of materials. In my case, gold, silver, platinum. I can't phase through any of them."

"So I won't be seeing you stealing any gold bars in the future?"

"No, but that's mostly because I'm no criminal."

"That's what you say." Alix leaned back in her chair. "What do you need, Wraith?"

"The Legion has sensors set up in some of those old warehouses in Fuego. Some of them have gone off. Since I'm meant to get acquainted with Heroics some more, I wanted to see if you wanted to go check up on it with me."

Alix shrugged. "Can't hurt. I was supposed to leave hours ago anyway. How did you even know I was here?"

"I called your base. Cass told me."

"Cass is on? She's supposed to..." A look of realization formed on Alix's face, and she smiled. "Ah. I think I might know who's breaking into those warehouses."

"Oh? Going to fill me in?"

"Nah." Alix stood up, putting on her black denim jacket. "Come on, Wraith. Sadly, we probably won't get to beat anybody up."

"Aw, man. I really wanted you to get to beat somebody up." Max reddened slightly. "I mean, I really wanted to beat somebody up."

"Trust me; that's the only reason I was going," Alix joked as she headed for the door, grabbing Max's hand and pulling him along with her.

"Thanks a lot," Max mumbled.

"No problem. Shut the door behind you."

"How did we end up the lookouts?" Jacob grumbled as he paced in front of the door of the sixth warehouse the group was exploring.

Riley, leaning against the wall of the warehouse, smiled humorlessly. "Maybe it's because you're being a miserable little jackass."

Jacob looked surprised. "What do you mean?"

"Come on, J. You can't tell me that you don't see that what you're doing to Aubrey is unnecessary."

"It's not my fault she decided to run off and get herself a job in the city," Jacob retorted.

"You mean like my father did?"

Jacob shuffled his feet awkwardly. "That's not what I mean. Justin earned his retirement. Same with Kara. Aubrey just..." His voice trailed off and he stared down at the ground.

Riley, frowning slightly, stepped forward and rested her hands on his shoulders. "J, what's wrong? Come on. You can talk to me."

Before Jacob could say anything, the warehouse door opened and the other kids walked out. "Not a damn thing," Ciaran grumbled in response to Riley's questioning look. "I'm starting to wonder if this is hopeless."

"I'm starting to wonder if we're just going to end up getting arrested," Isaac said as Aubrey worked on getting the door locked behind them.

"You wouldn't go to jail," Ciaran said. "Your mom's a cop."

"Is that supposed to make me feel better? She doesn't even *work* for the CCPD anymore; all she does is help them exchange training with Mexico City law enforcement."

"That's a *good thing*, Isaac," Matthias said. "She was missing her home country. She gets to go back occasionally while still doing her job here and being with her family."

"There's no point to that," Isaac snarled. "There's no point to missing home. It's just another place."

Rowan gave a quiet, scoffing laugh, and Isaac immediately rounded on her. "You think that's funny, Legion Girl?"

"Nothing about that is funny at all. It's sad, to be honest. That you care so little about what your mother cares about."

Isaac took a few steps towards Rowan, looking angry. "What do you know?"

"Not much. But I know a few things about missing a home country, and I know a few things about missing family. I know how your mother probably feels. I just think you should give her some patience."

"You don't know *anything*," Isaac spat. "All of you Legion heroes are the same. You're all spoiled brats from spoiled families who've never experienced anything bad in your lives. Why don't you go home to your life of luxury instead of harassing me?"

Logan, standing off to the side, looked furious, but before she could even say anything, Rowan lunged towards Isaac. Aubrey had apparently anticipated the reaction as she was on her feet, grabbing the other woman around the waist and dragging her backwards at the exact moment Rowan moved.

"*Jdi do prdele!*" Rowan yelled as Aubrey pulled her away.

"Rowan, stop!" When they were a decent distance away from the others, Aubrey's voice dropped to a whisper that she seemed to think only Rowan could hear, but that Brooke, who had also moved to intercept Rowan, was able to pick up. "Honey, *zklidni se. Zklidni se.*"

Something seemed to have snapped in Rowan and she ignored Aubrey completely. "You have *no idea* what you're talking about, you *bastard!*"

"I know he doesn't," Aubrey said gently. "But he won't learn a damn thing if he's unconscious, now will he?"

Isaac looked almost scared by the anger, but he decided to try to maintain his composure, scoffing and saying, "I'd like to see her *try* to knock me out. I'm not afraid of some Legion coward."

Rowan started towards him again, and it was such a genuine struggle for Aubrey to hold her back that Brooke hurried forward to help. "Isaac, I swear, shut your mouth before someone gets hurt," Aubrey snapped. "I'm serious, because she can kill you, and I'm half-tempted to let her."

"I finally get to tell one of these assholes the truth, and *I'm* the one who gets in trouble?" Isaac shook his head slowly. "What kind of bullshit is that? It's not my fault she can't take it."

"The *truth?*" Rowan gave a sharp laugh that was half-crazed. She looked furious, glaring at Isaac with pure hatred. "The *truth* is that my father was killed in those anti-hero riots when I was nine. The *truth* is that half of my maternal family line died in the *Zigeunerfamilienlager* in Birkenau. The *truth* is that the other half managed to survive in the Czech Republic for only a few generations until I was five and the assumption that Romani are thieving scum got them all burned alive by a vigilante mob backed up by the local police. The *truth* is that I had a little brother *until I was five*. The *truth* is that the only reason I'm still alive is because I was with my father, who they didn't want to kill because he was *white*. The *truth* is that my father had to bring me here from the Czech Republic because he could no longer trust his own country not to *murder his children*."

Rowan was actually shaking, from both anger and the tears that were starting to fall on her face. "So don't you *dare* tell me that I don't understand. Don't you *dare* say that to me, or say that I've never had anything bad happen to me or my family."

When she stopped talking, a heavy silence fell over the area. Isaac was staring at her, looking appropriately horrified. Rowan herself seemed surprised, as if she wasn't expecting to say what she had said. As she relaxed, Brooke let her go, but Aubrey lingered for a moment. "Are you good?" she asked softly.

"Y-Yeah," Rowan said in a hoarse voice.

Aubrey released Rowan, and the older woman stumbled backwards a few steps before just sitting down on the ground and putting her face in her hands.

"Rowan?" Thomas said hesitantly. "Rowan, are you okay?"

"I'm fine, buddy," Rowan mumbled.

"I-I thought you were just tan," Isaac said. He immediately seemed to realize what a stupid statement it was, so he just cleared his throat and looked at his feet.

"Shut up, Isaac," Aubrey said offhandedly. She crouched down next to Rowan. "You don't have to be here, you know. It's okay."

"I'm all right. Sometimes when that trigger flips I just... wear myself out."

"Trigger?"

Rowan looked up at Brooke. "My downside. I can keep my emotions under control just fine. I'm generally a pretty calm person. But there are certain topics that upset me, and when they do, I just..." She snapped her fingers. "It's like the trigger of one of my bombs is going off in my head, and I'm filled with every bit of anger I've ever felt in my life. It's exhausting, and it's dangerous, but I can't really stop it."

"Downsides are like that," Brooke said sympathetically. She was still restless on her feet, but the single track of her brain seemed to have slowed down. She gave Aubrey an odd look. "You seem to know when it's going to happen, sis."

Aubrey, who had been watching Rowan with a worried expression on her face, shook her head. "I've just seen it happen a few times, and I know that Rowan's family is a big way to set it off."

"I-I'm sorry," Isaac stammered.

"Yeah, well, what did I say about patience," Rowan joked weakly. She leaned back until she was laying on the ground and gave a soft groan. "Brooke, you're strong. I'm a hell of a lot more tired than I usually am, and that's all from fighting against you."

"Thanks a lot," Aubrey said dryly.

"Oh, don't be a sore loser, Aub," Rowan mumbled.

"I wasn't competing," Aubrey protested.

Brooke grinned and patted her sister on the shoulder. "That's what the loser always says."

"If we're all done," Jacob said stiffly, "we should probably get going before we actually *do* need to deal with the cops."

"We aren't making any progress this way," Brooke said. "We should break into smaller groups. Logan, Thomas, think you guys could figure out how to slip a lock open with your powers?"

The siblings glanced at each other and shrugged. "We've never done it before, but I'm sure we could manage," Logan replied.

"Good. Then Aubrey, you take Rowan, James, and Matthias, and handle the rest of the east buildings. Thomas, go with Ciaran, Rick, Riley, and Isaac and handle the west buildings. Logan, Jacob, and I will take the north buildings." Brooke reached down, holding her hand out to Rowan. "You good to go, Legion?"

Rowan smiled thinly. "I'll figure it out." She let Brooke pull her to her feet.

"Good. Come on, then."

The groups split up and disappeared further into the collection of warehouses.

"I don't get why we needed Aubrey if you knew we could've used the metal kids," Jacob grumbled as he followed Brooke and Logan into an old, abandoned Wechsler Industries warehouse.

"'The metal kids'? Seriously?" Logan shook her head slowly. "You are a *grumpy* teenager compared to how sweet a little kid you were. Snarky, but sweet."

Brooke laughed loudly. "Don't let him fool you. He's just pissed at Aubrey."

101

"Yeah, I've noticed." Logan squinted at her cousin as he pushed past Brooke to walk further into the building. "What is your deal with that, anyway? Who cares whether she does anything at all regarding Heroics? Richard probably isn't going to, either. He's going to go to school for film studies. I doubt that would be relevant to our interests."

"It's different," Jacob muttered.

"How is it different?" Brooke demanded. "I mean, come on, J, I'm irritated with her disappearing act, too, but you're on a whole other level."

Jacob turned around to face them. "Rick isn't the one who promised not to leave."

Brooke and Logan stopped walking, looking stunned. "What are you talking about?" Brooke asked.

"When Aubrey graduated high school, she *swore to me* that she'd always be there to help me; that she'd always be around for anything I needed. And then it's like something snaps in her head, and she disappears and gets herself her own apartment and stops hanging out at home and gets a job at WI and doesn't even associate herself with Heroics at all." Jacob put his hands in his pockets and looked down at the floor. "I can't talk to her about *anything* anymore. I can get her to do a few math problems for me, but only if I trap her and annoy her into it. Brooke, you were the protective big sister, the one I could talk to about science things. Logan, you were the cool sister, who was basically my age and who could help me know what to do when I was edging towards shy at school. But... Aubrey was the one who looked out for me when I had trouble getting letters and numbers straight in my head. She was the one who made me feel better about my head, and then she just left." His voice cracked as if he were about to cry. "So yeah, it *is* different. Aubrey didn't just abandon Heroics. She abandoned me. And I think I'm allowed to be mad at her for that."

Brooke swallowed. "J..."

"It doesn't matter." He turned on his heel and continued deeper into the warehouse.

Logan glanced at Brooke. "Little brothers, huh?" she asked softly.

Brooke gave a weak laugh and put an arm around Logan's shoulders. "I'll have to try that line on Aubrey."

"You really think Jacob is ever going to tell Aubrey what the real problem is?"

"No." Brooke sighed. "But I think I'm going to have to do it for him."

"Good luck with that. You haven't been talking to Aubrey, either."

"True, but I'm pretty sure I have a few things to talk to her about after today."

"Oh?"

"I need to think on it a bit. Right now we just need to worry about what we're doing." Brooke was bouncing on the balls of her feet again.

"Of course. I'll go catch up with Jacob. Make sure he's not getting himself into trouble."

"Thanks."

As Logan jogged off, Brooke looked around the warehouse. She started to follow her cousin, but she froze as a hard metal object pressed against the back of her head. She raised her arms slowly. "We aren't looking for any trouble," Brooke said quietly.

"Funny," a familiar voice said. "I thought that was your main hobby."

"*Son of a bitch!*" Brooke turned around quickly, coming face to face with Alix, who lowered her gun as she fell into a fit of laughter. "That wasn't funny, Al!"

"Pretty sure it was." Alix tilted the gun slightly. "Don't worry. Safety was on, finger wasn't on the trigger, and it's not even loaded." She snapped a magazine into the gun as if proving a point.

Brooke punched the older woman's shoulder. "How did you even get behind me?"

Alix pointed at Max, who was standing a few feet behind her with a confused look on his face. "Mr. Walks-Through-Walls can be pretty convenient at times."

Brooke looked at Max and said, "Next time? Don't let this one drag you into her schemes. She's a jackass."

"That hardly seems fair," Max replied. "You *are* breaking into WI warehouses, after all, and Thief *is* head of security."

"There? See?" Alix gave Brooke a mockingly arrogant look. "I was just doing my job."

"Worst aunt ever," Brooke grumbled as she turned and headed towards Logan and Jacob.

"Excuse me, *best* aunt ever," Alix corrected as she followed.

"Want me to tell Aunt Casey that?"

"Go ahead. She'd probably be willing to disown you three in a heartbeat."

"Seriously, Max, run while you still can. Tell Uncle Zach that you made a terrible mistake by becoming the liaison. It's your only hope."

Max shrugged as he headed after them. "You all don't seem that bad."

Brooke and Alix both laughed. "Trust me, Wraith," Alix said. "We're *worse*."

"I feel like you in particular are—"

Max was interrupted when both Jacob and Logan screamed. "*Brooke!*" Jacob yelled.

"*Jacob! Logan!*" Brooke sprinted towards where the screams had come from.

"Brooke, slow down!" Alix started running after her. "Damn kid's going to get herself killed," she grumbled.

Max, running next to her, said, "Like you'd do any different."

"No, but if we let her get killed, *I'm* the one who's going to have to explain it to Cass."

"You really *are* a terrible aunt," Max joked.

"I could be worse. You never met my creator."

"Creator?"

"Yeah, my—" There was a slight skip in Alix's step as she looked at him. "You don't... know what I am?"

Max frowned. "What do you mean?"

Alix paled, but before she could reply, they found Brooke. She was crouched down next to Jacob, who was sitting on the floor staring blankly ahead of him. "Logan," Alix murmured. She went over to the teenager, who was in the exact same position a few feet to Jacob's right.

As Alix crouched down next to her, Logan whispered, "They're all dead."

"What?" Alix turned Logan's head so that she was facing her. "Logan, sweetie, what are you talking about?"

Logan just whimpered. Alix was about to try again when Max said in a quiet, horrified voice, "*Thief.*"

Alix looked up at him and saw that he was staring deeper into the darker part of the warehouse, a stunned expression on his face. She followed his gaze until she saw a wide pool of blood. Five bodies were scattered inside of it, each with varying degrees of trauma. "Oh, hell," Alix whispered.

There was a quiet groan, and one of the bodies moved just slightly. Max rushed over and knelt down next to the teenage boy, ignoring the blood that immediately began to soak through his jeans. Diego de la Fuente's dark skin made it difficult to see the blood that was quickly drying on him, but he was clearly severely injured. His black hair was matted and sticking up in odd directions, and his brown eyes were glassy and unfocused.

"Hey," Max said gently. "Hey, kid. It's all right. We're going to get you some help, okay?" He glanced back at Alix, who pulled her communication glasses out of her pocket. "Just relax, kid. Don't try to talk." Max positioned himself so that the teen couldn't see the other bodies. "Just stay awake, buddy. You only have to stay awake."

Max looked up at Alix, and she saw her own sick horror reflected in his eyes. She pulled Logan into a tight hug, gently running her hand over the teen's strawberry-blonde hair. Then she put her glasses on.

Cass's voice came through clearly. "*What's up, Thief?*"

Alix swallowed, the words not quite able to come out.

"Thief?"

She swallowed again. "Control."

"Thief, what's wrong?"

Alix took in a slow, deep breath, her gaze shifting from Max to the body only a foot away from him, a brown-haired young man barely out of his teens. "We found the Galaxy Boys," she whispered. "We found Seamus."

7

Most of Heroics continued as usual after the massacre in the warehouse, though the three members who had been closest to Seamus Sullivan were put on inactive duty until further notice. Niall and Kate were busy attempting to comfort Andrew, his wife, Erica, and his daughter, Emma, while Ciaran had locked himself in his room at home, angry and frustrated and convinced that he could have done more. Rick, stunned into almost perpetual silence, lingered at the base, finding mutual comfort in Logan, who seemed shaken to the core by what she had seen. The horror of finding the bodies had also not been lost on Jacob, who could not be coaxed out of his bedroom by anyone, not even his mother.

"This is crazy," James said as he sat down at his kitchen table across from his mother, Claire. "I mean, this is *insane*. How could something like this happen?"

"That's what everyone's going to have to figure out," Kara said, next to him at the table.

"Speaking of things to figure out," Claire said slowly.

"Uh oh," Kara mumbled. "Run, Jimmy."

Claire smiled like she couldn't help it, but she quickly suppressed it as she gave her son a stern look. "What were you thinking? Going out there like that? You could've gotten yourself killed."

"I want to help people, Momma. I'm not going to say no when I'm given the opportunity."

"That's reckless, and it's irresponsible," Claire said. "You can't just run off half-cocked into something that you have no information on. You were looking for known criminals who had gone missing, in a section of Fuego that could have who knows what kind of people in it. Doing what you did was... You just can't do things like that, James."

"Mom did," James replied icily.

"Your mom had training and powers and she still almost died," Claire retorted. "That's not a good defense! I'm not going to sit here and say nothing while you—"

"Honey," Kara interrupted softly. "Calm down."

"How am I supposed to be calm when—"

"Claire."

There was a pause as Claire took a long, slow breath. She swallowed and said, "I know you want to help, James. I get it. I'm proud of you for it. If I wasn't proud of that kind of courage, I could never have married your mom. But four people *died* yesterday, son. All with powers, one the child of someone we know. If you're not careful, that could end up being you, and I... I-I don't think I could survive that."

James reached across the table and rested his hand on top of one of Claire's. "Nothing's going to happen to me, Momma. I promise."

Kara gave a soft laugh. "Oh, don't promise her that. I made that promise too many times when you were little. She might shoot you."

"So this is all *your* fault, Mom?" James asked, grinning slightly.

"Most likely. A lot of things are."

Claire gave a weak laugh. "You two are going to be the death of me."

"Haven't managed yet," Kara joked. She leaned back in her wheelchair and squinted at James. Her voice returned to a more serious tone as she said, "James, please just be careful. You don't realize how terrifying it is to know that you're doing stuff that can rather definitely get you killed."

"I'll be careful, Mom." James gave a small grin. "I promise."

Kara made a disgusted noise. "That was terrible."

"I know." James stood up. "I have to get to school. I think Rick, Logan, and Jacob are all staying home, but I'll swing by the mansion to pick up Thomas and double check with them anyway."

"Okay. Be careful."

"Always am, Momma."

Claire scoffed. "Don't start this conversation again."

James laughed, kissed both of his mothers good-bye, and headed for the door. Once he was gone, Kara said, "He'll be okay, you know, Claire."

"I used to say that about you," Claire said softly.

"Well, yeah, but it's not like I'm not *okay*."

"True. The stuff with Seamus and with James still wanting to be a cop are just sort of combining in my head and freaking me out right now."

Kara wheeled around to the other side of the table, positioning herself next to Claire. "*He'll be okay. Kid's got your blood, not mine. He's too smart to get himself killed.*"

Claire gave a genuine laugh and pulled Kara forward by the collar of her shirt, kissing her deeply. "You're not so dumb, you know."

"Please, I'm a *jock*. How smart could I possibly be?"

"Smart enough to marry me," Claire teased.

"See? Told you I was dumb."

Claire laughed again and rested her forehead against Kara's. "In case this was in question? I don't regret or resent the things you did for our city, Kar. Not one bit of it. I worry for James because he doesn't have the powers to protect him if things go wrong. How many times did your abilities save you? I've seen crime-fighting in this city take too many lives already. I don't want our son to be one of the casualties."

"I completely understand that," Kara said gently. "I agree. I just think we might not have much of a say in the long run."

"Curse of parenthood, huh?"

"Sort of the intended end result, really."

"Did I ever tell you that I'm pretty sure you're better at this parenting thing than I am?" Claire asked. "I know it's been seventeen years of this, but I'm still pretty sure."

Kara chuckled and kissed her. "Yeah, well, I'm better than you at a lot of things, Tyson."

Claire smirked. "Not running, though."

Her wife laughed and leaned back in her chair. "Oh, we're going for the low blows now? Why don't I remind you of that time when it was almost James's twelfth birthday and you forgot the actual date, and I had to tell you what it was? Despite the fact that *you're* the one who actually gave birth to him? I wasn't even dating you then, and I still remembered the date better than you."

"He's still your son, too," Claire grumbled. "When I forget these things, it's your job to remember them."

"It was his *birthday*, Claire. We have *one* child."

"I don't like this game anymore."

"Yeah, because you're losing," Kara snickered.

Claire yanked Kara forward again and kissed her until she couldn't quite remember what she was laughing about. Claire then stood up and headed for the bedroom. "I need to finish getting ready for work. So do you."

Kara was still for a moment, staring straight ahead blankly. "That was mean!" she yelled once she finally regained the ability to speak.

"I know!" Claire replied cheerfully.

"You're quiet this morning, Thomas," James commented as he drove his truck towards the younger boy's school. "Are you okay after last night?"

"I guess so," Thomas said softly. "I'm still trying to figure a few things out."

"About Seamus and the others?"

"Yeah," Thomas agreed, though there was hesitation in his voice, as if he wanted to say something more.

"Thomas? Is there something else?"

The boy paused, the blue eyes he had inherited from his mother narrowed in thought. "Why do people hurt other people?"

James gave a soft laugh. "Trust me, buddy, if I knew the answer to that I would've fixed humanity a long time ago." He glanced at the ring on his right hand, a circle of metal that he had made out of the remains of the piece that had gone through his mother's spine. In a whisper, he added, "I wish I knew."

112

"I'm scared."

"What of?"

Thomas fiddled awkwardly with his lunch bag. "I'm scared for Dad and Logan."

James ruffled Thomas's hair. "I know. I was always scared when my mom was out in the field. It's tough, being the guy who has to wait. But I think you can handle it a lot better than I could."

"You do?"

"Yeah. I was a complete baby about it."

Thomas paused, frowning slightly. "Hey... weren't you an *actual* baby?"

James pushed Thomas's head to one side playfully. "Yeah, but I was hoping you wouldn't remember that."

The boy snickered and ducked away from James's hand. "I'm smarter than *that*, James!"

"I wasn't sure," James teased. He fell quiet for a moment as he pulled to a stop outside of Thomas's school. "Hey. Can you keep a really big secret for me?"

"Yeah!"

"You know I turn eighteen in a few months, right?"

The boy nodded. "Four, right?"

"That's right. Well, for my eighteenth birthday, I'm going to change my name."

Thomas's eyes widened. "To what?"

"Prince Cornelius Bartholomew Evelyn III."

"Really?"

James laughed. "No, idiot. I'm changing it to James Tyson-Hall."

Thomas grinned widely. "*Really?*"

113

"Yep. My mothers never saw a reason to change it, because Mom was always my mom and they had nothing to prove, but... I'd rather have both of their names. Do you like that?"

"James Tyson-Hall," Thomas repeated slowly. His grin widened further. "I like it a lot."

"Good," James said, his grin matching the boy's. He messed up Thomas's hair again and said, "All right, enough of that. Get to school, kid."

Thomas groaned and started to get out of the truck. He paused before shutting the door. "James?"

"What?"

"Thank you."

"Never a problem, buddy. Now get out of here before we're both late."

James lingered long enough to make sure Thomas got into his school. Then he put his truck into drive and headed towards his own.

In the Wechsler Industries headquarters, the adult members of Heroics—minus Niall and Kate—held a meeting inside Casey's office.

"Where's Brooke?" Ray asked as he took a seat next to Kara.

"Keeping an eye on the kids that stayed home." Cass paused. "I'm also not sure she's... all that okay, either. I think she called Matthias and asked him to come over."

"Not a good week for her to deal with this kind of thing," Alix muttered.

"Never a good week for any of us to," Justin said quietly. He drummed his fingers on the arm of his chair. "Do we have any idea what happened?"

Kara sighed and leaned back, taking a sip of her coffee. "I talked to a doctor that Kate and I know who works at the hospital. Mara Jones. She said Diego de la Fuente remembers nothing about what happened to him, but he was beaten for several hours and then shot twice. One bullet managed to only graze him, which is the only reason he was still alive when he was found. The others were also shot, but their other injuries varied from repeated cycles of drowning and resuscitation, electrocution, stabbing in areas that would guarantee pain but not death, and suffocation. They were all dumped in that warehouse, still alive, about twelve hours before they were found." Kara paused for a long moment. "If the kids had been about two hours earlier... Galen Beitel, the sixteen-year-old, probably would've survived as well. He was the last to die."

"Hell," Max whispered. "We probably shouldn't tell them that."

"I certainly don't plan to," Zach said. He was repeatedly folding and unfolding a metal pen that was resting on the table in front of him. "If I had just..." He cleared his throat. "If we had bothered to look into this earlier..."

"Don't do that," Casey interrupted firmly. "We don't know what really happened here. Maybe you would've figured it out. Maybe you would've cleared that warehouse earlier and we would've never found them. Maybe whoever did this would've gotten you, too. There are too many maybes here. Don't over-think it."

"Andrew will blame me," Zach whispered.

Casey shook her head, but instead of saying anything she just leaned against him and took his hand in hers. AJ patted her on the shoulder briefly before saying, "Honestly, this is up to the rest of you, but I'm not sure we should patrol the abandoned district until we have a better idea of what's going on. Clearly numbers didn't matter. Five young men very skilled in superpowers were brutally murdered, and nobody knew about it until it was too late for four of them. I'd rather not risk sending anybody into the areas they frequented until we know more."

Justin gave a tired sigh. "Normally I'd argue with you, AJ, but I have to say that I can't. I don't see a run-into-the-fray game plan working out too well for us." His voice lowered to a whisper. "And I'd rather not see my daughter lose her life because I went overboard."

"I'm good with that plan," Ray said. "You know me; I like the safer plans. I might go for the risk, but only if I've thought out my options."

"I'm going to suggest that the Legion do the same." Zach glanced at Max. "Provided you agree."

"Absolutely. I saw what happened to those kids, too."

"What were you and Rowan doing there, anyway?" Zach asked curiously.

"Oh, we weren't together. I asked Thief to come with me to check on the alarms that were going off, since I'm supposed to be learning more about Heroics and whatnot. The kid was already with the others when I got there."

"She's friends with my niece," Casey said.

116

"Brooke?"

Casey frowned at Cass. "No, Aubrey."

"Aubrey was out last night too?"

"Yeah," Casey said slowly. "Didn't she talk to you?"

Cass shook her head. "I haven't talked to Aubrey since... Saturday?"

Casey hesitated. "AJ, has she talked to you since then?"

"No. Is something wrong?"

There was another pause as Casey sighed. "After this, I need to talk to you both."

"There isn't much more I can think of," Ray said. "We all just need to be more careful."

"We will. As careful as any of us *can* be, anyway." Zach kissed Casey quickly and stood. "I have to get out onto a patrol. You coming, Wraith?"

Max was having a whispered conversation with Alix, who was smiling slightly despite the seriousness of the meeting. It took a moment, but he looked up when called. "What was that?"

"Are you going to do your damn job today?"

"Oh. Yeah. Of course. Sorry." Max mumbled something to Alix, stood, and followed Zach out of the room.

In the elevator down, Zach chuckled and shook his head slowly. "You've got to be kidding me, Max."

"What do you mean?" Max asked, frowning.

"Gee, I dunno. You ask Alix specifically to go with you to check on the alarms. You have whispered conversations with her. You stare at her like a fricking idiot. It's been like *three days*; did you really fall that quickly?"

"I don't know what you're talking about," Max said innocently.

"You *cannot* date Alix Tolvaj," Zach groaned.

"Hypothetically, why not?"

"Because if you do, you'll be the second liaison *in a row* to have picked up a Heroics person. Either no one will ever want the position again, or too many people will."

"So you screw up and now I can't date anybody?" Max teased.

"Yes. That is exactly what I'm saying."

"Uh huh." Max smirked. "Your future recruiting troubles aren't really my problem, Kov."

"I figured." Zach hit the stop button on the elevator, preventing the doors from opening. He then grabbed Max's shoulder and lightly pushed him up against the wall. "All right, here's the deal, Max. I like you. You're a nice guy. You're talented. You're smart. But that won't mean a damn thing if you can't accept something extremely important about Alix."

"And what's that?"

"She's ace."

"You're right, she is quite awesome."

An irritated look crossed Zach's face. "I mean that she's asexual."

Max's calm expression didn't change. "Yeah, I know what you meant. Why the hell would that matter to me?"

"Because it could. And if it does, you're going to step off right the hell now, because I don't really feel like finding a new liaison, and if you hurt that woman, I'll kill you."

"Zach, I want to get to know her. And I think that when I do, I'll want to date her. And if she'll have me, that's what I'm going to do. The fact that she might never sleep with me has no impact whatsoever on that."

For a long moment, Zach just stared at him. Then, slowly, he turned and flipped the elevator back on, allowing it to complete its journey to the bottom floor.

"You guys care about her a lot, don't you?" Max asked softly. "You, Casey, Cass, AJ... all of you treat her like she's another one of your family."

"She is family," Zach replied. "Any one of us would die for her, and she'd return the favor."

"She's certainly not lacking in loyalty," Max commented.

Zach gave a thin smile as the elevator doors opened. "No; she's certainly not."

"You seem distracted, Fuse," Alex "Sketch" Wolfsong said, watching Rowan pace back and forth across the roof they were standing on. "Is everything okay?"

"I just had a long night," Rowan muttered as she formed a bomb in her hand and then made it disappear.

"The mother or the girlfriend?"

Rowan gave a dry laugh. "You ask that as if they're anywhere near the same level of stress."

"I wasn't saying that the girlfriend kept you up because of *stress*," the other hero teased.

"Oh, shut up." Rowan continued to pace, repeating the bomb creation and disposal movement as she went. "I was out with that group that was looking for the Galaxy Boys."

"I thought you were told to wait on that?"

"Yeah, well, sometimes things happen." Rowan bit her lip. "I was with Aubrey for a while afterwards, but then I went home and my mother was still up, and, well, that's never a fun experience."

"She still throwing dishes at you?"

"No; she ran out of them. Now she throws books."

Wolfsong shook her head slowly. "You need to get help with her, Fuse."

"Would if I could," Rowan said weakly. She handled one of her bombs incorrectly and it went off, lightly scorching one of the fingers on her left hand. She let out a short series of curses in Czech.

"Here." Wolfsong drew a bandage in the notebook she was carrying, tapped it once with her finger, and then held out her hand with her palm facing upward. In less than a second, a bandage formed in her hand.

"Thanks." As Rowan taped her finger, she said, "I've taken to consider it practicing. Y'know, for dodging."

"Girl, if you aren't an expert at dodging at this point, you're *never* going to be."

Rowan scoffed. "Thanks, Sketch." She felt her phone begin to vibrate furiously in her pocket and she pulled it out. "Aub? What's wrong? You never call me when I'm on patrol."

"*She's... gonna tell.*"

The other woman's voice was strained and breathless, and she sounded close to panic. Rowan's grip on her phone tightened. "What are you talking about? What's wrong?"

"I told Aunt Casey I'd tell Mom and Dad about my meds," Aubrey said quickly, now sounding like she was crying. *"And I was supposed to do it by end of yesterday. And I didn't. She's gonna tell them, Rowan."*

"Where are you?"

"Office."

"I'll be there in five minutes. Just breathe, okay? It's going to be all right." As Rowan hung up, she shot Wolfsong an apologetic look. "I need to go. I need to take care of something. I'm sorry."

"It's okay. Go ahead." Wolfsong watched as Rowan headed for the ladder down to the street. "Oh, but, Fuse?"

"Yeah?"

Wolfsong looked almost sad. "Try to take care of yourself sometime, yeah?"

Rowan gave her a weak grin. "I imagine I'll have the chance to when I retire." She hopped onto the ladder and climbed down out of sight.

Rowan pushed Aubrey's office door open and shut it behind her, squinting to see in the dark. "Aubrey? Did you turn the lights off or are you not in here and I'm an idiot?"

"Couldn't take 'em bein' on. Head hurts," Aubrey mumbled. She was sitting on the floor with her knees up to her chest and her back against the wall. Her breath was quick and ragged, right on the edge of hyperventilation.

"That's okay," Rowan said as she got on her knees next to Aubrey.

"It hurts," the other woman managed, her fist tightly gripping a clump of her shirt near her heart. She was sweating and shaking, her free hand tapping furious sets of three against her knee.

"I know, *miláček*," Rowan said softly. "But it'll pass." She gently stroked Aubrey's hair. "You'll be okay. Just let it work itself out."

Aubrey leaned into Rowan, letting the other woman run her hand up and down her back comfortingly. After several minutes, Aubrey's breathing began to calm, and Rowan felt her start to relax.

"There you go," Rowan whispered. "There you go. *Zklidni se.*"

Aubrey gave a quiet sigh and buried herself in Rowan's shirt. "Thank you," she murmured. "For putting up with me."

"It's not 'putting up with' you, Aub. It's being there when you need someone to be there. That's not a burden." Rowan lifted Aubrey's chin so that they were looking at each other. "You're not a burden."

"Sometimes it feels like I am. I think Brooke feels like that too on her bad days. Our brains have given us a lot, but not all of it has been good." Aubrey rubbed her eyes. "Aunt Casey has to tell Mom and Dad about my medication. I promised her. I made a deal."

"That's okay. It'll work out."

"I can't go back on them, Ro. I *can't*. They just make me slow down, and where will I be then? I already feel tired from trying to keep up with what I'm doing here. If I go back on the meds, it'd be a complete disaster."

"Then tell them that," Rowan said gently. "Aubrey, you can *tell them that.* I know your head is telling you otherwise, but try to ignore it just this once. They're worried about you. *I'm* worried about you."

Aubrey took in a shaky breath. "You're always worried about me."

"Force of habit." Rowan slowly pushed Aubrey's hair off of her face. "It'll be okay, Aubrey. You'll get through it. You know Mrs. Carter wouldn't do anything that would hurt you."

"Doesn't make it easier."

"It probably never will. Luckily for you, you're strong enough to push through it. And you have people to help you when you struggle." Rowan put her hand on top of Aubrey's. "I'm not going anywhere, *miláček.* I promise."

Aubrey pulled her forward and kissed her lightly. "Thank you." She set her head against the wall and closed her eyes. "You know what?"

"What?"

"I'm going home."

Rowan gave her an incredulous look. "At noon on a Tuesday?"

"Yeah. I have plenty of off time I can use, and I really don't feel like being here anymore. Plus I'm really, really tired. I was having trouble sleeping last night. Too much running through my head."

"We could form a club," Rowan joked as she stood and held out a hand to pull Aubrey to her feet.

Once she was standing, Aubrey hugged Rowan tightly. "Thank you," she repeated.

"Never a problem. Now come on. Talk to whomever you need to, and let's get out of here."

"I can't get the image out of my head," Brooke murmured as she laid on the couch, her head resting in Matthias's lap.

Matthias gently ran his fingers through her hair. "It'll fade. It may never go away, but it'll fade."

"Can you invent brain bleach?"

He scoffed. "I'm just a computer guy. You're the genius, Hamil."

"Mm. One of us should've gone into something more productive than engineering or math. It would've been more helpful in the long run."

"Oh, you mean you aren't brilliant enough to branch out? I'm disappointed."

"Hey, I might not know everything about..." Brooke trailed off, frowning. She elbowed him. "I know you're just trying to distract me, jackass."

"I don't know what you mean," Matthias said innocently, pushing his thick-framed glasses up on his nose.

"Yeah, okay."

Matthias closed his olive green eyes and pinched the bridge of his nose. "What time is it?"

Brooke glanced at her watch. "Four."

"AM?"

She laughed. "No, PM. It can't feel that late to you."

"I'm exhausted, so it does a little bit." He absentmindedly linked his fingers with hers. "Also, I haven't done any of my schoolwork."

"That's not *my* fault," Brooke said, smiling slightly. "It was *your* idea to go to grad school."

"You could've told me not to."

"As if you would've listened." Brooke leaned up and quickly kissed him on the cheek. "Thank you for coming over here, Mat. As you've probably noticed, the others are a bit... off."

"So are you."

"Yeah, yeah. Do you think you could do your work here? I have something I want to do, and I don't want to leave the younger kids alone."

"That's fine. I'll stay as long as you need me to."

She grinned. "Best friend in the world, Matthias."

He paused. "Hey, Brooke, are you okay?"

"Yeah, why?"

"You're not as..." Matthias hesitated. "Okay, this is going to be worded *incredibly poorly*, so I apologize in advance, but you aren't as... depressed... as I was expecting."

Brooke laughed softly. "You *want* me to run a razor blade up my wrists again, Hobbes?"

"No, no, absolutely not, I just... You went through a lot. You *saw* a lot. And usually when something like that happens, you swing as far away from manic as you can get and stay there for weeks. It's actually a bit concerning that you haven't, and I'm worried that you're trying to hide it."

"Relax, Matthias, I know what you meant. And trust me, a lot of the thoughts are in there. But I can't fall apart yet. Not when my siblings are coming apart at the seams." Brooke bit her lip. "I doubled my medication. And since my version of bipolar disorder is a downside, I can hold it in just a little bit. I can't afford to go off the rails right now. It's exhausting, but I can't afford to let it out."

"You should sleep, Brooke," Matthias said softly. "You still haven't slept properly."

"Can't. The medication has never worked very well to combat the insomnia, and luckily for me that's managed to be a symptom in me in both manic *and* depressive episodes."

"Does anyone actually sleep around here?"

Brooke gave a short, sharp laugh. "I honestly don't think so." She rolled off of him and stood up. "I should head out."

"Are you leaving?" Jacob asked, having suddenly appeared in the doorway.

"Yeah, J. I need to go have a talk with Aubrey."

Jacob scoffed. "What for?"

"Because she's our *sister*, and I want to *have a conversation with her.*"

"Good luck. I already told you that she doesn't talk to us anymore."

"She was talking to us last night, wasn't she?"

"Yeah. Look how well that went. Apparently she's bad luck."

"J, that's unreasonable."

"I know it is. But at the moment, I'd rather not think about whether any of this is *reasonable*," Jacob snarled.

126

"Come on, buddy…" Brooke started, but he had already turned on his heel and left. She shot a helpless look at Matthias.

"At least he left his room."

"Yeah, but he'll probably just go right back."

"It's okay. I'll keep an eye on him."

"Thank you, Matthias."

"You owe me one," he joked.

"I'll do your next assignment for you," she said, lightly pushing his head back as she turned and headed for the door.

"Don't kid. I'd take you up on it," Matthias called after her.

"Don't be surprised if you get kicked out of grad school for it," Brooke replied.

"You wouldn't do that to me," Matthias said hesitantly.

Brooke smirked at him. "Keep telling yourself that."

"If anyone knocks on my door, you're gonna have to hide in my closet," Aubrey said casually, squinting in at her assortment of clothes.

Rowan, sitting on Aubrey's bed, raised an eyebrow. "Aw, come on, I was already in the closet for like five years."

"That was a terrible joke."

"That was a *great* joke."

Aubrey picked a softball up off of her desk and tossed it at Rowan, who caught it easily. "You have a terrible sense of humor, then."

Rowan shrugged. "I can accept that." She looked back down at the book she was reading, one of Aubrey's old college textbooks. "*Nenávidím matematiku*," she mumbled.

"You *hate math*?" Aubrey looked offended. "Rowan, I'm sorry, but we have to break up."

Rowan gave a sharp laugh. "I love your love of the subject, but it makes absolutely no sense to me. Chemistry? Physics? Fine. Calculus? Not a chance in hell. Senior year math might have been the only time in my entire school career that I got anything higher than a D, but that doesn't mean we exactly got along."

"You aced history that year, too. And isn't chemistry basically math?" Aubrey asked, turning back towards her open closet.

"Well, yeah, but it's still different." Rowan paused. "Honey, maybe you *should* consider going back on your meds."

"Why?"

"Because you're organizing your closet so that every clothes hanger is exactly three centimeters apart."

Aubrey blinked and looked down at the ruler in her hand. She slowly set it back down on her desk. "Oh."

"Is it usual for people with OCD to do stuff like that without even realizing it?"

"I'm not sure. The illnesses that Brooke, Jacob, and I have don't quite work the same way as they work for regular people. I think it's because for us, they're downsides, not necessarily natural mental disorders or disabilities."

Rowan gave a small nod. "I'm familiar with the fun, bizarre nature of downsides." She hesitated again. "And your anxiety disorder?"

A strained smile formed on Aubrey's face. "That's a full-fledged, honestly obtained one. Lucky me." She sat down in her desk chair. "I'm a mess, Ro. You should've given up on me a long time ago."

"You give up on yourself enough. There's no reason for me to add to it."

Aubrey laughed softly. "You're far too good for me, Rowan."

Rowan smirked. "I know. I guess I just have a soft spot for charity cases."

"Jerk."

"That *is* the reputation I was *trying* to maintain. You just keep making it difficult." Rowan walked over and put her hands on the arms of Aubrey's chair. "I'm worried about you, *miláček.*"

"You don't need to be."

"Like that will stop me." Rowan kissed her forehead lightly. "I love you."

"I love you, too."

Brooke glanced at her watch as she walked down the hallway towards Aubrey's apartment. It was 5:10 p.m., which meant it would probably be a while before her sister showed up at home. As she came up to the door, Brooke noticed a light shining from under it, which normally indicated that Aubrey was back from work.

"Weird," Brooke mumbled. On a whim, she knocked.

There was a quick sound of muffled and unintelligible conversation from the other side of the door, and a faint smirk formed on Brooke's face. She waited for a moment, then the door swung open and Aubrey looked out at her.

"H-H-Hey, sis." Aubrey cleared her throat and adjusted the way her shirt was laying. "What's up?"

"I thought maybe we needed to have a chat," Brooke said, pushing past Aubrey and into the apartment. "Did you leave work early?"

"U-U-Uh, yeah. I had some time I could take, and I needed to do it for mental health reasons."

"OCD acting up?" Brooke asked sympathetically.

"Among other things." Aubrey watched as Brooke paced around the empty apartment. "What do you want to chat about, Brooke? This is sort of a bad time."

"I thought it might be." Brooke ran a hand through her hair. "Why don't you talk to us anymore, Aub?"

"I was talking to you yesterday."

Brooke snorted. "Geez, do you and Jacob have a few things in common."

Aubrey frowned. "What do you mean?"

"Nothing. My point, kid, is that you haven't been *talking* to us. Sure, you'll tell us random and unimportant things, but you won't say anything that actually matters. I don't know how you are. I don't even know a single thing that's going on in your life."

"Work," Aubrey said with a shrug.

"Yeah, see, but it's not *just* work. You realize that you can talk to us about, like, important things, right? *Legitimately important things?*" Brooke opened the

130

closet, pulled Rowan out of it by the collar of her jacket, and shut it behind her. "Like *this*, for example?"

Rowan and Aubrey exchanged a quick, scared look. Aubrey swallowed. "I-I-I don't know w-w-what you think—"

"For hell's sake, Aub, you really expect me to believe you're just friends? I *saw* you in that club. You were about half a second away from making out with her. Then when she was about to kill Isaac, you called her 'honey.' And seriously, the entire night you were staring at her like a love-struck idiot. I cannot believe that anyone who has ever seen the two of you together could possibly *not* know that 'friends' isn't exactly the best description of your relationship."

Rowan, who was standing next to Brooke with a stunned and confused look on her face, stammered, "I-I... uh... Wh-What are you... talking... about?"

"It's okay, Rowan," Aubrey said quietly. There was a soft resignation in her light green eyes. "Brooke, I-I-I didn't tell you because I... didn't want you to be mad at me."

The smirk on Brooke's face vanished. "*Mad at you?* Hell, Aubrey, I'd never... Did you really think I would be mad at you for dating another woman?"

Aubrey rubbed her temples. "I don't know. I don't know what I think anymore."

"I would *never* be mad at you for being who you are, Aub. *Never*," Brooke whispered.

"You haven't showed much of that towards me avoiding Heroics," Aubrey replied, though there was no fire in her retort.

The sisters stared at each other for a long moment until Rowan quietly said, "I'm going to go. I think you two need to talk." She headed for the door, pausing next to Aubrey. "Do you need me to come back later?"

"No." Aubrey kissed Rowan directly on the mouth, as if she was daring Brooke to protest. "It's okay," she said once she let the other woman go. "I'll call you."

Rowan squeezed Aubrey's hand briefly, nodded, and left.

Aubrey spun the ring on her finger in three sets of three before asking, "How the hell did you even know she was in there?"

"I heard you talking to someone before you opened the door. And whenever I was grounded and I snuck Matthias over, I always hid him in my closet."

Aubrey snorted. "And you wonder why Jacob, Logan, and I always assume you two are dating. And now you also know why I didn't let Kaita meet Rowan for as long as possible. She would've figured it out immediately if she had seen us together. She's got like a nose for this crap." She walked over and sat down on her couch, resting her elbows on her knees. "What are you going to do now, Brooke?"

"Nothing but talk to you. That's what I came here for." Brooke walked over and sat down on the table in front of Aubrey. "We used to talk. Sure, when Jacob got old enough you talked to him more, but for a long time it was just the two of us. Two stupid kids with brains that didn't quite make sense to anyone around them." She pushed Aubrey's hair behind her ear and rested her palm against Aubrey's cheek. "I just need to know that my siblings are okay. Jacob's mad at the world right now because he's scared and jumping at shadows and *still* pissed at you for leaving him. I can't get through to him. I know that. But I can do something about you."

"Jacob's mad at me for leaving?"

"Yeah. That's why he's so pissy whenever you go near him."

"I thought he was mad because I'm not working with Heroics."

"That's a part of it, but it's more abandonment issues."

"But that... that doesn't make any sense," Aubrey said, confused.

Brooke gave her a sympathetic smile. "Aub, you told him you wouldn't leave and then you did. You can kind of see his point."

Aubrey looked down at the floor. "Honestly, I didn't really think anybody would care if I left."

"Why wouldn't we care?"

"I'm the odd man out, Brooke. Always have been. Hell, you and Jacob even got Dad's darker South Italy/Greek skin, and I got Mom's pale Irish. I have *nothing* in common with you two. With *any* of our family."

"That doesn't make you less a part of it, Aub," Brooke said softly. She gave a small laugh. "You know what's funny? You're *just like Mom.*"

"What? No I'm not."

"You're so much like Mom I'm shocked she and Dad didn't see all the signs of 'definitely has secret relationship going on' already. Which, by the way? From what I've seen of how you and Legion interact, your relationship is almost exactly the same as Mom and Dad's."

"You've lost your mind, Brooke," Aubrey muttered.

"And you're in denial. We're quite the pair."

"I guess I just don't see how anything I'm telling you has anything to do with Mom."

Brooke folded her arms across her chest. "Have you not paid any attention to our parents? Like, ever? Mom's a mess of self-esteem issues and impulse control problems. She spends an awful lot of time convinced that she doesn't deserve the life she has. Does any of that sound even a little familiar, kid?"

Aubrey closed her eyes and bowed her head. "Yeah," she whispered. "It does." She shook her head slowly. "But none of it will matter after tomorrow. Mom and Dad are going to kill me."

"Why?"

"I haven't been taking my prescription. And judging by the number of missed calls on my phone, Aunt Casey told them about it today. They're going to kill me."

"They won't kill you. They care too much. That's *why* they're calling you." Brooke lightly messed up Aubrey's hair. "We all care, Aub. That's what you need to get that brain of yours to believe for once."

An hour or so later, after Brooke had left, Aubrey called Rowan.

"How did everything go?"

"It was good," Aubrey said. "It was... It felt good."

"I'm glad. What's the plan now?"

"Well, I'm going to have to face the music eventually. Might as well do it after work tomorrow."

"I think that's a good idea. It probably won't be too bad. Let me know how it goes."

Aubrey smiled slightly. "Yeah, see, that's the thing... I have a question."

"Shoot."

"What are you doing tomorrow afternoon?"

8

"I sometimes forget that you're rich," Rowan muttered as she and Aubrey walked through the front door of the Heroics mansion.

"*I'm* not rich. *My mom* is rich," Aubrey corrected.

"Same thing in the long run," Rowan said softly.

"Hey." Aubrey bumped her shoulder against Rowan's. "You okay?"

"Hm? Oh, yeah. Just a bit of a rough night."

"You ever going to talk to me about those?"

"Thinking about it," Rowan said tersely.

"Good." Aubrey headed towards an elevator, but before she got there, Alix stepped out of a side room.

"Well, look who decided to make an appearance." Alix folded her arms across her chest. "I heard you've been making quite the disturbance for someone who's never around."

Aubrey winced and started spinning her ring around her finger. "How mad are they?"

"They aren't *mad*, Aub. You know better than that." Alix glanced at Rowan. "Wow. She brought you along? She *must* be worried."

Rowan shrugged. "I go where I'm needed."

Alix laughed. "I'd believe that." She clapped a hand down on Aubrey's shoulder. "You'll be fine, Aub. Go on up. Last I saw them, they were in the library. Once you're done, do you think you could do me a favor?"

"Anything for you."

"Talk to Jacob."

"Just not that."

Alix grinned and playfully pushed Aubrey's head to one side. "He keeps holing himself up in his room. I think he's a bit traumatized. I would recommend therapy, but the last time I did, I was told that it apparently didn't do much for *me*, so what's the point."

"Ouch. If he's throwing that low of a blow at you, I can't *imagine* what he's going to do to me," Aubrey said.

"He loves you. Just maybe not to the best of his abilities right now. Look, he won't even open his door. He came down *once* to steal food and yell at Brooke, and that's it." Alix rolled her eyes and sighed. "This is what your Aunt Casey gets for having a house where the bedrooms have their own bathrooms attached."

"You think he's going to listen to *me? Really?* Come on, Al."

"Well, maybe he'll open the door to throw a shoe at your face?"

Aubrey rolled her eyes. "Thanks a lot, Al."

"Always trying to be as helpful as possible, kiddo."

"I'm sure." Aubrey headed past her, continuing towards the elevator.

Rowan went to follow, but Alix grabbed her arm. The younger woman immediately flinched, fear lighting in her eyes. Alix's brow furrowed in concern, but she simply let go. Rowan shifted awkwardly before saying, "What do you want?"

In a soft voice, Alix said, "Keep an eye on her. Cass and AJ would never do anything to hurt her, but they don't always see things that they should. And Aubrey won't tell them everything they need to know unless she's pressed."

"What if she just doesn't want to talk about it?" Rowan asked.

Alix smiled slightly, a sad look in her eyes. "Nobody ever wants to talk about it. That doesn't mean they shouldn't." When Rowan looked down at the ground, Alix frowned. "Are *you* okay, van Houten?"

"I'm working on it."

"You know that if you need anything, my door's open, right?"

"Perks of dating a Hamil?" Rowan joked in a somewhat weak voice.

"Perks of being someone who seems like they could use it," Alix replied seriously.

Rowan looked surprised, but she nodded. "I-I'll... think about it. Honestly. And I'll keep an eye on Aubrey. I always do."

"Good. And for the record? I won't touch you again unless you have fair warning and I have permission."

A grateful glint formed in Rowan's dark blue eyes. "I-I'm sorry about that. I can shake somebody's hand, but—"

"You don't need to explain it. Or apologize. Understand?"

Rowan swallowed and nodded again.

"Now go on. Don't make her wait too long. It's a bad enough day for her without worrying where you've disappeared to."

"I'll just blame you," Rowan replied dryly.

"That's the spirit."

Aubrey froze outside the door of the library, her hand hovering over the doorknob. "I'm sorry you've been yanked around the past few days. With people randomly finding out about us."

"I've never had a problem with people knowing about us. I don't mind."

"Your patience is astounding."

Rowan gave a quiet laugh. "It's not so much 'patience' as it is 'being fair.'"

"You're ridiculous and you sound like a book of clichés."

"You're one to talk."

Aubrey leaned against Rowan briefly. "Yeah, I know. It's bad."

"What's bad is you stalling."

"You're no fun," Aubrey grumbled. She took in a deep breath and opened the door.

Cass and AJ were on the couch. AJ was looking at something on his tablet while Cass, her head resting on his lap, was apparently sleeping. It took only a moment before AJ raised his head, and he immediately set his tablet down on the table next to him. "Aubrey."

"Hey, Dad."

As Rowan shut the library door and leaned against it, allowing Aubrey to step further into the room alone, AJ gently shook Cass's shoulder. "Honey, wake up."

"M'awake," Cass mumbled as she opened her metal-gray eyes slowly.

"Yeah, I can tell," AJ teased.

"Oh, shut up." Cass turned her head slightly, noticing her daughter in the corner. She immediately sat up. "Aubrey."

"Uh-huh. That's what Dad said." Aubrey folded her arms across her chest. "I-I-I, uh, I expect that Aunt Casey talked to you yesterday."

"She did," AJ said calmly. He glanced past Aubrey. "Before we get to that, who's this?"

"Oh, u-u-uh, this is Rowan van Houten."

"Ah, the friend who was with you and the others looking for the Galaxy Boys." AJ nodded at Rowan. "Nice to finally meet you, since you've apparently been around for a while, despite my daughter never mentioning you before."

Rowan cleared her throat uncomfortably. "She does that, sir."

Cass laughed. "I like this one."

"I'd like to know more about you, Rowan, but at the moment I think there's another conversation that needs to occur first," AJ said.

"I'm aware," Rowan said softly. She leaned forward and gently pushed Aubrey, moving her closer to her parents.

Aubrey shifted her weight back and forth between her feet. "W-W-What exactly did Aunt Casey tell you?"

"That you haven't been taking your medication," Cass replied, her voice quiet and even. "And that you were visibly worse when she talked to you about it."

"She's not... wrong," Aubrey said carefully as she began spinning her ring.

"Aub, you said that stuff was helping. That, and the fact that neither you nor your sister will even *consider* therapy—which I still say is probably the better option—are the only reasons I let you stay on it." AJ leaned forward, resting his elbows on his knees. "You said it was calming down the compulsions, and with them, the anxiety."

"It *was* helping with that."

"Then why stop taking it?"

"*Because*, Mom! It dulls my brain. It makes it harder for me to get from Point A to Point B as fast as I usually do. I know it's probably just a normal person's speed, but I can't tolerate that. I can't give up my edge."

"Aubrey, I don't like telling you what to do," Cass said. "And I'm not going to *tell* you to do anything. But, sweetheart, your edge isn't worth what it puts you through."

"I can't afford to lose it," Aubrey replied. "I need it."

"*Why?*"

"Aub, just tell her," Rowan said quietly.

"Shut up, Rowan," Aubrey snapped.

"Tell me *what?* Aubrey?"

"Aubrey, I—" Rowan cleared her throat again, shooting a nervous glance at Cass and AJ. "You're my best friend, but if you don't tell them, I will."

"Why does it matter?" Aubrey demanded, giving Rowan a look of pure betrayal.

"Because it's going to kill you one of these days, and I don't want that," Rowan murmured.

Aubrey's glare softened and she turned back to her parents, who were now staring at her with confusion and worry. In a very low voice, she said, "I-I-I... I can't lose the edge because I do my work *and* my boss's, and if my brain doesn't work fast enough it'll completely overwhelm me and get me fired."

"It's already overwhelming you," Rowan said, her arms folded across her chest as she leaned against the door. "You barely get any sleep, and you're at work all the time."

"Shut up, Rowan," Aubrey repeated in a hoarse voice.

"Let me get this straight," Cass said slowly. "You went off your meds, subjecting yourself to the worst of your compulsions, because of *my company*?"

"It's a bit more complicated than that," Aubrey muttered, staring at the floor.

"No. It's not." Cass's voice held barely suppressed rage. "That... That *jackass* Lattimer accused me of nepotism the day you started, and I told him that you'd earned your job fair and square. If he thinks he can take his suspicions about me out on you, he's *incredibly* mistaken."

"Aubrey," AJ said, "I can adjust the prescription so that you can take it without losing as much of your brain as you do. But you have to sleep, baby. Everything just gets worse when you don't sleep."

"I hope she listens to you," Rowan said softly, watching Aubrey carefully. "It's like talking to a brick wall sometimes."

"She'd better listen." Cass walked over to Aubrey and took her face in her hands. "Oh, kid. You're too much like me for your own good, you know that?"

Aubrey swallowed, her green eyes glistening as if she was trying not to cry. "I just want it to stop, Mom."

Cass pulled her into a tight hug. "Trust me, baby. I wish I could stop it."

AJ stood as well, walking over to his wife and daughter and stopping next to them. "Why didn't you just *say* something, Aub? You know I could've fixed the meds long before you had to resort to stopping them entirely."

"I wasn't... completely sure you'd... care," Aubrey said awkwardly.

There was a long pause. Cass backed out of the hug, resting her hands on Aubrey's shoulders and looking her directly in the eye. "Sweetheart, why wouldn't we care?"

"I'm the black sheep, aren't I? Middle child who won't join the family business, has nothing in common with anybody else in the family, doesn't deserve half as much of the attention her siblings get..." Aubrey shrugged and averted her gaze. "I'm the one you aren't supposed to care about."

"Aubrey, not being involved in Heroics means you're probably the only *white sheep* in this whole family," AJ said. "As for not having anything in common, have you checked your sarcasm meter lately? How about the fact that you look just like your Aunt Casey? Or, I dunno, that terrifyingly smart brain in your head that is a common denominator between you and your siblings?"

"The terrifyingly smart brain has a habit of ignoring things like that, though," Cass murmured. "Doesn't it?"

Aubrey gave a stiff nod. "It didn't help that you two always seemed to give Brooke and Jacob more attention when we were growing up," she mumbled.

Cass and AJ looked at each other, surprised. "What are you talking about?" Cass asked.

"You guys always sort of... left me to my own devices. And it was nice some of the time, but... sometimes it would've been nice to have some focus, instead of all of it being concentrated on Brooke and Jacob."

AJ closed his eyes briefly. "Sweetheart, I... When you were growing up, we concerned ourselves with Brooke and Jacob more only because we thought they needed it more. You seemed to always have everything under control. We never felt like we *had* to worry about you, but those two? Hell, thrice a week we were trying to prevent them from accidentally blowing themselves up. Your mom and I used to joke that you were the only responsible person in the whole damned house, occasional bouts of sibling-accompanied mischief aside."

"We never meant it as any sort of negative indicator against you, Aubrey," Cass said gently. "We honestly thought you were fine."

Aubrey gave a weak laugh. "You guys are idiots."

Cass and AJ both echoed her laugh. "Yeah, this family isn't too great in the communication department," AJ said. He rested a hand on Aubrey's cheek. "I'm sorry, sweetheart. We didn't know. And we'll do anything we can to fix it. Just tell us where to start."

Aubrey hugged her mother again, trying not to break down. "This works."

As AJ tightly hugged Aubrey as well, Rowan looked at the floor, smiling softly. Cass, who had pulled away to give AJ space, squinted at her. "So, did Aubrey drag you along as moral support, or so you could rat her out when she decided not to do it herself?"

"Her idea was moral support," Rowan replied. "Al— *my* idea was to rat her out."

"Wait a minute, you weren't going to say 'my.'" Aubrey turned and gave Rowan a suspicious glare. "You started to say something else. That sounded suspiciously like the beginning of 'Alix.'"

"I... plead the Fifth?"

"You aren't even an American, van Houten."

"I still have rights!" Rowan protested. She hunched her shoulders slightly, a grumpy look on her face. "And I *have* citizenship, thank you very much."

"I had a feeling you weren't from around here," AJ said.

"Why's that, sir?"

"The accent."

"Oh," Rowan said with a laugh. "Honestly, I forget I have it sometimes. I moved here from the Czech Republic when I was just a little kid, but my dad had a heavy accent, especially when he was at home, and I barely spoke outside of the house, so I just sort of somehow kept it."

"Come, sit, let's talk. It's been a stressful couple of minutes, and I think we could all use a bit of an easier conversation." AJ sat back down on the couch with Cass, and Aubrey and Rowan took chairs opposite each other on either side of it.

"Zach says you're one of the Legion heroes," Cass said.

Rowan nodded. "Fuse. Volatile constructs." She fidgeted with the leather strap on her wrist. "Same power as my dad."

"Is he in the Legion too?" AJ asked.

"He was," Rowan said shortly.

There was a moment of silence, broken only when Cass said, "Oh, hell. Now I remember."

AJ frowned at her. "What is it?"

Cass was staring at Rowan, looking horrified. "Janek 'Svetlo' van Houten. Volatile constructs. Killed during the anti-hero riots. He was your father, wasn't he?"

"Yes, ma'am, he was."

"I'm sorry."

Rowan shifted in her seat. "It's okay. It was a long time ago."

"I'll say." Cass glanced at Aubrey. "You were only… eight?"

"Turned nine a few days later," Aubrey whispered.

"That's a lot of history for one person to have to deal with," AJ said.

"I've seen worse." Rowan leaned back in her chair. "Aub, remember that you were supposed to go talk to Jacob."

Without noting Rowan's change in subject, Cass turned to her daughter. "Talk to Jacob? What, to try to get him out of his room? Good luck."

"I said that, but you know how Alix gets."

Cass considered it for a moment. "Annoyingly persistent and somehow usually right?"

"That's the one."

"Funny, you *are* named after her, Aubrey Alexandra Hamil."

"Ugh, don't remind me. That woman's a pain in the ass," Aubrey said, grinning.

Cass laughed. "Trust me, you should've seen her when she was younger."

"I'll be back in a few minutes, Rowan. Think you can survive that long?"

"Depends; are your parents as aggravating as you are?" Rowan asked with a smirk.

"Oh, we're much more so," AJ deadpanned.

"Fantastic."

Aubrey shook her head slowly. "Unbelievable. I invite you along and all you do is harass me, van Houten."

"It's a special talent of mine," Rowan said. "I'm nice, but I'm also a complete jerk."

"Yeah, that pretty much sums you up." Aubrey headed for the door, but stopped before she reached it. "You know, I *could* make my time away talking with Jacob utter hell for you, Ro."

"How's that?" Rowan asked, confused.

"Mom, Dad, the grumpy yet wonderful jackass sitting in this chair over here is *not* a friend of mine."

AJ frowned. "What do you mean?"

"Aubrey," Rowan said warily, "what are you doing?"

The younger woman went over to Rowan, kissed her directly on the mouth for several seconds, and then, with a smirk on her face, walked out of the room. Rowan sat frozen in the chair as Cass and AJ, stunned, just stared at her.

"Well," Cass finally said. "Several things suddenly make a lot more sense."

"I... I-I'm not sure what I'm... supposed to do right now," Rowan stammered.

AJ stood slowly and headed over to a small fridge hidden in what had appeared to be a set of drawers. "Do you drink bourbon, Rowan?"

"O-On occasion, sir."

He poured some of the amber liquid into a glass and handed it to her. "Then my personal suggestion would be to drink some, because you probably deserve it."

Aubrey banged on Jacob's door loudly. "Hey! Let me in. We need to talk."

"I don't want to talk to you," Jacob's muffled voice said.

"Tough luck. Let me in anyway."

"You aren't Mom!" Jacob protested. "I don't have to listen to you!"

Aubrey rolled her eyes. "First of all, you haven't been listening to her, either. Second of all, me not being Mom means that I'm allowed to pick this lock, come in there, and *kick your ass*."

There was a pause from the other side of the door. "You wouldn't do that."

"You're right, because you're upset right now and you have every right to be. But don't sit in there and mope. Talk to me, little brother."

"Oh, you're actually going to talk to me now?" he asked rebelliously.

"I'm sort of talking to you already, aren't I?"

"I mean *really* talk."

"Yeah, J, we can *really* talk."

"... Prove it. Tell me something completely unrelated to your stupid job."

Aubrey paused. "The Legion girl I was with the other night? Not my friend. My girlfriend."

After a surprisingly short moment, the door opened and Jacob squinted out at her. "Are you serious?"

"I'm serious."

He opened the door fully and let her into his room. "Okay; let's talk."

Aubrey scoffed and ruffled his red hair. "You're a pain in the neck, you know that, boy?"

"Family trait," Jacob deadpanned.

"Well, you're not wrong."

Jacob shut his door and sat down on his bed. "You're dating someone from the *Legion? Seriously?*"

"First of all, our *uncle* is from the Legion. Second of all, *that's* what you're concerned about?"

He frowned at her. "First of all, Uncle Zach is an exception. Second of all, what else could I possibly be concerned about?"

"I can think of a few things," Aubrey said slowly.

"Yeah, well, then you're an idiot." Jacob leaned back on his bed, staring up at the ceiling. "If they sent you in, they must be getting desperate to fix me. Hell, they must be *really* desperate if they actually convinced you to do it."

"You say that like I don't care about you."

"Of course you don't," Jacob muttered. "You're the one who left, not me."

There was a long, silent moment as Aubrey struggled to gather her thoughts. "I left this house because of my own problems. It had nothing to do with you. And I've been slowly realizing just how little it really did concern you. How much of it was really my own head telling me things. That's not on you, but please don't place all of the blame on me, either. I still come here as often as I can. For all intents and purposes, *I still live here.* You shut me out just as much as I left. I can make it right, Jake, but I need you to meet me halfway here."

"Don't call me that," the boy grumbled. "You know I hate that."

Aubrey smiled slightly. "Aw, come on, I've always been allowed to call you Jake."

"Yeah, that's before you became a button-up accountant."

"Oh, please. Like you didn't become a surly teenager at the same time, Jake."

Jacob shifted so that his weight was resting on his elbows and he was glaring at her. "My name's not Jake."

"What are you going to do about it, *Jake*?"

Muttering curses that would definitely get him grounded for a month, Jacob bolted off the bed and attempted to tackle his sister. Unfortunately for him, while Aubrey was nowhere near as physically skilled as Brooke, she was definitely better than her brother. She easily stepped out of the way, twisted him around, and grabbed him in a gentle—if solid—chokehold.

"Y'know, I go rock climbing for fun," Aubrey said casually. "I could totally just drag you out of your room right now."

"Get *off* of me, Aubrey!" Jacob yelled, struggling futilely.

"Sure. Just promise me that you'll leave your room sometime today."

"I don't negotiate with terrorists."

"That's a shame." She tightened her grip as he fidgeted. "Hang from boulders. For fun. I could stay here for a good, long time, boy."

"Yeah, and I'd still be in my room," Jacob retorted.

Aubrey laughed. "Oh, trust me, I'd throw you out of here long before it got to be a victory for you."

"You're a pain in the ass, and I wish you hadn't come home."

"*Now* we're getting somewhere," Aubrey said gleefully.

"What the hell is wrong with you?" Jacob demanded. "You're such a *freak!*"

Aubrey immediately threw him back onto his bed, the amused look on her face vanishing in an instant. To his credit, Jacob seemed to have already realized that he had gone too far, as a horrified look was spreading across his face.

"I-I didn't meant that," he stammered.

The hard look in Aubrey's eyes softened slightly. "What's *wrong*, J? This isn't like you. I know you saw something horrible, but even then, you usually bounce back from the terrible reality of vigilantism faster than this."

"I just..." Jacob bowed his head. "It made me realize that..."

Aubrey walked over and sat down next to him. "Made you realize what?" she prompted quietly.

"We're so *vulnerable*. Usually when something awful happens, it's a fluke. Or one person alone, and that's how they get killed. The Galaxy Boys were an entire group that got systematically taken out. They were a *team*, and they basically all died. What hope do we have against something that can do *that?*"

"I don't know," Aubrey admitted. "But I do know that this team has faced some pretty awful things before and come out of it okay."

"There's a first time for everything, Bree," he whispered.

Aubrey hesitated. Ever since Jacob had turned ten and 'became a grown-up,' he had only called her Bree when he was wholeheartedly scared. "Yeah, there is. It doesn't need to be now, though."

Jacob gave a weak laugh. "That's not exactly your most compelling argument ever constructed, sis."

"It needs some work, to be sure." Aubrey lightly bumped her shoulder against his. "Doesn't mean I'm wrong."

"There are plenty of other reasons for you to be wrong. Like the fact that you always are."

Aubrey grinned and ruffled his hair again. "Yeah, okay. How about you give me this one?"

"I think I can do that, just this once," Jacob murmured.

"Good." Aubrey put an arm around his shoulders and kissed the side of his head quickly. "Now, how about we get out of here before Mom gets fed up and sends Brooke in?"

Jacob scoffed. "Brooke already tried and got nowhere."

"I'm going to take a moment to be proud of that."

"Don't bask too long in your own glory or I won't leave."

"Okay, okay." Aubrey stood. "Come on, little brother. Let's get out of here."

Jacob paused for a long moment, then got to his feet. "Sounds like a plan."

When Aubrey got back to the library with Jacob, her girlfriend was halfway through a glass of bourbon and her father was halfway through a story.

AJ was grinning. "So at this point, this kid has Jacob by the front of his jacket, and he has a fist raised. And I'm pretty sure that I'm about to watch my kid get his face beaten in, but I'm all the way across the parking lot so there's nothing I can do. I tell Aubrey to get out of the damn car and do something since she's a lot faster than I am, and she just laughs. This is really weird to me, as Aubrey's never been so cavalier with her brother's safety. But then I look up, and Brooke has sprinted all the way over from the soccer field and she grabs this kid and decks him. Like, *floors* him, right in the face."

Rowan grinned. "Aubrey saw her coming?"

"Worse. I realized that this kid was the same kid Jacob had been complaining about. Apparently he had said some things about Jacob and his siblings being freaks, but Jacob was never one for fights, so no matter how much it bothered him, he wouldn't do anything. It turns out, my *wonderful* children, jackasses that they are, planned the whole damn thing. Actually, scratch that. *Aubrey* planned the whole damn thing, and all three of them carried it out. Jacob egged this kid on until he was physically threatened, giving Brooke an excuse to punch him without getting in trouble for it, while Aubrey was in the car with me making sure that I couldn't intervene."

"That kid deserved it," Aubrey said, crossing the room and sitting down on the arm of Rowan's chair.

"He really did, Dad," Jacob replied, taking the chair opposite her. "Besides, it was a brilliant plan."

Aubrey shrugged. "And we needed a plan like that, because Brooke had already been suspended like six times, and she really couldn't afford another fight."

AJ gave a long, slow sigh. "I've raised monsters."

"Yeah, you did," Cass said.

"They got this from you."

Cass snorted. "Not all of it, sweetheart."

Aubrey gave Rowan an awkward smile. "So, uh, how are you?"

Rowan took another sip from her glass. "*Jdi do prdele.*"

"That's not very nice."

"Speaking of which, are we going to talk about what happened here?" Cass asked her daughter casually. "Or are you going to just pretend it never happened?"

"I'm not sure yet," Aubrey replied.

"Well, tough, we're deciding for you," AJ said. "Because we like her." He leaned forward, resting his elbows on his knees. "So, why don't we talk?"

"I can't believe you did that to me," Rowan grumbled as she walked next to Aubrey through the streets of Caotico City.

"Aw, come on, my parents aren't *that* bad," Aubrey teased.

"No, your parents are great. And very understanding. And your father is very aware of the fact that dating women in your family sometimes requires alcohol." Rowan dodged out of the way as Aubrey tried to elbow her in the side. "But you *would* out yourself to your parents and leave me to deal with it all by myself."

"They weren't mad."

"You almost seem surprised."

"I'm not... really. I mean, they care a lot about Kara, so it's not like I was expecting... I don't know. It's just weird. And that's not exactly how I meant to go about it."

Rowan raised an eyebrow. "Gee, really?"

"Oh, shut up."

"Never." Rowan bumped her shoulder against Aubrey's gently. "You're stuck with me now, Hamil."

"I think I can live with that. Even if you *are* an utter bastard."

"You're the one who ditched me with your parents half a second after revealing that we're dating."

Aubrey scoffed. "Yeah, and *you're* the one who almost blew me up the first time we met."

"It was *one bomb*," Rowan protested. "Will you *never* let me live that down?"

"Probably not," Aubrey replied brightly.

Rowan sighed. "I never really thought my life was going to be quite this hard."

Aubrey smirked and patted Rowan on the back. "Yeah, well, you're stuck with me now."

9

"I think my ribs are broken," Max groaned from his spot on the floor in the Heroics training room.

Alix laughed and held out a hand to help him to his feet. "You're a terrible fighter."

"Am not," Max protested. "You just hit really hard."

"You're capable of letting my fist go *right through you*, and it's *my* fault that you suck?"

Max straightened his t-shirt in irritation. "It's the ring."

Alix looked down at the black and silver ring she was wearing on her right hand. "Aw, hell, I forgot I was wearing that. I'm sorry."

"It's not really the immense pain that made it awful. That's real silver, isn't it?"

"Oh, right, the gold, silver, and platinum thing."

"You mean you really didn't do it on purpose?"

"I'm not *that* mean." Alix considered her ring for a moment. "Now, how does that work exactly? If I was wearing this ring and you tried to pull me through a wall, would the ring stay on the outside, or would you just not be able to go through the wall at all?"

Max paused. "Y'know, I've never tried it. I'm worried that it would result in like, you getting your hand ripped off, or me somehow getting my face bashed into a piece of concrete."

"Fair enough. No experimenting, then."

"Not if you want to be sure you're going to stay in one piece." Max wandered over to a large contraption shaped like a wheel. "Do you guys have really big hamsters?"

Alix gave a thin smile. "We used to have a speedster. He died during the anti-hero riots. That wheel was the only way he could get any run training in."

"Smart setup."

"Casey's a smart woman."

"She designed all of this stuff?"

"Most of it. Everything; until the Hamil kids started toying with mechanics and she was no longer the only whiz kid."

Max laughed. "Must suck to be the normal genius in a house of super-geniuses."

"I think she handles it pretty well. Honestly, I'm not sure Case even considers herself a genius. She absolutely is one. I've seen some of the stuff she's come up with, but I don't think she sees it in herself."

"Shame."

Alix shrugged. "Depends on whether she needs that to feel good about herself. Aside from a particular time in her life when Casey... had a bit of a rough time of things, she's typically been pretty good with herself. Especially after her mom was gone, and the constant emotional stress—*stress* being a nicer word for 'abuse'—wasn't hanging over her head anymore. She's got a slight guilt complex, but she's probably the person on this team who's the most okay with themselves." Alix paused, frowning slightly. "Except for Logan. I'm pretty sure Logan absorbs the confidence of the people around her."

"What about you?"

"What *about* me?"

"You're a part of this team too, aren't you?" Max asked softly. "How do *you* feel about yourself?"

Alix stared at him for a long moment, as if her mind had suddenly gone blank. "I... haven't really thought about that in quite a while." She sat down on a nearby bench and started adjusting the laces of her boots. "I used to be fine. Then something happened to me that screwed it all up. I started to hate myself. To hate everything that I was. Now I just... don't really care. I like where I am, what I'm doing, what I'm able to do. I'm good with what I am. And I guess I'm good with who I am. But I don't think I'll ever get back to the way I was before." She shrugged. "To be honest, I'm not completely sure I *want* to."

"This might be a bit forward," Max said slowly, "but can I ask... last week, you said something about 'creator'..."

"Ah. Right." Alix cracked her knuckles absentmindedly, avoiding eye contact. "That's uhm... Do you know who Alice Cage was?"

"Of course."

"I'm her clone."

Max gave her a stunned look that he quickly adjusted into a sympathetic one. "That must be pretty tough."

"It never used to be. Not really. I hate her, obviously. I *hated* her. But I know that I'm me, whether the blood that runs through my veins is solely my own or not. It just became a bit difficult when my powers started to kill me and everything in my head started coming apart."

Hesitantly, Max sat down next to her. "Are you okay now?"

"Yeah. I think so. I have bad days, but I've elected not to let her ruin my life after she already did such a damn good job of trying when she was actually alive."

"Sounds like a good way to go about it."

"It's honestly easier now that I'm forgetting things."

"What do you mean?"

"Alice programmed the memories of a bunch of other clones she had created into my head. It sort of screwed my mental age up a bit, and to be honest, my age has always been a bit screwy anyway. Ever since I got rid of my powers, I've been slowly losing those extra memories. At this point, pretty much the only ones I have are ones I created on my own terms."

"Is that a good thing?"

"Y'know, I think it is. Like I said, it's making everything easier."

"Good, then." Max leaned forward, resting his elbows on his knees. "How old *are* you, anyway?"

"The best answer I can give you is that, in terms of my own mind and my own memories and the way my physical aging has adjusted, I'm thirty-four."

"Same as me," Max commented.

Alix laughed. "I bet you came about it in a much easier way."

"Probably not as interesting, though."

"It might have been. I'd have to judge that for myself." Alix glanced at her watch. "I have to get upstairs. There's a meeting." She stood and playfully pushed his shoulder. "Don't you have actual Legion work to do, Legion?"

"I'm confused, am *I* Legion or is *Rowan* Legion?"

"Every one of you Security people is Legion around here until you've earned the use of your actual name."

"But you always call me Wraith," Max protested.

"Well, if that's what you like, I can definitely call you that instead of your real name." Smirking, Alix turned and left the room.

"I can't believe I fell for that!" Max yelled after her. As he sat alone in the training room, Max shook his head slowly. "I think what I like is fairly obvious," he muttered.

Cass looked up as Alix joined her, Brooke, Kara, AJ, Casey, Kate, and Ray in the meeting room of the Heroics mansion. "Nice of you to join us, Al."

"Ah, you know how punctual I am," Alix joked as she took a seat.

"Yeah, especially when meetings follow your little daily rendezvous with Mr. Oakley," Brooke teased.

Alix frowned at her. "Why are you saying it like that?"

Brooke gave her a patient look. "Why do you *think* I am, Al?"

After a rather long moment, Alix flushed pink. "It's not like that," she muttered.

Casey snorted. "Pretty sure it's exactly like that."

"I... It's... I've only... I've only known him for like *two weeks*," Alix stammered.

Cass leaned forward, grinning. "Yeah, but you're *hetero*romantic, not *demi*romantic. Timeline shouldn't make all that much of a difference."

"Wh-B-"

"Put it this way; you should at least be able to tell if you think he's cute," Brooke said. She looked at her mother and aunt expectantly. "Is that not a fair question?"

"Oh, absolutely," Cass and Casey agreed simultaneously.

Alix groaned and rested her head on the table. "Kara, can I come live with you?"

Kara took a sip of her soda and shrugged. "It wouldn't help."

"I'm pretty sure there was an actual topic to today's meeting, and it wasn't Alix's love life," AJ said with a laugh.

"I don't *have* a lo—"

"You're *right*, honey, we *did!*" Cass cut Alix off with obvious glee, shooting the younger woman a mocking glance. Her amusement died as she glanced at Brooke. "Uh, sweetheart, didn't you have a lunch with Matthias scheduled today? In a few minutes?"

Brooke shrugged. "One of his classes got moved, so he had to cancel. What's the difference?"

There was an uncomfortable silence in the room. Brooke looked around slowly. "Hang on. I know why Niall's not here. And I know Justin's busy at work. But why am I the only kid here?"

"They're all on patrol," Ray said.

"Then why have a..." Brooke narrowed her eyes. "What's going on?"

When silence answered her, she turned to her father, her eyes narrowing further. "Daddy? What's going on?"

AJ groaned softly. "Why do you do this to me, girl?"

Cass snorted. "The better question is, why do you always give in to her."

"As if you don't give Jacob whatever he wants," AJ muttered.

"Now we know why Aubrey feels ignored," Alix mumbled.

"Shut up, Al," Cass snapped. "Now's not the time."

"I think it's something we should discuss, because she wouldn't even tell *me* what was going on, and that's not—"

"*I'm doing my best!*" Cass rounded on Alix, looking furious. "I *did* my best! Maybe that wasn't good enough, but I am not going to sit here while you—"

Brooke slammed her fist down onto the table so hard everyone jumped. "Stop!" she growled. "Just stop. You can all argue over parenting and whether you screwed Aubrey up later. Right now? Right now, you're going to tell me what the hell is going on."

Her parents and Alix just glanced at each other and stared at the table. The others were avoiding looking at her as well, seeming uncomfortable. Casey was the only one who finally met Brooke's gaze.

"Fine," she said softly. "If nobody else is going to do it, I will." She faltered, swallowing and pushing her glasses back up on her nose.

"Aunt Casey," Brooke whispered. "Please."

Casey swallowed again and took in a deep breath. "You know what happened when Jay died and Kara and Justin had to retire, right?"

Brooke shrugged. "Heroics was down to only two people on the field team. Kate and Ray couldn't do everything by themselves, so we were barely an active team until Ciaran, Isaac, and Logan were old enough."

"Right. But the thing is..." Casey glanced down guiltily.

For a long moment, Brooke just stared at her aunt. Then realization jolted into her brain. "You didn't *want* to get an active team back." She looked around at the uneasy expressions on the other Heroics members present. "*None* of you did."

"Can you blame us?" Kate asked softly. "The job ruined our lives, Brooke. We don't want the same thing to happen to you and the others."

"That's not your decision to make."

"Yes, sweetheart, it is," AJ said, his voice gentle.

"No. It's not." Brooke shook her head slowly. "None of you get it. We all *grew up with this*. We saw what it did to all of you, and we're still here." She gave a sarcastic laugh. "I *watched you get shot*, Dad, and it was because of this life; and look at me. I ended up with the same kind of life that put you in that position." AJ, now fidgeting uncomfortably with his tie, opened his mouth to interrupt, but Brooke didn't let him. "All of you still treat us like kids, but we aren't. Not when we're doing Heroics work. We're part of this team, because you *let* us be a part of this team, and none of you are allowed to back out on that just because it's more convenient that way." She pushed her chair back and stood up. "I get that you're trying to protect us. I get that you've all seen a lot. Far too much. But it's too late to push us out of this team now. And if you don't like it? Go ahead and run away. See how many of us run with you." With a furious glint in her hazel eyes, Brooke turned on her heel and stormed out of the room.

Raymond Lattimer straightened his suit jacket as he approached the desk of Justin Oliver's secretary. "Excuse me, miss," he said in a serious voice. "I have an appointment with Mr. Oliver."

The secretary raised an eyebrow at him. "Okay. For what time?"

"Fifteen minutes from now."

"You're Ray Lattimer?"

"*Raymond* Lattimer," he corrected briskly.

"Uh huh." The secretary picked up her phone and hit a speed dial. "Mr. Oliver? I have your eleven o'clock here for you." She paused and smirked. "Yes, sir. Right away, sir." Once she had set the phone down, the young woman said, "Mr. Oliver will see you now, Mr. Lattimer."

"Thank you. If I were you, miss, I'd be a bit more polite and energetic when speaking with Mr. Oliver's appointments. You seem to be arrogantly assuming many things about me, and I do not appreciate it."

The secretary now looked like she was seconds away from laughing hysterically, though it did nothing to temper the deep sadness in her blue eyes. "Of course, sir," she said in a tightly-controlled, professional voice. "If you would, please mention that to Mr. Oliver, sir. It would be very helpful for me."

"I will," Lattimer said. He walked past her and through the door into Justin's office.

The blond-haired CEO was sitting behind his desk, studying something on his computer. Lattimer walked up to the desk and cleared his throat. "Mr. Oliver. Your rather rude and disinterested secretary sent me in here."

Without looking up, Justin said, "My rather rude and disinterested secretary is my sister's niece. She's usually more polite, but she's going through a bit of a rough time right now. She just refuses to miss any more work than she already has, despite me offering to let her take more time off. It doesn't matter much. She has free range to act however she wants towards people I'm about to fire, because I find it amusing."

Lattimer felt his blood run cold. "E-Excuse me, sir? Fire?"

Justin ignored him as the door opened again, and Lattimer's second-in-command, Ariane Nikorak, walked in. "You asked to see me, sir?"

"I did, Mrs. Nikorak. Please, both of you, sit down."

Nikorak took a seat in one of the chairs in front of Justin's desk, but Lattimer stayed where he was. "What do you mean by 'fire'?" he demanded.

"What?" Nikorak looked alarmed.

Justin held up a hand in Nikorak's direction, as if putting her on hold while he looked directly at Lattimer. "Your department was missing a significant portion of work for the month of September, Mr. Lattimer."

"So, what, you're going to fire us both just because our department happened to be behind one month of the year?" Lattimer scoffed. "That's no way to run a business."

"Actually, Mr. Lattimer, I'm only planning on firing *you*."

Lattimer gaped at him for a solid minute. "For *what?*"

"The only work that was missing from your department was all *yours*. You're the only person who failed to do their job."

"I see what this is," Lattimer said with a dry laugh. "You're all just covering your asses to make up for the fact that the Hamil kid can't do *her* damn job."

Nikorak looked uncomfortable, but instead of speaking, she just bowed her head. Justin glanced at her. "Have something to say, Mrs. Nikorak?"

"I-I just..."

"Go on," Justin said gently. "It's okay."

"Well, Raymond, you didn't exactly give the girl a chance, did you? You gave her twice the work of a person normally in her position, and then on top of that you expected her to do all of your work while you were on vacation. And you explicitly told me that if I gave her any assistance at all while you were away, you'd fire me."

"She needed to learn how real companies work!" Lattimer replied furiously.

Nikorak scoffed. "No; you just needed to teach her the lesson that you couldn't teach her mother."

"I refuse to work for a company that so blatantly hires using a standard of nepotism," Lattimer said, folding his arms across his chest.

"Well, two things," Justin said. "First of all, you not working here is sort of the point of this meeting. Second of all, Aubrey Hamil applied for a job here just like everyone else. She went through the same hiring process as everyone else. She's a bright kid, and she was put in your department because it was believed that she could be useful to you. And you'll *notice* that she did absolutely all of the work that was assigned to her position, even though, according to Mrs. Nikorak, it was way more than she should've received."

"You probably fudged the numbers," Lattimer sniffed.

"We didn't." Justin leaned against his desk. "Mr. Lattimer, the department under your command missed its deadline. You went on vacation when you knew your work was not finished, which people with your title are not supposed to do. You assigned your work to an employee who was not qualified to do your work. You intentionally overworked an employee for the sake of revenge. I do not want you working at Wechsler Industries anymore. You're fired."

"You'll regret this," Lattimer snarled. "I'm much more useful than some brat kid whose rich mom got her a job."

"That brat kid graduated college with honors at nineteen and has an IQ of 137," Justin replied calmly. "Plus, y'know, she's not an egotistical jerk. I really don't think I'm going to regret my decision. Please leave my office before I have security escort you out."

Muttering curses under his breath, Lattimer stormed out of the office. Justin looked at Nikorak. "Thank you. For being honest with me."

"Aubrey really didn't deserve what Lattimer was giving her," Nikorak said softly. "I was just too afraid of him to do anything about it. I guess that makes me a coward."

"Not necessarily. You need your job, and you prioritized that. It's understandable, though I think you could do better." Justin smiled slightly. "Think you could do *Lattimer's* job better?"

Nikorak looked surprised. "Run the department?"

"Yes, ma'am."

"I-I could absolutely do that, sir."

"Just, please don't be afraid of Aubrey Hamil. She really doesn't want to get anyone in trouble. She just wants to work in peace."

"I believe that. That poor girl couldn't be convinced to report *anything* that Lattimer was putting her through."

"That's how she is. Can you handle that?"

"Absolutely," Nikorak said quickly. "And if she's as good as I think she is, I think I know how I can use her a lot better than Lattimer was."

"Good." Justin stood and held out a hand. "If you need anything, Mrs. Nikorak, just let me know. Talk to Emma on your way out; she can change your profile over to a higher status."

"T-Thank you, Mr. Oliver."

"Thank *you*, Mrs. Nikorak. Trust me when I say that the Hamil family—and associates—has needed some good to come their way for a while. If today goes according to plan, they, and we, may just have exactly what is needed."

Logan frowned as Riley crouched down on the edge of a roof and began assembling her rifle. "Y'know,

Sniper, one of these days you're going to have to explain to me how that's easier than a bow and arrow."

"Ease is relative," the other girl replied. "I can use a gun with one hand."

"That's what crossbows are for. Besides, you certainly can't use *that* gun with one hand."

Riley looked back at Logan. "Why do you have to try to ruin all of my fun, Eisen?"

"It's a special skill of mine." Logan pushed her sunglasses further up on her nose, in the exact same motion that her mother always adjusted her regular glasses. "Does anyone know how Diego de la Fuente is doing?"

"Slipped into a coma the day after he was brought in," Ciaran replied through the communications system. *"They aren't sure if he'll come out of it."*

Logan swore, loudly and colorfully. "Orion, I swear, if we find the bastards that did this, we're—"

"Mugger," Riley muttered, interrupting Logan's rant.

"Where?" Logan crouched down, squinting out in the general direction Riley's rifle was pointed in.

"Intersection of Kettle and 8th."

"Damn." Logan leaned back, resting on her heels. "That's the Legion's patrol zone."

"So? You were all fired up not four seconds ago, Eisen."

"Blitz, you know the rules," Ciaran said warily.

"Nobody's here to stop us. Don't be such a girl, Orion."

"Uhm, *excuse* me?" Riley scoffed. "I could shoot you before anybody noticed, Blitz. Don't push your luck."

170

"Oh, shut the hell up, Sniper!"

Logan gave an irritated sigh. "Orion, remind me later to have Blackout clear up who exactly is in charge when he and Targeter aren't around, because clearly the old method isn't working."

"You mean the 'hope for the best' method?"

"That's the one."

"I'm going to go take care of the bad guy," Isaac said. *"If all of you cowards feel like hanging out here doing nothing all day, be my guest."*

"Blitz, it's not our—"

"Let's just go, Eisen."

Logan pushed her glasses up again. "Repeat that, Orion?"

"Let's go."

"Why?"

Ciaran's voice was quiet. *"Because the disjointed behavior of the teams hasn't done anyone any good lately, has it?"*

Logan hesitated and glanced down at Riley, who shrugged. "I've got everyone covered if they want to go," the younger girl murmured.

"Fine," Logan said through gritted teeth. "But we take this guy down and get back to our own patrol route. Everyone got that?"

"Who put you in charge?" Isaac demanded.

"Shut up, Blitz," Ciaran said softly. *"Come on."*

"I told you that would be a good idea," Isaac said in a smug voice as he stood over a small teenage boy who looked furious, struggling against rope bindings.

171

"Yeah, whatever," Logan muttered. "Can we go back now?"

"You're acting like we don't have a responsibility to the *whole* city, not just a part of it." Isaac folded his arms across his chest. "Why are you such a baby, Eisen?"

"I'm *not*. I just think we need to respect patrol borders more than this. And for the sake of curiosity, if it was really about protecting the whole city, who do you think is patrolling *our* routes while we're over here? The Legion does a fine enough job on its own. We don't need to intrude on their territory."

Isaac rolled his eyes. "Typical."

"Typical of *what?*" Logan asked dangerously.

"Typical of some half-Legion, half-Heroics bastard who doesn't know where she wants to belong."

There was a long moment of horrified silence. Even the mugger seemed surprised. Before Logan could even react, however, a stun bullet smacked into Isaac's chest and sent him sprawling onto the ground.

"Man have I wanted to do that for ages," Riley's voice snarled in Logan's ear.

"You shouldn't have done that, Sniper," Logan said softly as she looked down at her unconscious teammate.

"Yeah, well, he shouldn't be an asshole. We're even."

Ciaran shook his head and dragged the mugger over to a nearby lightpost, propping him up against it. "And now we have to carry him back to base ourselves. Great plan."

"I'm all the way over here. It works out just fine for me."

"I'm glad you're so—"

"What the hell are you three doing over here?"

Ciaran and Logan looked up as Davi "Chuva" Esteves and Jesika "Teleka" Ramone approached them. "Chuva," Ciaran greeted slowly.

"You didn't answer me," Davi snarled. "Why are you here?"

Logan held up her hands defensively. "We just happened to notice a mugger while we were patrolling our route, and we thought we'd take care of it. It's not that big of a deal, Chuva."

Davi grabbed Logan by the front of her vest and dragged her forward, getting in her face. "This is *my* patrol area! I don't give a *damn* who your daddy is; stay the hell out of it!"

"Let go of me," Logan said calmly.

"You come in here like some sort of savior, acting like you're doing us a *favor*, but I know you're just rubbing it in my face that you got here before I did!"

"Let. Go. Of. Me," Logan repeated, her voice gaining a touch of a growl.

"Chuva, come on. They weren't doing anything wrong," Jesika said. She was frowning at Davi, clearly wondering what was going on with her teammate.

"They broke the rules, and if they don't admit to that, they're going to pay for i—"

A nearby street sign suddenly bent in half, swinging down at Davi and stopping mere inches from his face. "I'm going to tell you one more time," Logan whispered. "Let me go."

A nervous glint formed in Davi's eyes, but instead of backing down, he sneered. "You don't have the guts, girl."

"You've met both of my parents," Logan replied. "You really think that's true?"

The closest water hydrant began to tremble. "I could put you down before you even *thought* about moving that sign again, kid."

"Oh, is that so?"

"Eisen, stand down," Ciaran said quickly as Jesika whispered into a communications device on her wrist.

"Why should I, Orion? Chuva certainly isn't going to."

"He should." Ciaran took a few steps forward. "Chuva, we can't turn on each other. That's not going to help anybody."

"The Legion can take care of itself. We don't need you. We don't need to work with you. Heroics can be exterminated for all I care." Davi snorted. "It almost was a few years ago. Shame the riots didn't take all of you out."

The street sign immediately started dropping again, but it came to a sudden halt less than an inch from Davi. Logan, confused, looked around.

"That's enough!" Zach yelled as he jogged up to the group from a nearby alley.

Logan immediately flushed red. "S-Sorry, Kov," she mumbled.

"I'll accept your apology only after Chuva lets go of you," Zach said, his voice cold.

Davi stared at Zach for a long moment before releasing Logan so roughly that she fell back against

Ciaran. "Keep your brat out of my patrol territory, Kov," Davi said. "Or else I won't take it easy on her." He grabbed the mugger, pulled him to his feet, and dragged him away.

Jesika shot Zach a nervous look. "I'll keep an eye on him."

"Good luck with that," Zach replied. Once Jesika had left, Zach turned to Logan. "Are you okay, kid?"

"I'm sort of wishing I had asked Sniper to shoot him, but yeah."

"Come here." Zach led Logan into the alley, while Ciaran stayed with the still-unconscious Isaac. When they were out of the way, Zach removed his sunglasses and turned back to Logan. "What were you thinking? You know this is Chuva's patrol route. You know he's a miserable jackass."

"Yeah, I know," Logan said as she pulled her own glasses off. "But I was dealing with Isaac, who is also a miserable jackass. He was going to come over here whether the rest of us joined him or not, and I figured it was better to not let him get into a fight by himself."

Zach sighed. "All right. Just be a bit more careful, okay? Why are the others not with you, anyway?"

Logan shrugged. "We were told to patrol for a bit and that Control might not be available while we did."

"Hm. I don't like that."

"Well, you're going to have to take that up with the adults."

Zach smirked. "Am I not an adult?"

"I'm honestly not sure."

"Brat," Zach said affectionately as he messed up Logan's hair and then kissed her on the head.

"It's in my blood."

"Don't I know it." Zach glanced at the watch on his wrist. "You guys should probably start heading home soon. Finish up your patrol and head back."

"Okay." Logan paused. "I love that you haven't even asked what's up with Isaac back there."

"I was assuming he was being a jerk and Riley got fed up and shot him."

Logan nodded. "That sums it up."

"Have fun explaining *that* to Ray."

"I... don't plan on trying," Logan replied slowly. "*I* didn't shoot him."

"Uh huh. Let me know how that works out for you."

"I imagine it won't, but I'll let you know." Logan kissed Zach on the cheek quickly. "I'll talk to you later, Dad."

"Absolutely. Try to stay safe."

Logan snorted as she headed back towards Ciaran and Isaac. "You first."

Raymond Lattimer cursed loudly as he put his belongings back into his car in the parking garage of Wechsler Industries. He slammed the trunk shut and headed for the driver's side door, but before he could open it, a hand rested against it.

"Leave me alone," Lattimer snarled.

"Is there a problem?" the black-haired man in a military uniform asked calmly.

"Yeah," Lattimer spat. "That... That *incompetent idiot* Oliver *fired* me."

"I'm sorry to hear that," the man said sympathetically. "If you'd like, I can help you make that incompetent idiot pay. I just need a little bit of information from you about Wechsler Industries, Mr. Oliver, and the Wechsler women."

Lattimer studied the man for a moment. "Can you make them regret making such terrible business decisions?"

"That's the goal."

A vicious grin spread across Lattimer's face. "I'll tell you whatever I can, sir."

"Very good. You're doing your country a great service." The military man smiled and put an arm around Lattimer's shoulders as a black SUV skidded to a stop next to them. "You may never know just how great a service it is."

10

By Saturday morning, the story about the incidents that had occurred at the intersection of Kettle and 8th had made its way through the ranks of Heroics. While most of the issues had already been dealt with quietly, there was one that hadn't been handled yet.

"I would really like you to explain to me why you can't get along with your teammates," Ray asked as he sat down at his kitchen table across from his son.

Isaac slumped in his chair and crossed his arms. "The better question is why *they* can't get along with *me*."

"You're avoiding the question, Isaac," his mother, Olivia, said quietly as she took a seat as well. "It doesn't matter whose side it's on. You're the only one who seems to be having problems. What's going on?"

"What's going on is that Riley likes shooting people," Isaac grumbled, rubbing his chest where the girl's stun bullet had hit him.

Ray leaned forward. "You called Logan a 'half-Legion, half-Heroics bastard.' I'm not saying that Riley should've shot you, but I can't say that I'm surprised she did."

"You're the best dad ever," Isaac said sarcastically.

"Isaac!" Olivia looked stunned. "Don't talk to your father that way!"

"Why shouldn't I? He's not doing anything but bowing down to the almighty Olivers and Wechslers. What the hell respect does he deserve?"

Ray frowned, confused. "What are you talking about?"

"You're the damn *team leader!* But all you ever do is take advice and orders from Casey and Kate and Cass and all the rest of them! What's the point of being a leader if you never do any *leading?*"

"I have direct field command," Ray said slowly. "If there are any immediate choices that need to be made, it's my job to make those choices. But Heroics doesn't have some boss or commander, Isaac. We're a *team.* A *unit.* Casey and Cass run the base operations, Kate and I run the field, but none of us are 'in charge.' Especially not after what it did to Kate."

Isaac scoffed. "So Kate can't handle a little pressure, and suddenly nobody runs Heroics? Please. They just didn't want to give you command."

"A little *pressure?*" Ray slammed his hands on the table and stood up. "My sister was suicidal because of the stress of watching people she cared about get themselves hurt, and knowing the whole time that her orders were putting them into those dangerous positions. Being leader almost killed her. It ruined her marriage, and it almost ruined her relationship with her sons. I'm not sure why you *want* that for me, but I refuse to fall down that rabbit hole. I refuse to have my life be ruined in the name of status, and if you don't like that? That's just too bad. Learn to be on a team, or you're off of it."

Isaac stared up at his father, shocked. "You can't kick me off Heroics."

"I'm the field leader," Ray growled. "I can sure as hell bench you until further notice."

"I *hate* you!" Isaac spat. He threw a bolt of electricity at Ray, but it was harmlessly absorbed into the man's chest. The teen jumped up, knocking his chair over in the process, and stormed out of the room.

Ray sat back down slowly. After a long moment, he murmured, "I probably could've handled that better."

"Maybe," Olivia said. "I'm honestly not sure. It's stuff he had to hear."

"I'm not sure how you put up with either of us."

Olivia scoffed and reached out, resting her hand on top of Ray's. "It's the trips to Mexico. Getting miles and miles away from you two is the only way I survive."

"Seems reasonable." Ray ran a hand through his black hair. "I'm not sure what to do with him. It's like he thinks the others believe they're better than us, or something."

"He doesn't know what he thinks. He's a seventeen-year-old boy."

"I was a seventeen-year-old boy once, and I take offense to that."

Olivia stood, walked over to Ray, and kissed him quickly. "You probably didn't actually know anything at the time either, sweetheart."

"Gee, thanks."

"You're welcome!" Olivia leaned against the table and took Ray's face in her hands. "Are you okay?"

"I'd be better if our son wasn't the problem child of my team."

"It's Heroics. You're all problem children."

"You're not exactly making me feel better, Via."

His wife chuckled. "I've never had much luck at that with you, to be honest." She straightened from the table. "I'm going to go defuse Isaac. Maybe I'll have better luck with him." After shooting a small smile at Ray, Olivia turned and walked out of the room.

The library of the Heroics mansion was crowded when Zach walked in. AJ was on the couch, Casey was in one of the chairs, and Logan, Aubrey, and Rowan were having a conversation in the middle of the room.

"So you're actually my cousin's *girlfriend*," Logan was saying slowly, looking at Rowan through narrowed eyes.

"Uh... yes?"

Logan gave Rowan a once-over and then smirked at Aubrey. "You have very good taste." She glanced at Rowan again, nodded, and left the room.

Rowan looked at Aubrey with a mixture of confusion and panic. "W-What... uh... h... why is... uhm..." She cleared her throat and rubbed the back of her neck. "Uhm?"

"Don't mind Logan," Zach said as he walked past Rowan and Aubrey, kissed Casey, and took a seat in a nearby chair. "I'm pretty sure her sexuality is 'whatever,' and she really doesn't care about showing it."

Casey pushed her glasses further up on her nose as she studied a document on her tablet. "Zach and I have a bet going over whether she's bi or pan."

"Is that a... normal... thing for people to do?" Rowan asked carefully as Cass walked in and joined AJ on the couch.

"No," AJ said.

"Normal? In this house? You *must* be new, kid," Cass joked.

181

"Oh, leave her alone," Aubrey said grumpily. "She doesn't need the whole hazing ritual, okay?"

"Relax, Aub," Rowan said with a smile. "I can take whatever they throw at me."

"I knew I liked this one," Cass said brightly. She pulled out her phone and narrowed her eyes at it. "Aubrey, have you heard from your sister today?"

Aubrey shook her head. "I don't think I talked to Brooke yesterday, either."

Cass sighed. "I thought not. Damn. Are you heading out?"

"Yeah."

"Could you call Matthias and let him know Brooke's gone off radar?"

Aubrey gave a grim nod. "Absolutely."

Rowan's brow furrowed. "What's going on?"

"Brooke sometimes does what we call 'going off radar.' It's when we suspect she's in a full break—one way or the other—and she goes out of communication with the rest of us." Aubrey glanced at her parents. "Usually we don't need Matthias to find her unless there's a reason she'd freak out if she saw one of us."

AJ fidgeted with his tie. "Your sister isn't very fond of us right now. And given certain things that occurred the last time we spoke to her, she probably doesn't want to talk to you, either."

"Oh, great. What did *I* do?"

Cass winced. "It's more the fact that Alix and I started to get into an argument while Brooke was upset, and then Casey was talking, and basically I'm pretty sure your sister is mad at her entire family at the moment."

"Not me," Zach protested. "I didn't do anything."

"Guilt by association, babe," Casey said.

"Aw, damn. She was the only person in my family who actually liked me."

"I like you, Uncle Zach."

"Thanks, kid."

Aubrey smirked. "Somebody's gotta."

Rowan sighed and put her face in her hand.

"Oh, don't act like you're the responsible one here, van Houten," Aubrey complained. She grabbed her girlfriend by the collar of her jacket and started to drag her out of the room.

"What did I do?" Rowan asked, baffled.

"Started dating me in the first place," Aubrey replied with a grin. "Now come on. I need to call my sister's not-boyfriend."

Once the two young women had left the room, Cass smiled softly. "It's nice to see Aubrey actually happy. It's been a while."

"Fuse is a good kid," Zach said. "Bit troubled deep down, I think, but a good kid. If I'd trust anyone with my niece, I'd trust her."

"You know," Casey said, chuckling, "Rowan actually reminds me of someone."

"Who?" AJ asked curiously.

Casey raised an eyebrow at him. "*You.*"

"*Me?*"

Zach smirked. "Well, they do say girls end up with people who are like their fathers."

"I hope not," Cass and Casey said simultaneously.

"Oh. Right. My bad."

Alix walked into the room, studying something on her phone. "Finn's on her way back from her parents' house."

"Good," Casey said. "Is Kaita with her?"

"Please," Alix scoffed as she fell onto the couch next to Cass. "That would be too obvious. They have to deny everything all the time, remember?"

"Speaking of denial, where's your shadow?"

Alix raised an eyebrow at Cass and tiredly asked, "Who?"

"Max."

Alix groaned and slumped down in her seat. "Will you shut up about that? There's nothing going on."

Cass reached over and ran her hand through Alix's shoulder-length hair, putting it just enough out of its careful alignment to irritate the other woman and have her jerking away until she was half-buried in the corner of the couch.

"Get off," Alix grumbled.

"You're *miserable*," Cass laughed. "I cannot *believe* how miserable you are right now. Are you really that much in love with him?"

"Why do you care?" Alix snarled.

"After all the crap I went through when I was dating AJ, getting to do the same thing to any of you is what I *live* for."

Alix shot an annoyed look over Cass's shoulder at AJ, who just shrugged. "Gee, thanks, that was very helpful," she said dryly.

"You don't have to sleep with her tonight," AJ deadpanned.

"You don't, either," Alix shot back. "Not knowing that is probably how you ended up with three kids."

Casey and Zach both snorted loudly. "That was the best thing I've ever heard," Casey snickered.

"You idiots had *two* kids without meaning to."

"Thomas was intentional," Casey protested.

"Sort of," Zach mumbled. He was immediately hit in the face with a pillow.

Alix gritted her teeth. "How about, instead of talking about which of your children were or weren't accidents, we talk about the one I know for an absolute fact wasn't?"

Cass's grin died. "I don't know what you want me to say about Aubrey."

"*Anything*, Cass. For hell's sake, it's not even her decision not to talk to you about Lattimer, or her not wanting to admit that she wasn't taking her medication. She wasn't even comfortable telling us she's *gay*. For some reason, she thought that, despite Kara and Claire, despite me, despite Logan, despite Kaita and Finn, despite *Casey*—because I swear, woman, if you're straight I'll eat my boots—Aubrey felt like she couldn't tell us. And even though I know there are things in her head telling her that she doesn't matter, it *hurts* that those things don't trust us enough to let her talk to us."

Casey frowned. "How did my... *flexible* sexuality get dragged into this?"

Cass glared at her sister. "Stay out of this."

"I'm *trying* to!"

"Look, Al, I have no idea what Aubrey's brain's been telling her. I have *no idea*. And blaming me for it isn't going to help anything, so why don't you just—"

Alix hit the side of the couch with her fist. "*I don't blame you, I just want to!*"

Cass stared at her for a long moment. "What do you mean?"

"If you blame us," AJ said slowly, "you'll stop feeling so guilty. Isn't that right, Al?"

Alix ran a hand through her hair, rested her elbows on her knees, and stared at the floor. "She's my goddaughter," she whispered. "I'm supposed to protect her."

"Yeah," Casey said sarcastically. "Because I've done such a *great* job with Brooke."

"You're both missing something important," Cass murmured. "I'm their *mother*. What good have I been? I didn't notice Aubrey was almost at a mental breakdown because of my own company, and Brooke? Hell, I have no idea how to help Brooke. Every time I try I just make everything worse. That's why I always wimp out and let Matthias deal with it. He at least knows what he's doing."

"Honey, we *both* do that," AJ said, his voice gentle. He swallowed tightly. "We're *both* useless."

"Shut up," Zach growled. "Shut up, all of you."

Casey looked up, startled. "Zach—"

"No. You don't get to do this to yourselves. You don't get to drown yourselves in guilt. They're twenty years old. You have time. You have a chance. *Fix it.* I'm not saying you run out there and try to drag Aubrey back here—she's starting to open up, and she needs to do so in her own time. I'm not saying you immediately try to talk Brooke down, either. She's still going to be far too pissed at any of us to talk right now. But you can all *get better.* We can all pay more attention to things. We can

186

make sure our kids are okay. We just need to decide to do better."

AJ smiled slightly. "That sounds like one of my speeches, Zach."

"Yeah; I was saving it for when you were the one who needed his ass kicked."

Casey shifted so that she was kneeling in her chair, leaned across the table that separated her from Zach, and kissed him. "It was a good speech, darlin'."

"I'm not kissing you," Alix said flatly. "But it wasn't bad."

"Awwwwww." Zach stood up and walked towards the couch. "Come on, Al. You're making me feel bad."

"Get away from me."

"Nope." Zach lifted Alix up by her jacket and kissed her on the cheek. "I'm He Of The Good Speeches. I do what I want."

"Gross, get off, asshole." Alix shoved him backwards and wiped her cheek with the back of her jacket sleeve.

"Don't take offense, Zach," Cass said, the humor returning to her bright gray eyes. "You know how it is."

"Oh, right." Zach grinned. "*I'm* not the Legion hero she wants to kiss."

"*Son* of a *bitch!*" Alix looked torn between laughter and fury as she lunged in Zach's direction. Unfortunately for her, her awkward position on the couch skewed her aim, and in a moment Zach had her around the waist and was holding her a good foot off the ground.

"Man, Tolvaj, you really are short."

"I'm five foot five," Alix grumbled as she tried to kick him.

"Yeah, but I'm six foot three. You're *miniscule* from my perspective."

"Casey, did you *have* to marry this guy?" Alix complained.

"Absolutely. How else would I pin you down so we could throw you in the lake?"

Alix froze. "You wouldn't."

Cass shrugged. "I don't know; it seems like a really good idea right now."

"Have I mentioned lately that I *despise* the fact that I ended up with you all as siblings?" Alix muttered.

AJ laughed and stood up. "That's not helping your case, Al." He opened a nearby window and held his hand out. "And what do you know, it's *warm* today, so 'it's October it's cold' isn't going to save you."

"Guys. Come on. Guys."

"Come on... do it? Okay! Lead the way, Casey." Zach's grin widened as Casey, snickering, moved to open the door.

"*Nobody?*" Alix asked with a yelp as Zach started to drag her out of the room. "*Nobody* is on my side?"

"That's the curse of being the youngest, my friend," Casey said gleefully. "You're the one who gets ganged up on."

Downstairs, Rick and Logan looked up from the couch as a small cluster of adults and a loud cluster of laughter and cursing made their way down the steps and out the front door.

Rick glanced at Logan and raised an eyebrow. "What is happening?"

Logan sighed, shook her head, and laid down across his legs before going back to her book. "I don't even ask anymore."

On a secluded field deep in the forest next to the University of Fuego, Matthias found Brooke leaning up against the posts of a soccer net, a can of beer in her hand and a truly alarming number of empty cans surrounding her.

"Usually alcohol is a manic thing for you," he said quietly as he took a seat on the ground across from her.

"It seemed like a good idea at the time," Brooke muttered as she finished her drink.

"And now?"

Brooke shrugged and tossed the can towards the recycle bin a few yards away. It landed inside perfectly. "At least my aim's still good."

Matthias glanced around. "Brooke Hamil on a soccer field and she's not showing off? What's the world coming to?"

She shrugged again. "At the moment it doesn't seem fun. At all. Which is probably bad, but I honestly don't care." She cracked open another beer and started to drink it.

"Your sister called me. She was worried."

Brooke snorted. "Not worried enough to find me herself."

"It seems she was under the impression you'd be mad at her if she found you."

There was a pause as Brooke took a long sip from her can. "I wasn't mad at Aubrey. I was mad at everyone else, but not her."

"Are you still mad?"

"... No."

"What are you now?"

Brooke paused. "I don't really feel anything. I just kind of feel empty." She started toying with the tab of her beer can. "And worthless."

Matthias leaned forward, his voice softening. "How could you be worthless?"

"All of this is my fault, Mat. I should've stopped Aubrey from leaving. I should've been a better sister to Jacob. I should've sided with Ciaran four years ago when he asked us to go out there, kick Seamus's ass, and bring him home." She finished the can and crushed it in her hand. "I apparently can't even drink myself to death. I should've tried something harder than the crap Uncle Zach keeps in his office." She threw the second can at the bin like the first, but this time it bounced off the side of it.

"That's enough, Brooke," Matthias said softly, putting his hand over the new beer can she was trying to open. "None of that was your fault. Aubrey got an apartment, but she still has a room at the mansion—something everybody seems to be ignoring, but that's for another day. She wouldn't have been happy staying only at home. She has her own demons. She needs some peace sometimes. The mansion just can't give that to her. As for Jacob, please. He's a fifteen-year-old boy, Brooke. Maybe you didn't see what was bothering him, but he did a pretty good job of passing his sadness off as teen angst bullshit. That's not your fault."

He shifted closer to her, pushing the can back down onto the ground. "And as for Seamus? Seamus and the other Galaxy Boys were *murdered*, Brooke. Someone kidnapped them, tortured them, and *murdered them*. That's not your fault. That's the fault of the person or people who killed them." Matthias gently took her hands in his. "Brooke. You were fine the last time I saw you. Or, as fine as you can be when you swing out of a manic episode. What happened? What spiraled you downward?"

"They're giving up," Brooke whispered. "The real adults. They're giving up."

"What do you mean?"

"Apparently they wanted to stop Heroics back when Kate and Ray were the only ones on the field team, but they lingered, and then Ciaran and Isaac and Logan got old enough to drag them back into a fully active team. And now they're giving up, and they want to force us to join them."

Matthias paused. "Did you ask why?"

Brooke gave a sarcastic laugh. "Because they don't respect us? They see us as nothing more than kids, Mat. They let us into the hero world and they still don't treat us like we belong there."

"Did they say that?"

"No." Brooke folded her arms across her chest. "I don't need to hear them say it. I know it's the truth."

"I'm not so sure."

Brooke glared at him. "Why not?"

Matthias linked his fingers with hers. "They were broken, Brooke. This job *shattered* them. And Kate and Ray were the only ones left active in the field. They couldn't do it all by themselves. Ray's wife's job was taking off, so he was taking more care of Isaac. Kate..." Matthias took in a deep breath. "Kate was slipping, badly, because of guilt over what happened to Jay and Kara. It almost destroyed her life. It ripped apart her life. Her self-destructive madness pulled her marriage into pieces, and she had to let her sons go so that she wouldn't hurt them. Not that she'd want to, but she was a mess. And that was her tunnel vision downside whispering her failures in one ear, and depression whispering the worst things a person could think about themselves in the other. That depression was caused by a few things, but a lot of them were because of the job."

"Everyone always talks about what this job does to a person," Brooke whispered. "The bad things. What about the good things? Without this job, my parents would never have even met. Aunt Casey and Uncle Zach might not have ended up together. I wouldn't know everyone that I know. I wouldn't even *exist*. How can I hate this job?"

"They aren't ignoring the good, Brooke," Matthias said softly. "They just can't cope with the bad anymore."

Brooke nodded stiffly, drumming her fingers against one of the empty beer cans. "So. Depression makes it impossible to have a life?"

"Absolutely not. Kate was a specific case. And she's repairing her life. It's getting better, slowly." Matthias took Brooke's face in his hands and lightly kissed her on the forehead. "But it's not the same case.

It's never the same. You know that. You can have a life, Brooke. You *have* a life. It might be a bit confusing right now, but I promise you. If I can do anything to make it as easy on you as possible, I will."

She gave a soft laugh. "You're a good guy, Matthias."

"So I've been told." He stood up and started throwing her beer cans into the recycle bin. "Come on, Hamil. Let's get out of here."

"I don't want—"

"We're not going to your house. We'll go to my apartment, okay?"

Brooke nodded, looking relieved. "One problem, though."

"What's that?"

"My entire body hurts and I'm a bit too tired to move."

"That's okay." Grinning, Matthias picked her up. He swung her around so that her waist was behind his neck, her legs were over one of his shoulders, and her arms and head were over his other. "We'll get there."

Brooke laughed and lightly hit him. "This is ridiculous, Mat."

"Nah. You barely weigh anything."

"Gee, thanks."

Matthias's grip on her tightened. "Just relax, Brooke. You carry enough. Let somebody carry you for a change."

"All right, fine. Just let me get into a better position, jackass."

He let her down so that she could get on his back, her hands linked on his chest. "Better?"

"Better," Brooke murmured. She rested her chin on his shoulder. "Hey, Mat?"

"Yeah?"

"I'd be careful. I could fall in love with you."

Matthias snorted. "That'll be the day."

She smiled slightly and tightened her grip. "Well, you never know."

Logan glanced down at her phone as Thomas walked into the living room. "Looks like Matthias found Brooke. She's going to stay at his place until her head readjusts."

Thomas scoffed. "What was she drinking this time?"

"Uh... Dad's beer."

Rick grimaced. "Gross. Your dad has terrible taste."

Logan elbowed him in the side.

"Not... that we would know."

Thomas rolled his eyes as he sat down in a chair across from them. "You're both weird."

"Takes one to know one, bastard," Logan growled.

"Hey, *I'm* the *legitimate* child."

Logan laughed loudly. "As if Mom wasn't pregnant with you the day she and Dad got married."

"They were married when I was born," Thomas said pointedly. "That counts."

"Only in your mind, little brother." Logan set her phone down on her chest and ran a hand through her hair. "I guess if we see Jacob, we'll have to tell him where Brooke went. Aubrey's gone back to her apartment, but I'm sure she'll get a text."

"Jacob's out, too," Rick said. "Riley was mad at him for something and she dragged him out of the house to make it up to her."

"He really needs to figure out if he's dating her or not. This is getting ridiculous." Logan frowned. "Wait, let me get this straight. Brooke is ambiguously dating someone, Aubrey *is* dating someone, Jacob has *some* sort of thing with Riley, and Alix totally has a denial-hidden crush on that Legion guy." She looked at her brother through narrowed eyes. "I think we're a bit behind in the game in this family."

Thomas shrugged. "I'm too young to care, honestly, which means you're the only one who's a loser."

"Thanks a lot."

"No problem. Besides, I thought you and Rick were dating."

Logan laughed. "No."

Rick frowned down at her. "Thanks for that speedy denial, Carter."

She patted his cheek. "You're welcome."

"I thought Riley was gay."

"*Is* she?" Logan blinked up at Thomas, surprised. "If so, my radar for these things is *way* off."

"Honestly I never thought she was interested in Jacob. I thought she was interested in *you*."

Logan chuckled and picked up her phone as it vibrated. "Well, in fairness, who wouldn't be?" She glanced at her phone screen and went pale. "Oh... hell."

"What is it?" Rick asked.

"Jacob." Logan rolled off of Rick and the couch and started sprinting towards the elevator.

Rowan pulled her jacket tighter around her as a brisk gust of wind blew past her and Aubrey. "I like fall, but I think I'd like it more if I wasn't in this wind tunnel of a city."

"We don't have to live here," Aubrey said. "I think I'd like to *work* here, but I have no particular love for *living* here for the rest of my life." She paused when she noticed that Rowan had stopped dead and was now staring blankly at her. "What's wrong?"

"Nothing, I just… I don't think I've ever heard you saying anything about the future before."

Aubrey flushed and started spinning her ring around her finger. "Sorry if it's assuming a bit much; it just came out."

"No; it's absolutely fine. You just surprised me. I don't think I've ever seen you this relaxed."

"I guess I'm… happy? Like completely, honestly happy. The anxiety is still there, I still have that voice in my head, but having my family know everything that's going on has just made everything easier, somehow." Aubrey rubbed the back of her neck awkwardly. "It's not that I wasn't *happy* before then, of course, but—"

"*Miláček*, relax," Rowan said with a laugh, putting her hands on Aubrey's shoulders. "I get what you mean."

"Good," Aubrey sighed, relieved.

"And for the record? If I take issue with the fact that you feel *happy*, you should dump me, because I'm not worth it."

Aubrey laughed and kissed her. "I'm glad we agree on that."

Rowan grinned, but before she could respond, all of the lights in Caotico City went out.

"What the hell?" Aubrey wondered, looking around.

"Oh, *zatracený*," Rowan muttered.

"What's wrong?"

Instead of answering, Rowan took off at a run down the street.

"I still don't understand why you're mad at me," Jacob grumbled as Riley pulled him through a crowd in the center of Caotico.

"I'm really not," Riley replied. "It was just the only way to get you to come with me."

"You're a horrible person."

"You like me anyway."

"Because I need a best friend who doesn't want to sleep with my cousin."

"Well," Riley said fairly, "your cousin *is* hot."

Jacob groaned and rolled his eyes. "Remind me later to shove Logan in the lake or something."

Riley raised an eyebrow at him. "She would kill you. You're smarter than that."

He sighed. "This is why it's really difficult to be me."

"Yeah, I'm sure it's super hard." Riley squinted ahead of her, where she saw her parents walking down the street towards them. "Look, there's my mom and dad. It's just one lunch, J. You can survive one lunch."

"If it's so easy, why are you making me come?"

"Uh, because my parents are *boring*?"

Jacob rolled his eyes again. "Whatever you say, Riley."

"Damn straight." When Justin and Erin met them, Riley said, "Hey, Mom and Dad."

"Hi there," Erin greeted. She shot Jacob a bright grin. "You got suckered into chaperoning, Jacob?"

"Apparently I was in fake trouble until it was too late for me to turn back."

"You need to look out for those," Erin said. "She's good for them."

"I've noticed." Jacob looked at Justin. "Please ground her."

The older man rubbed at the scruff on his face. "It sounds more fun to let her torture you."

Erin laughed loudly. "You should've known better, Jacob."

"I really should have," Jacob sighed.

Justin chuckled and kissed Riley on the top of the head. "Try not to go overboard, though, okay? He really is quite useful, on occasion."

"Rare occasions," Riley agreed.

"You do know that I'm *right here,* right?" Jacob complained.

Erin put an arm around his shoulders. "They don't care, honey."

"Excuse me, Mr. Oliver?"

Justin turned around and frowned as he came face to face with Raymond Lattimer. "Can I help you with something, Lattimer? Because we're done talking about your job."

Lattimer stared straight ahead, his gaze glassy and unfocused. His voice sounded strained, as if his words were being fed to him. "This isn't about my job," Lattimer said slowly. "It's about your old one."

"My what?"

"Your... old job."

"I'm really not sure what you—"

The former manager pulled a gun out from behind his back, aimed it, and shot Justin twice in the chest.

11

The crowd in Caotico's city center dissolved into panicked fleeing masses the moment the gunshots registered. It only got worse when Raymond Lattimer turned the gun on himself.

No one close to Justin seemed to notice the shooter fall. They were too busy focused on the victim.

"*Dad!*" Riley screamed. She started to fight her way through the crowd to him, but Erin, who looked on the verge of panic, grabbed her and shoved her towards Jacob.

"Get her out of here!"

"Mom, no!"

"Riley, *go!*" Erin yelled before running over to Justin.

"Ry, come on," Jacob said urgently. "*Come on!*" Hating himself for it, Jacob dragged Riley away from her fallen father and pushed her through the crowd into the nearest alleyway. He continued to lead her as he ran further and further away from the chaos until he was near Casey's bar. He came to a stop in the alley just behind it, panting to catch his breath. "Riley?" he whispered.

The girl was just staring blankly at the ground. She didn't even seem to hear him say her name.

"Riley, I'm sorry. But that wasn't somewhere you needed to be."

"I-I need to... W-We need to... What if he's..."

"Hey." Jacob put his hands on her shoulders. "The best we can do is stay out of the way. We'll get information as it comes in, all right? Come on. Let's go into my aunt Casey's bar." As he followed Riley into the back door of the building, Jacob noticed that his hands were shaking. He knew why.

What he had neglected to tell Riley was that he was almost completely positive that her father was already dead.

"Jacob! Riley! Are you both okay?" Kaita asked urgently as she met them in the back room of the bar. "I already heard what happened. It's been all over the Heroics communications system. Not sure how it got there so quickly, but it did."

"I think Riley needs to sit down," Jacob murmured.

"Of course. Come here, sweetheart."

As Kaita pulled over a chair for her, Riley whispered, "Is my dad still alive?"

Kaita gave a small, sad sigh and crouched down in front of the girl. "No, honey. I'm afraid he's not."

Riley swallowed, nodded, and broke down sobbing. She collapsed forward, hugging Kaita around the neck and crying into the woman's shoulder.

"Shhh," Kaita said soothingly, rubbing Riley's back. "It's all right, sweetheart. It's gonna be all right." After a long moment, Kaita carefully extracted herself from Riley's grip. "I'll be back in just a minute," she whispered. She glanced at Jacob. "Keep an eye on her."

Once the boy, his eyes red as if he was moments from crying, nodded, Kaita disappeared into one of the other rooms.

Finn was sprawled on the couch, sound asleep. Kaita's four-year-old daughter, Mila, whom Kaita had once described as 'the only good thing to ever come from being with a man,' was sitting on top of the sleeping woman, watching a movie on Finn's phone.

Kaita smiled and pressed a soft kiss to Finn's forehead. She hadn't had the heart to wake the other woman up earlier, but now she had no choice. She ruffled Mila's light-brown hair and said, "I need you to do me a favor, baby. Think you could play in your room for a bit? I need to talk to Whitney."

The little girl looked up at her with wide blue eyes. "What's wrong, *Majka?*"

"There's some bad stuff going on, and we need to go deal with it, okay?"

Mila nodded. "Can I keep Whit's phone?"

"That'll be up to her." Kaita reached down and started to pick her daughter up.

Finn snapped awake and grabbed the little girl by the waist in a quick, jerking motion. Her breathing was fast and almost panicked, and her brown eyes were lit with fear.

"Whitney, it's me," Kaita said, confused.

After a second, the blonde recognized her. Finn flushed pink and relaxed, though there was still a faint edge of terror in her eyes. "Sorry," she mumbled.

"Whit, you okay?" Mila asked, worry in her voice.

"Yeah, kid," Finn sighed. "Yeah. I'm okay."

The girl clambered further up on Finn and kissed her on the cheek. "Y'sure?"

Finn gave a weak laugh. "I'm sure."

"Okay. Can I keep your phone?"

"Go ahead."

"Thanks!" Mila scrambled off the couch and bolted towards her room.

Finn took in a deep, shaky breath and sat up on the couch. Kaita sat down next to her. "Are you actually okay?"

"Sure." Finn ran a hand through her white-blonde hair. "I'm sorry."

"What was that about?"

"You started to move Mila, and I just..."

"Just what?"

"I panicked. I didn't know it was you, and I panicked." Finn fidgeted with the strings of her sweatshirt. "Alice Cage kidnapped me when I was ten years old, Kay," she whispered. "I don't want anything similar to happen to your child. I care about her too much."

"Caring is still a bit new for you, isn't it?"

Finn snorted. "I never quite know what to do with it."

Kaita laughed softly. "You do a fair enough job." She took Finn's hand and interlocked their fingers. "She's safe as long as she's with us, at the very least. At the moment, we have other things to worry about."

"What happened?"

"Justin was murdered. Jacob and Riley watched it happened. They're in the other room."

"Oh, hell," Finn sighed. She pinched the bridge of her nose and closed her eyes. "What do we do?"

"Take care of them."

"I don't understand teenagers."

Kaita smiled slightly. "You were one once."

Finn raised an eyebrow.

"Right. You were a jackass teenager who slammed people's faces into bar counters."

"It's not something most can relate to."

"Remind me again why I'm sleeping with you?"

Finn shrugged and stood. "I'm still trying to figure it out."

"Har har. You're *still* a jackass."

"I wasn't joking," Finn said flatly.

Kaita gave a weary sigh and got to her feet as well. "Forty-six. I'm forty-six. Why am I still doing this to myself?"

As the two women joined Jacob and Riley in the other room, the television suddenly switched from a calm music station to a news alert. A man in a military uniform was sitting behind a desk, looking into the camera with a serious expression on his face.

"People of Caotico City," he said in a somber voice. "My name is General Henry Reznik. Some of you may already know me. I came to this city to calm the anti-vigilante riots, and I have stayed here to ensure your safety while the vigilantes struggle to decide whether they are criminals or honest citizens.

"It is my duty to inform you—and I take no pride in doing this—but I must inform you that today, a short time ago, the vigilantes chose to be criminals. The group you know as Heroics carried out a public execution against Justin Oliver, the CEO of Wechsler Industries. He was murdered in front of his family, in a hit ordered by unempowered civilians who have been helping Heroics get away with their unjust acts.

"Cassidy Hamil, Casey Carter, and Alix Tolvaj, three high-ranking Wechsler Industries employees, are now considered fugitives. They are armed and dangerous, and they should not be confronted directly. If you see any of them, please inform the nearest military personnel. These three women ordered the assassination of Justin Oliver in order to get him out of their way, and they used their personal army of vigilantes in order to do it.

"As of today, all vigilantes in Caotico City, be they Heroics or Security Legion or independent actors, must surrender themselves at the army base in Fuego Village. There, it will be determined whether they are complicit in the horrific crimes committed by certain members of Heroics, whether they committed other crimes, or whether they are innocent and free to become regular citizens.

"Caotico City and Fuego Village are now under total military lockdown. No communication will come in or out of the city. No one will be permitted in or out of the city. There will be a curfew in place starting at nine o'clock every night and lasting until five o'clock every morning, and anyone caught outside during these times will be arrested and interrogated.

"The purpose of this lockdown is not to treat any honest citizen of Caotico City as a criminal. But these so-called heroes must be stopped at any cost, or they will continue to prey upon you all until it is too late. I beg you to be patient with us while we work to put an end to this vigilante menace. If we work together, we can make Caotico City a place free from corruption and violence. We can make this city a beautiful place to live.

"Stay home. Stay safe."

Reznik disappeared from the screen. As soon as the television went dark, the entire city went with it.

"Rowan, slow down!" Aubrey called as she chased her girlfriend into the poorest section of Caotico, a block near the prison that was known for foreclosures and crime. Rowan didn't seem to have heard the request, but she came to a stop in front of an old apartment building. The red paint was faded and crumbling, and one of the windows on the first floor was boarded up with decaying wood.

"Where are we?" Aubrey asked softly as she came to a stop next to her.

Rowan glanced at her but didn't respond. She looked embarrassed and afraid, with tears in her eyes that were so far out of character for her that Aubrey couldn't even ask any other questions. Rowan walked up to the front door of the building and went inside, with Aubrey close behind.

The inside of the building was just as decrepit as the outside. A few steps on the staircase in front of them were missing entirely, and the wall to their right had been ripped away until the internal structure could be seen.

"Don't look at it," Rowan mumbled. "Just... please, don't even look around."

Yelling was echoing from most of the apartments, but Rowan didn't acknowledge it at all as she hurried up the stairs to the third floor. She took out a key and started opening the door of an apartment towards the back of the building.

"Ro, what—"

Before Aubrey could finish her question, Rowan pushed the apartment door open and stepped inside.

"*Daj?* Are you okay? *Daj!*" Rowan walked into the kitchen, where a woman was sitting in a wheelchair, bent over and muttering to herself.

"They are coming for us, Kaja," the woman said in Czech. She had an accent that was similar to Rowan's but significantly stronger, so much so that, when combined with her hoarse and cracked voice, it was difficult for Aubrey to mentally translate her words.

Rowan crouched down in front of the woman and started speaking Czech as well. "No one is coming, *Daj*. I promise you. Nobody is coming."

The woman yelled quickly in a language Aubrey didn't recognize, and Rowan flinched. "*Daj*, please, I have trouble following along when you speak Romani. Can you—"

She was cut off when the woman slapped her across the face. The woman then started screaming various obscenities in Czech so rapidly that Aubrey couldn't keep up at all, though she caught several variations of the phrase *worthless child*.

"I-I am sorry, *Daj*," Rowan said over the woman's yelling. Her voice was thick and heavy, as if she was trying not to cry. "I will do better next time."

"*Useless* girl," the woman snarled. "Where is Janek?"

There was a pause as Rowan swallowed and took in a shaky breath. "*Daj*, you know Father is dead. He has been dead for years."

"Oh, Janek," the woman sighed. "Why did you leave me with this mediocre child? Why could they not have killed her instead of Einar? He was a good child. He would have helped me."

Rowan was trembling, her expression somewhere between fear, anger, and bitter sadness. She slowly started to stand, but the woman grabbed her by the wrist and screamed, "*I need light!*"

"Y-Yes, *Daj*, I will find light for you," Rowan said.

"Get the light, Kaja! Before they find us and burn us all!"

"I promise, *Daj*." Rowan stood stiffly and stared in Aubrey's direction, her head bowed.

As Rowan walked away, the woman raised her head slightly, allowing Aubrey to see her face, which her white hair had been obscuring. Aubrey's breath caught in her throat. The woman was badly burned, enough that one side of her face seemed completely unusable. Her pale blue eyes had a dead note to them, and they stared ahead at nothing.

Rowan walked right past Aubrey, avoiding eye contact with her. She dug through a nearby drawer and pulled out an old battery-powered lantern.

"This should last for a few hours, *Daj*," Rowan said, setting it on the table a small distance away from the woman. "I will come back and replace it for you."

"You had better," the woman snarled.

"Yes, *Daj*."

Rowan led Aubrey back out of the apartment, though she still wouldn't look at her. "I-I'm sorry," she stammered, switching back to English. "She just gets... she doesn't like when the power goes out."

"Is that your... mom?" Aubrey asked quietly.

"Yes. It is." Rowan rubbed her cheek where her mother had struck her.

Aubrey paused. "Is that where you live, then?"

"Yeah," Rowan murmured. "All my life."

They started down the steps towards the ground level in awkward silence until Aubrey said, "I-I-I thought your mother died in that fire."

Rowan fidgeted with the leather cuff around her wrist. "I never said that she did, but I never told you that she didn't. That's a cop-out, I know, and I'm sorry. It's just that she might as well have." She toyed with the cuff again, still not looking at Aubrey. "That was one of her better days, actually. Usually she throws things at me."

"Honey..."

"It's not her fault," Rowan said stiffly. "She's not... right. Ever since that fire. Ever since then, she's been a complete mess. She's paranoid, she's delusional, she forgets damn near everything except for that day. She can't remember that my father's been dead since I was nine, and she still thinks she's in the Czech Republic and people are coming after her to kill her."

Aubrey reached over and took Rowan's hand gently. "I'm sorry."

"So am I," Rowan whispered.

"God, how could you even listen to me complain about my family? When you have all of this going on in your life?"

"Pain and personal problems are not competitions, *miláček*. Just because your issues might not be the same as mine doesn't mean that they aren't valid in their own right." Rowan leaned against Aubrey, looking exhausted. "I should've told you about this stuff sooner. It's been hard, dealing with it by myself. I guess I just didn't want to trouble you with it when you had other things on your mind."

"Honey, you aren't the only one in this relationship who's allowed to be supportive. Let me in a little, okay? Let me help when I can. At least talk to me when you need to talk."

"I think I might," Rowan murmured.

"Good." Aubrey raised an eyebrow at her. "And for the sake of clarification, why does she call you Kaja?"

"Because it's my name."

Aubrey stopped on the bottom step as Rowan continued towards the door. "Whoa, hold on, you can't just drop that on me as if it's not a big deal."

"It's *not* a big deal," Rowan said. "My name was legally changed to Rowan van Houten when we moved to America. But I was born Kaja Ctvrtlanik."

"I literally know *nothing* about you, do I?"

Rowan gave her a sheepish grin. "I love you?"

"Yeah, yeah, suck up." Aubrey put her hands on Rowan's shoulders. "Are you okay? With your mom and living here and everything? I mean seriously, Rowan, I'm asking you to tell me the truth. *Are you okay?*"

"I-I think so," Rowan stammered.

"If you ever aren't, I need you to tell me. Please. Even if I can't help, I want to do whatever I can for you. All right?"

"All right. But you have to do the same."

Aubrey grimaced. "Aw, man. I don't like this trade."

"Tough luck, Hamil," Rowan said with a grin, kissing Aubrey quickly. "It's too late to renegotiate."

"It's been like half a second!"

"Like I said," Rowan teased. "Too late."

"You're the worst."

"You love me anyway."

"It's true." As they stepped out the front door, Aubrey pulled out her phone. "Jacob's calling," she muttered. She raised the phone to her ear. "Hey, buddy, what's up?"

Kaita looked down at her Heroics communications sunglasses. A light on the side of them was glowing red. "Oh, hell," she whispered. "Whoever's working Control just sent out an order for all Heroics operatives to go underground."

"What does that mean?" Jacob asked.

Finn squinted at him. "Do you not read *any* of the general memos?"

Jacob tapped a finger on the side of his head. "Dyslexic."

"Fair enough." Kaita stood up to get Riley a glass of water. "Whitney, explain."

Finn leaned back in her chair. "Basically, whoever is at your house wants everyone from Heroics to stay off the streets, keep away from their homes, and stop all communication via the network until further notice."

"Doesn't that mean Riley and I should get away from here, too?"

"Most likely," Kaita said.

"But where should we go?"

Kaita shrugged. "I don't know. But I'm certainly not letting you go alone, so we'll figure it out together."

Jacob shook his head. "You two can't come with us, Kaita."

"And why not?"

"If you're gone from here, and military goons come knocking on the door, they'll assume you're involved. You aren't actually a member of Heroics. You have no powers. They have no reason to arrest you unless you give them one. Riley and I can't put you in danger like that."

"It's not your decision to make, J."

"Kaita, please," he said. "If something goes wrong, I don't want to know that you ended up in prison—or worse—just because you were worried something might happen to us. I wouldn't be able to live with that."

The bartender bit her lip, but nodded.

"What about me?" Finn asked.

"There's no reason for you to leave here, Finn. You have just as little external connection to us as Kaita has, and this is a bar. There's no reason anybody should have a problem with you being here." Jacob's voice softened. "And we both know you want to stay."

Finn's expression twitched slightly as she glanced at Kaita. "Alix would kill me if I let anything happen to you, Jacob."

"Nothing's going to happen to me," Jacob insisted. "And trust me, Finn. She'd understand."

The woman bowed her head awkwardly, putting her hands in the pocket of her sweatshirt. "Thanks," she mumbled.

"So what's your plan?" Kaita asked.

Jacob hesitated. "Brooke is out of the picture, but I wonder if..." He took out his phone and dialed Aubrey's number. After a few rings, she picked up.

"*Hey, buddy, what's up?*"

"Did you see the announcement on the news?"

"Announcement? No. The power's out, though, so that's not completely surprising."

"It's not a power outage, Bree," Jacob said grimly. "The city's on full military lockdown. Some general named Reznik wants to arrest everyone from Heroics, specifically Mom, Aunt Casey, and Alix, and the city's on a full blackout—power, communications, and travel—until he gets us all."

"That's insane. What the hell's his excuse for that?"

Jacob lowered his voice. "Justin was shot and killed. Reznik's blaming us for it."

There was a long pause. "Please tell me this is a sick joke, Jake."

"I wish it were."

Aubrey gave a slow sigh. "Okay. Uhm. Okay. Where are you?"

"The bar, with Riley. We're going to leave soon, though. Can I meet you somewhere?"

"Absolutely. How about the normal—" Aubrey's voice cut off.

"Bree? Bree!"

When her voice returned, it sounded breathless and full of fear. "Jake, just run. Just go. Run!"

"Bree!"

The line went dead. Jacob lowered his phone shakily and slipped it into his pocket.

"Jacob?" Kaita prompted hesitantly. "What's wrong?"

"I don't know," Jacob said hoarsely. "But I feel like I just lost my sister."

Cass and AJ stared at the computer screens as, one by one, the Heroics communication devices that were out in the field went offline.

"How did this happen?" AJ whispered.

"I have a feeling this Reznik guy's been planning this for a very long time," Cass replied in a murmur.

"What do you want to do?"

Cass spun her wedding ring around her finger slowly. "Casey and I have already talked about it."

"That's terrifying."

"I'm serious, AJ. We're going to let them arrest us."

"*Why?*"

She sighed. "They already know where we are, AJ. It's only a matter of time before they catch up with us. We're who they're *looking for*. You and the kids don't need to be here."

AJ took in a long, slow breath, surprisingly calm. "Do you really think they're just going to ask you a few nice questions and let you go?"

"Absolutely not," Cass admitted. "But we can't hide forever, and Reznik *can* keep this lockdown going basically forever. We'd be killed on the streets long before running became the better option."

"Just so we're clear, this feels very similar to the last time you surrendered yourself to someone who probably wanted to kill you."

"This is different," Cass said, absentmindedly rubbing her wrist, where long ago her father and Alice Cage had affixed a painful mind control device on her.

"Oh? How?"

"I'm actually telling you about it before I commit to it this time."

AJ sighed. "That's not *better*."

"It's a *little* better." Cass started fixing AJ's tie. "We'll be fine. We always are."

"Cass, these guys murdered Justin in cold blood," AJ murmured. "Forgive me for not being okay with you being arrested by them."

"I know." Cass kissed him softly. "I know. But I really don't know what else to do. We can't run. It'll put all of you at risk. It'll put the kids at risk. I can't let that happen."

AJ smiled slightly. "I know you can't. It's not who you are."

"That sounds about right." Cass yanked him forward by his tie, kissing him more firmly this time. She then moved her hands to his shoulders and rested her forehead against his. "Hey, AJ?"

"Yeah?"

"I think I'm in love with you."

AJ laughed. "Well, good. We've been married for over two decades, so that's probably the preferred way to feel."

Cass grinned and pushed against him lightly. "I figured it might be something that would interest you."

"It does." AJ closed his eyes briefly, his head still resting against hers. "Hey, Cass?"

"Yeah?" she whispered.

"I think I'm in love with you, too."

"Rick," Casey said softly as she walked into the living room. "Could I have a minute with my kids, please? Alone?"

"Absolutely." Rick, who had been sitting on the floor with Logan and playing Double Klondike with Thomas to keep the boy's mind occupied, stood, ruffled Thomas's hair, and headed towards the kitchen.

"What is it?" Logan asked, staring up at her mother.

For a moment, Casey just stared back, unsure of what to say. Logan noticed, and she quickly pieced together what was going on.

"Mom, no. You can't."

"Can't what?" Thomas prompted.

"She's going to surrender to that Reznik asshole."

"Logan," Casey admonished softly.

"It's true, isn't it?" Logan retorted fiercely, getting to her feet.

Casey sighed. "Yes. Your aunt and I are going to let him arrest us."

"*What?*" Thomas stood up alongside his sister.

"We *have* to, honey. I can't explain it very well. Not in a way you'll accept. But we *have* to do it."

"Mom, please," Logan begged. "They'll kill you."

Casey gave her a weak smile. "Nah. Why would they bother? I'm no superhero." She looked at Thomas, who didn't seem capable of forming words. "I'll be okay. It's going to be okay."

Thomas moved forward and hugged her tightly. Logan quickly followed suit.

"Geez," Casey said with a strained laugh. "You'd think I was handing myself over to a military prison or something."

Her children chuckled weakly before falling silent. They just stood there for a long moment, holding each other. Then Casey pressed a soft kiss to the top of Logan's head. "I love you guys," she whispered. "I love you. I know I don't say it enough, but I need you to know that." Casey tightened the hug, trying to keep either child from noticing how much she was shaking. "I just really need you to know it."

In an alley in Caotico, Max watched as Alix, her hair damp and wavy, paced back and forth. "What can I do, Thief?" he asked softly.

"I'm not sure there's anything any of us can do," she replied. She fidgeted with her jacket. "I shouldn't have left the mansion."

"Don't do that. You were soaking wet and irritated. You were all just fooling around, and you came out here to complain about them. It's a normal thing, Thief. You couldn't have imagined what was going to happen."

"I know. It doesn't make me feel any better."

Max nodded and put his hands in his pockets. "What are you going to do?"

"I have no idea," Alix admitted. "I need to find out what's going on, but I know I can't go back to the mansion. I need..." She paused. "Help."

He grinned. "Luckily for you, help is something I'm rather good at."

Alix frowned at him. "Why would you want to help me?"

"Uh, because you're my friend?"

"It's not for any... other reason?" Alix asked hesitantly.

Max paused for a long moment, until an embarrassed look spread across his face. "Zach told you."

"No, but apparently everybody but me knew, so it got filtered down to me from quite a few different sources." Alix's voice lowered. "You probably shouldn't have a crush on me, Max."

"Why's that?" Max flushed. "I'm sorry. That's not an appropriate question. You don't need to have a reason not to be interested. I apologize."

"I'm not..." Alix cleared her throat awkwardly. "... *not* interested. But I... You'd have to be okay with the, er, asexual thing, and—"

"And what? If that's a deciding factor in a relationship, I don't deserve to be in it."

Alix's jaw tensed. "You're serious?"

"Absolutely. I'm also serious about you being my friend, and you'd be my friend no matter how you felt about me."

"Can I... stick with that, at least for now?"

"Of course," Max said quickly.

"And that's really okay with you?"

Max gave her a three-fingered salute. "One hundred percent."

Alix laughed. "What are you, a Boy Scout?"

"Eagle Scout, actually."

"Somehow I'm not surprised." Alix started to walk past Max, but he lightly tapped her arm to stop her.

"If my crush developed too fast for you, I'm sorry," he said softly. "I just… you're too fascinating for it not to."

"I was aware of you rather early on too, Max. I just don't know yet whether or not what I'm feeling is a crush."

"Let me know when you figure it out?" he asked.

"Well, you said you were going to help me with this lockdown, so it's not like I won't probably be in your presence when I do, anyway."

She walked away and Max, smiling, followed.

An hour and a half after Caotico City had gone on lockdown, Reznik and a group of his soldiers kicked down the door of the Heroics mansion. They found Cass and Casey sitting calmly in the library, drinking tea and reading books.

"Gentlemen," Casey greeted casually. "Ladies. Welcome to my humble home. Can I interest you in some coffee? Tea? Hot chocolate? I have marshmallows."

"Cut the crap, Carter," Reznik snarled. "Where is everyone else?"

"Everyone else?" Casey looked at Cass. "Have you seen anyone else, dear sister?"

"Certainly not, dear sister," Cass replied. "I believe the only people I've seen all day are you and these soldiers."

Reznik chuckled. "Oh, so you're difficult ones. I don't know why I'm surprised." He looked at one of the lieutenants. "Johnston, take these two to the van. We're going to see how quippy they are after a week in our care."

Cass laughed as the lieutenant pulled her to her feet. "Trust me, General Reznik. I've met people much scarier than you."

"You really think so?"

"I *know* so."

"Hm. Somehow I don't think it will matter much."

Reznik gave a short nod, and Cass and Casey were escorted out of the mansion in handcuffs.

12

Zach slammed open the door of the tenth Heroics safe house that he had gotten to. He still hadn't found anyone, but, by luck, on this try he found the two people he was most desperate to see.

"*Dad!*"

Thomas and Logan both tackled him around the waist, hugging him tightly. He hugged them back, letting out a ragged sigh. "God, I was starting to think I'd never find you guys," he murmured.

"We were worried something had happened to you," Thomas said.

"To *me?* Please. Who do you think I am?"

Logan raised an eyebrow at him. "A Carter."

"This is a very good point." Zach stepped further into the safe house. "Who are you with?"

"*Tell me* you weren't just wandering around the streets like a damned idiot."

Zach grinned and went over to hug AJ as well. "Have you ever known me to be anything *other* than a damned idiot?"

"Not at all."

"I had to get a look at what was going on, and I had to find my kids," Zach said.

"Yeah, but that's reckless, Dad. What's the rule about recklessness?"

Zach looked down at his son. "Only when AJ's not around to yell at you?"

"Hey!" AJ folded his arms across his chest. "Why am *I* the spoilsport?"

"Uh, because you always are?" Zach patted AJ on the back. "Try to keep up, brother."

"Dad, they have Mom," Logan said urgently.

Zach went pale and sat down on the nearest chair. "What?"

AJ bowed his head. "And Cass. They thought it would be best to surrender to Reznik so he wouldn't tear up the entire city looking for them. They figured it would be better than risking him arresting all of us just to get to them. I have no idea whether he has Alix, too."

For a long moment Zach was silent, his eyes closed and his head resting in his hand. Then he sighed. "Those Wechsler girls are too damn noble for their own good."

That got a soft laugh from AJ. "I think they got all of the decency their parents were lacking. Combine that with pure concentrated stubbornness and here we are."

"We have no idea what's happened to them?"

AJ swallowed, looking close to tears. "None."

"Oh, hell," Zach sighed. He glanced up at his children, noting the fear on their faces. "Don't worry, guys," he said quickly. "Your mom and your aunt Cass have been through a lot. They'll get through. They always do."

"You don't believe that," Logan said softly.

"I have to try, don't I?"

Logan nodded stiffly and put a protective arm around her brother's shoulders.

"What's going on outside?"

Zach looked up, finally noticing Rick standing in the doorway. "Oh, hey, Rick. What was that?"

"What's going on outside?" the teen repeated.

"It's ugly. A few of the Legion heroes tried to go out on the street to calm down some of the looting that happened right after the blackout. They were all killed." Zach paused. "One of them was Paul Cartwright."

Logan's jaw dropped. "*Kilowatt?*"

"Who was he again?" Rick asked, frowning.

AJ looked stunned as well. "The *leader of the Legion.*"

Rick gave a low whistle. "Then who the hell's in charge."

Zach shifted uncomfortably in his chair. "Uh, yeah, about that..."

"Shut the hell up," Logan said.

Her father didn't even bother to correct her. "Yeah. I was the highest-ranking Legion member still around. So I was made the leader."

Thomas shook his head slowly. "We're all going to die. That's it. The city's doomed. Everyone's going to just die."

"Thanks so much for the confidence, son."

"No problem, Oh Great Leader," Thomas replied, grinning.

"There's something else," Zach said. He hadn't even laughed, which was a key indicator that something was deeply wrong. "AJ, I'm not sure how to say this."

"Say what?"

"After we confirmed who was dead, I sent an order out for every Legion hero to check in." Zach met AJ's gaze steadily. "Rowan was the only one who didn't do it."

AJ's blood ran cold. "You're telling me," he said slowly, "that the only Legion hero still missing is the one who is not only dating my daughter, but who was with her not a half-hour before everything went to hell."

"Yes."

AJ took a seat in the chair across from Zach's. "I-I don't... I don't know what I'm supposed to do, Zach."

"There's nothing we *can* do," the other man said softly. "But you deserved to know."

"I hate this," AJ whispered. "I hate not being able to do anything."

"So do I." Zach reached out, resting his hand on AJ's shoulder. "So do I, brother, but I promise you. If we find *anything* that we can do, we'll do it. Got that?"

AJ nodded. "I just hope we have time to figure it out."

Kaita was washing glasses in the bar when Reznik walked in with a few of his soldiers. "Can I get you men anything?"

"Kaita Dragovic?"

"I'm not on the menu."

Finn, sitting at the end of the bar, snorted a laugh into her soda. Reznik's serious expression didn't change.

"This building is owned by Casey Carter, correct?"

"I believe so." Kaita shrugged. "I just work here. I get paid. I don't really care who signs my checks as long as they keep coming."

"Have you seen Alix Tolvaj today?"

"Who?"

Reznik leaned against the bar. "Alix Tolvaj. Head of security at Wechsler Industries."

"If you gave me a picture I might be able to tell you if she's been in, but I see a lot of people on a lot of days, General. I don't learn all of their names. I'm a bartender, not a teacher."

"Of course." Reznik turned towards Finn, who was watching the proceedings out of the corner of her eye. "You're Whitney Finnegan, aren't you?"

"Maybe." Finn continued drinking her soda. "Why do you want to know?"

"You're Alix Tolvaj's second-in-command. Have you seen your boss today?"

"It's Saturday. I don't work on Saturdays. Neither does Tolvaj."

Reznik glanced at one of his soldiers and nodded. The lieutenant dragged Finn off of her barstool and moved her over so that she was standing in front of Reznik.

"I'm sorry, was I not clear?" Finn asked coldly. "I don't know where Tolvaj is."

"Yes, and I'm sure you'd tell me if you did."

Finn just shrugged.

"*Majka*, what's goin' on?" Mila asked, coming out of the back room to squint at the soldiers.

"Get back in your room," Kaita said through gritted teeth.

"But—"

"*Milanka Gemma Dragovic, go to your room!*"

The girl, looking scared, started to leave, but before she could, Reznik said, "Why not let the girl stay? We won't be much longer anyway." He smiled at Mila. "Can *you* help me, little one?"

"Don't talk to her," Finn growled.

Without warning, Reznik drove a solid punch into Finn's gut that put her onto her knees.

"*Whitney!*" Kaita exclaimed. She started to come out from behind the bar, looking furious, but another soldier stopped her.

Reznik crouched down next to Finn. "I'm going to find Alix Tolvaj. With or without your help. How much you're going to regret it when I do depends on whether you help me."

"I don't know what you want me to say," Finn said through gritted teeth.

"Have it your way." Reznik slammed Finn's head into the nearby barstool before standing and leaving the bar with his soldiers.

"Whitney!" Kaita hurried over to the other woman, who was groaning on the floor. "Whitney, are you okay?"

"Tell Casey that she's right. The materials in her bar are of too high a quality to go bashing people's faces into."

Kaita smiled in spite of herself as she knelt down, pulling Finn into a sitting position. She brushed the other woman's white-blonde hair out of the deep gash in her temple. "You should get that looked at."

"The city's gone to hell. I'm fine."

"Is this going to be as annoying as it was to get you to take an ice pack for a black eye?"

"Probably worse. I'm fine."

Kaita shook her head and rested her chin on Finn's shoulder. "You're going to be the death of me, Finnegan."

"I keep trying."

"Was that a *joke*, Whitney?" Kaita asked, shocked.

"An attempt at one."

"I'm impressed."

Mila crept around the bar, staring at Finn with a worried look on her face. "Whit? Are you okay?"

"Trust me, kid, I've had worse."

The little girl climbed into Finn's lap and hugged her tightly.

"Ow," Finn muttered. "I did get punched in the ribs, you know, kid."

Mila ignored her and continued to hug her.

"Typical."

Kaita continued softly brushing her fingers through Finn's hair. "You could've dodged that. Your power is reflexes. You had to have seen those blows coming."

"I did."

"Then why didn't you *do something about them*?"

"I couldn't," Finn murmured.

The bartender swallowed, realization creeping in. "Because you didn't know how Reznik would react."

Finn shrugged. "Wouldn't've mattered if he ended up hurting me worse. But..." She shot a short, embarrassed glance at Kaita.

"Oh, you idiot," Kaita whispered affectionately. She turned Finn's head and kissed her quickly.

"I've been known for it."

Kaita gently rested a hand on Mila's head. "If that guy finds out who we are to Heroics, I have a feeling it's going to be quite painful for us anyway," she murmured to Finn.

"Well," Finn said slowly, "I guess we'll just have to hope that Alix doesn't run off in the direction of danger and get herself arrested."

"So, no chance, then."

"Not a one."

Kaita smiled slightly. "I've heard Serbia is nice this time of year."

Finn laughed and gently hugged Mila. "If it were possible, Dragovic, I think I'd take you up on that."

Rowan woke up to pain.

It took her a few minutes to figure out why, but eventually the fuzziness in her head focused enough for her to realize that the chair she was chained to was attached directly to a power outlet.

"No fair," she mumbled.

"Well then! Good morning." Reznik took a seat in a chair across from hers. "Do you remember me? We met yesterday."

"*Jdi do prdele,*" Rowan muttered.

"That didn't sound very nice." Another jolt of pain ran through Rowan's body. Reznik leaned back in his chair and crossed his legs. "You know, I've been following your little girlfriend for quite a while. She's the weak link in her family, so I knew that if I ever needed to take someone as leverage, it was going to be her. But *you*... you're interesting to me."

Rowan gritted her teeth. "Why's that?"

"When I realized that she hung out with you a lot, I did some research into who exactly you are. Rowan van Houten. Daughter of Janek van Houten. Now, my sources tell me that he used to be a Legion hero. He died in those riots a few years back."

"What's it to you?"

228

"Well," Reznik said slowly, "I *caused* those riots so that I could institute a military control in this area. So one could argue that I'm the one who *caused* your father's death." He picked up Rowan's leather jacket, which had been removed and tossed onto the floor. "This was his, wasn't it? It's too big for you, and I don't see why that would happen unless it wasn't yours. You want so *badly* to impress him, don't you? Even though he's dead and buried."

An explosive immediately started to form in Rowan's hand, but before she could even think to use it, a Middle Eastern woman stepped out from behind Rowan's line of vision, grabbed Rowan's wrist, and forced her hand closed around the tiny bomb.

Rowan screamed as her own construct burned into her skin. The woman who was holding her made a quiet scolding noise. "That's not the best idea in the world, Legion Girl."

Panting, Rowan tried to ignore the pain in her hand as she asked, "What did you do with Aubrey?"

"Oh, don't worry. I'll be paying a visit to your associate shortly. Right now, I need something from *you*."

"And what's that?"

"Information."

"Go to hell."

Reznik laughed. "I figured you would say that." He stood up, tossing Rowan's jacket onto the chair as he vacated it. "That's okay. We have plenty of time, and I have plenty of options. This is Lieutenant Colonel Sarah Amirmoez. She's going to spend some *quality* time with you while you consider just how much information you don't want to tell us."

"I think you'll find I'm tougher than I look," Rowan snarled.

"Be that as it may," Reznik said patiently, "I think you'll find that everyone gives in eventually. The question is whether you'll still be in one piece when you do."

13

Nothing happened in Caotico City for a whole week after General Reznik put it on lockdown. The military put a stop to any looting or riots during the blackouts, and the curfews kept everyone too afraid to go out at night. The members of Heroics were spread throughout the city with no method of communication— the mansion being shut down disabled all of the sunglasses, and cellular reception had gone out minutes after Jacob's phone call with Aubrey. No one knew where anyone was, or how anyone was doing. Which meant that few knew just how long Cass and Casey had been missing.

Reznik had asked them both a long list of questions the moment they were brought back to his military base, but when they refused to answer any of them, he had them put in a single simple cell for the rest of the week. On that next Saturday, Cass and Casey were pulled from their prison cell, tied to chairs in the middle of a large, empty room, and left for an hour before Reznik bothered to show up.

"Ah, the Wechsler girls!" the general greeted cheerfully as he walked into the room. "I hope your week here hasn't been too terrible."

"It was really boring, honestly," Cass said. "If you're trying to be threatening, it isn't working."

"You don't look like you've gotten much sleep, at least," Reznik said.

"That wasn't your doing. I get nightmares sometimes." Cass shrugged. "Personal flaw, I suppose."

Reznik raised an eyebrow. "You have nightmares for a week and I'm not supposed to assume that it was my doing? I'm insulted, Mrs. Hamil."

Cass snorted. "I used to have them all the time. They stopped when I started seeing my husband. Seriously, don't flatter yourself."

"You must be joking. You get nightmares if you aren't sleeping next to AJ Hamil?" Reznik laughed loudly. "Your father really did ruin you, didn't he?"

"I'm coping," Cass said angrily. "It's not always easy and it's not always pretty and it doesn't always work, but I'm trying my best, and you don't get to tell me that I'm not."

Reznik chuckled. "I'm sure. If it'll make you feel better, I can always bring Dr. Hamil into this fine establishment and let him join you. I'm not sure what would make you feel worse. Him being here, or you not being with him."

"Go to hell."

Before Reznik could reply, Casey cut him off. "Is this your master plan for getting us to tell you things? Be incredibly boring and leave us in cells until we're driven mad from *boredom.*"

"Oh, don't worry. That was just a test to see whether you were afraid of prison. Which, clearly neither of you are."

"Not really," Casey said.

"That's a shame. That means I have to break out the more... *exact* methods of getting you to talk."

"For hell's sake," Cass sighed. "Am I going to get tortured *again*?"

"This is already like the eighth time you've been tied to a chair," Casey pointed out. "Really, at this point you could start going for world records."

"I'm getting too old for this." Cass settled back in her chair and sighed again. "All right, look, why don't we just skip a few steps? Whatever you do to us isn't exactly going to change anything, okay? We don't care. We have no answers for you. We know nothing about Heroics, and there's nothing you can do to us that will make a difference."

"Seriously," Casey said, "we have no idea what you want us to say. We can't answer questions that we don't have answers to."

Reznik smirked. "I think your opinion on what information you 'don't' have and mine are very different."

Casey rolled her eyes and looked at Cass. "I wonder who this guy thinks he is."

"I'm not sure, but I know that what he *is,* is wasting his time."

"Cute," Reznik growled. "But I know you're lying." He pressed a button on a remote in his hand and a large tank full of water was wheeled into the room by two corporals. "So I'm going to give both of you a choice. Cooperate with me, or you'll become intimately familiar with the feeling of water pouring into your lungs."

"You're going to *drown us?*" Cass asked incredulously. "I don't really see how that's going to help you much."

"Trust me, Mrs. Hamil. I have quite a few ways to make sure you survive long enough to tell me what I want to know. Think about that." Reznik turned and left the room with his soldiers.

Casey swallowed. "Cass, I don't think I want to do that."

"You won't have to."

"Do you have a plan?"

"Yeah. I go first."

"That... That's not a good plan."

Cass shrugged. "What do you want me to do, Case? I'm out of options."

Casey gave a short, scoffing laugh. "So am I, but there's no way in hell I'm watching my little sister be drowned right in front of me, either."

"You might not have a choice," Cass muttered.

Kate walked partway down the stairs of one of the safe houses she had set up years ago and sat down next to Niall, who was staring at the front door. "Erin's asleep," she said quietly. "I finally convinced her to get some rest when we heard that Ciaran had found Riley and Jacob."

"Good. She needs some sleep." Niall ran a hand through his hair tiredly. "I'm not sure Andrew's slept since Seamus died. I wish I knew whether he was okay. I wish I knew whether *anyone* was okay. I don't know where anybody is."

"It's just luck that I was even able to find you and Ciaran. I think I set up too many safe houses."

Niall chuckled. "It's entirely possible. But it ended up being for the best."

"True."

"I can't believe I came back from dealing with one tragedy just so I could deal with another."

"Isn't that the Heroics way?" Kate gave a ragged sigh. "I don't know what to do, Niall. I really don't. I can't..." Her voice cracked. "I've lost so many siblings already, but I never thought I'd ever lose Justin."

Niall put an arm around her shoulders and hugged her tightly. "It's okay to not know."

"What I really want to know," Kate whispered, "is how I can get to Reznik to make him pay for this."

"Don't go and get yourself killed, Kate. That won't help anyone."

"I'm not going to do that. I promise. I'm not going to do that to you or the boys again." Kate leaned against him heavily. "But I'm not going to let this guy win, either. He's wrong about us. About all of us. We're good for this city. We may not be perfect, but we help people at great risk to ourselves. Lori, Julian, Jay, Kara, Justin... they sacrificed so much for people. Except for Kara, they all lost everything. I'm not going to let any of their sacrifices fade away or be covered up by claims that we were all criminals. I can't let that happen."

"I understand." Niall kissed the side of her head gently. "Just remember that you've made sacrifices, too. You don't need to give everything."

"I won't."

The front door opened and Ciaran, Jacob, and Riley walked into the safe house. Riley nodded once at Niall and Kate before walking into the living room. Ciaran followed her, hugging his father quickly and completely ignoring his mother. Kate's eyes were glazed with sadness, but she swallowed and glanced at Jacob. "How's Riley doing?"

"Not great," Jacob said. "Which isn't shocking, of course."

"Everything okay with you?" Niall was frowning. "You look like something's bothering you."

"I was talking to Aubrey right before everything went to hell. She sounded terrified, and the line went dead. I-I... I don't know where she is, or if she's okay."

"She's a strong kid," Kate said softly. "All of you Hamils are. She'll be okay." She put her hands on Jacob's shoulders. "You have to believe that, okay?" She ran her hand through his hair and walked into the living room to check on her son and niece.

"How did you know we were coming, anyway?" Jacob asked Niall.

Niall tapped his fingers against a walkie-talkie that was hooked onto his belt. "Low tech trumps high tech every time, boy."

"You're a computer nerd and you're going to give me that speech?"

"Shhh. Let me have my moment."

Jacob laughed and shook his head. "Okay, Niall, whatever." He bit his lip. "So you've... heard *nothing* from my family?"

"No, Jacob, I'm sorry, I haven't. But believe me, you Hamils could survive anything."

"Nobody can survive anything," Jacob murmured.

"That's true. But if anybody could give a damn good try of it, it's you guys." Niall got to his feet. "Come on, kid. You're probably hungry, and we have food."

"I'm not sure I can eat anything."

Niall led Jacob towards the kitchen. "That's too bad. You're going to anyway."

Matthias sat on his desk chair, watching silently as Brooke slept in his bed. It had taken a few days for her to finally be able to pass out, and he was going to do everything he could to make sure she got as much sleep as she could possibly get.

Once she woke up, he knew it was going to be hard to get her to go back. She had spent four straight days battling the depression as it mixed with terror for her family. The brief phone call from Jacob that confirmed that Aubrey was missing had done nothing to assuage the insomnia.

She was useless at the moment, and they both knew it. Brooke Hamil, big sister, who couldn't tolerate guilt or failure, and who prided herself on fighting for her siblings, was powerless to do anything for them.

Brooke couldn't do anything but wait and maybe—*maybe*—catch up on some of the weeks of sleep she had been missing. If the only thing Matthias could do was watch over her and make sure she was okay while she tried, he was going to make sure he did it well.

Max walked into his living room and found Alix sound asleep on his couch, just like he had found her every morning for the past week. He'd offered to take the couch himself, but she had blown him off. At first he thought it was a lack of trust, but he quickly realized that the woman legitimately didn't care.

"Time to get up," he said as he nudged her knee with his foot.

"Go away," she grumbled in response.

"You *told* me to wake you up at this time, Thief."

"Tell myself to shut up."

Max smiled slightly and sat down on the coffee table. "I would, but I walk *through walls*, not *back in time*."

Alix grunted something under her breath and sat up. "What good are you, then?"

"Hey! You come to *my house* and insult *my lack of relevant skills*..."

"Damn right I do."

"Y'know, I wasn't sure I believed you, but you really *do* like sleeping on the couch, don't you?"

"Yeah."

"Why?"

She laughed, and the sound sent a chill down his spine. "It's pretty simple, really. A little while after I first started staying at the mansion, I tired myself out and fell asleep on the couch in the library. I woke up the next morning and there was a blanket on top of me."

Max started to catch on. "And you hadn't had one before you fell asleep."

"Nope. Casey put it over me in the middle of the night. It was the first time anybody had ever done anything remotely maternal—or even *friendly*—towards me in a long while. That was the first time I actually felt like I belonged somewhere." Alix gave a small smile. "So I like sleeping on couches. I'd have one as my bed in my room if Cass and Casey wouldn't kill me for it."

"They love you."

"Yeah," Alix sighed. "More than I probably deserve. But I love them back, so I guess it balances out."

"Do you feel like you belong now?"

"With them? Absolutely. They torture me all the time. It's the best indicator that somebody in this stupid family I ended up a part of actually cares."

He grinned widely, put an arm around her shoulders, and joked, "Oh, so you *care* about me?"

"Yeah. More than I figured I would," Alix murmured.

Max hadn't been expecting a serious answer, so he just stared down at her for a long moment. "Do you, uh... need anything?"

"Think I can borrow one of your insane number of glasses to have water?"

"It's not an insane number," Max protested as he followed her into the kitchen.

"Max, you have two of everything."

"It's a Jewish thing."

"Ah, right. That's why you have your fridge separated into dairy and non-dairy shelves."

"Right. It's enough to keep my mother from disowning me, but not quite so much that I have to really worry about it that often."

Alix shrugged. "Fair enough." She leaned against the counter and took a sip from her glass. "I'm going back out onto the streets today. I think I'm going to head over towards the military base."

"What the hell for?"

"I'm worried, okay? I haven't found any of the Hamil kids other than Brooke. She's still resting at Matthias's, so I know she's safe. But I don't know anything about Aubrey or Jacob, and I also don't know about Cass, AJ, or Casey. Even Zach doesn't know where they are, and I can tell he's worried. I don't like it. I need to find them, and if they're at that base, I'd rather know sooner rather than later." Alix took another drink. "Especially if it's Jacob or Aubrey. I don't want anything to happen to them if I can help it."

"You're a pretty good aunt, Thief."

Alix frowned. "I'm not their aunt. Casey is."

Max smiled slightly. "I'm pretty sure you're *both* aunts, whether you know it or not. Besides, you've always referred to yourself as their aunt."

"I'm not really though," Alix mumbled. "I joke about it sometimes. But I'm not."

"Doesn't matter. You're one of them. You always will be." He sat down at his kitchen table. "You're pretty great, you know, Alix."

"Oh, so it's *Alix* now?"

"I thought you liked Thief. I can stop if you want."

"No; I like them both." Alix sat down across from him. "Do you mind when I call you Wraith?"

"I kind of like it, honestly."

Alix smirked. "Maybe I should stop."

Max gave a sharp laugh. "You can if you want." He lowered his voice. "They're going to be okay, Thief. They're tough kids."

"They shouldn't have to be. Their mom went through enough suffering that her children shouldn't have to go through any at all." Alix bowed her head. "I can't do this, Wraith."

"Can't do what?"

"I can't handle my friends getting hurt anymore. I really can't."

240

"From your reputation, I would've assumed that you could handle anything."

Alix gave a soft chuckle. "I've lost my fire over the years. Too much pain."

Max reached over and rested his hand on top of hers. "It's still there."

"The pain?" Alix asked dryly.

He laughed. "The fire, you idiot."

"I certainly hope so. I'm going to need it." Alix spun her empty glass on the table carefully. "It's the only thing I have going for me without my powers."

"I don't think it would be so bad," Max said quietly.

Alix looked at him curiously. "What?"

"Losing my powers. It's not like I couldn't still help people without them. You're a hero without them."

She gave a low laugh. "I'm no hero."

Max frowned. "Of course you are. You've helped a lot of people."

"I won't deny that. But honestly, Wraith, I'm not sure any of us are heroes. We're just a bunch of desperate souls delaying the inevitable so that maybe one or two people in this world live longer than they would if we weren't helping them." Alix looked down. "We can't really save anyone. We're no heroes. We're just an annoyance."

"Maybe we can't save everyone. Maybe we barely do any real good. I don't know. What I do know is that you've risked your life for other people time and time again. Whether it changes anything in the end or not, it still matters, Thief."

"What if it doesn't?" Alix asked in a near whisper. "What if it doesn't really matter to anyone?"

"It matters to me," Max offered with a slight smile.

Alix laughed weakly. "Oh, well, if it matters to *you*..."

"It does," he said seriously. "Trust me, Alix. It does."

"Because you're in love with me?"

Max hesitated. "Yes."

"You shouldn't be."

"I'm sorry."

Alix stared down at her empty glass. "I'm not worth the time, Max."

He gave a sharp, sarcastic laugh. "I'm sure the Hamils and Carters would totally go for you talking about yourself like that. And for the record, I think it's bullshit, too."

"Wraith—"

"Thief."

She gave him a frustrated look. "Are you always such an asshole?"

"Only towards people who deserve it."

Alix snorted. "I've done nothing. I'm right."

"You're not."

"What are we, six?"

"Seems so." Max absentmindedly ran his thumb along the back of her hand. "Alix, you're afraid of me, and I don't know why. I'd really like to know why."

"This past week I've started to sort a few things out in my head." She sighed. "And I... sort of... *might* have feelings for you, but we don't want the same thing."

"How do you know?"

Alix didn't reply, but she started playing with the black ring on her hand.

"For hell's sake, Thief, I told you, I don't give a damn whether or not you're going to sleep with me."

She looked up at him quickly, startled.

"Yeah, I got the subtle symbolism of you fiddling with the ace ring while trying not to talk to me. Seriously, Alix, I really don't give a damn about any of that. I'm in love with *you*, not the hypothetical future sleeping habits we feasibly could or could not get involved in."

"I-I don't want you to—"

"To what? Make my own choices in that department? Or do you think I'd try to force you to make certain decisions that you don't want to make? I'm not a dick, Alix." Max paused, flushing red. "Okay, not the best choice of words right now."

Alix laughed, loudly. She stood up and walked over to the other side of the table to gently kiss him on the forehead. "Dammit, Wraith. You're such an asshole."

"But not a dick. We're establishing that."

"But not a dick," she agreed. She shook her head slowly. "I don't know what to do with you, Wraith."

He smiled slightly. "You could invite me along on your stupid suicide mission."

She laughed again. "Well, if you're really that desperate. Think maybe you want to come along? Help me out?"

"Of course. I was hoping you'd ask."

"Good." Alix put her glass in the sink and set her silver-lined ring on the table. "Then let's go raid a military base, shall we?"

"So, have you two made your decision?" Reznik asked as he walked back into the room Cass and Casey were being held in.

"I have," Cass said. "You're going to have to torture me, or whatever the hell you're calling it. Because I swear to you, I don't have the answers you want. I can't name anyone from the Security Legion. I've never *met* any of them."

"You're involved in Heroics yet you've never met anyone from the Legion?" Reznik snorted. "How dumb do you think I am?"

"Incredibly dumb," Cass retorted. "First of all, Heroics and the Legion are two separate teams. They interact on separate radars, so I'd imagine that if they've met, they've all kept their identities secret. There's not *that* much trust in the hero community. Second of all, like I've said time and time again, *I'm not involved in Heroics.*"

"That's truly a shame, Mrs. Hamil. Especially because I don't believe you."

"Why *not*?"

"Because *everyone in this city* knows where the Heroics base is," Reznik said patiently. "Do you really think nobody noticed when suddenly a group of people who looked almost exactly like heroes were set up in one conveniently large house that was off the main power and communication grids? Please. When you all stopped pretending that you didn't live together, most intelligent people figured out pretty quickly who you all were. The problem was that nobody *cared*. Heroics members weren't controlled by John Wechsler and Alice Cage.

Heroics members weren't committing murders. Heroics members weren't causing anti-vigilante riots. Heroics members didn't participate in that hero strike a few years back. The Legion, on the other hand? They were involved in *all* of it. It would be *easy* to turn the public against those idiots. But you all? Going after you in the position you were in would've been making you martyrs. It would've lost all of the respect and power I've gained in this city over these past few years. I needed the perfect time and the perfect way to turn everyone against Heroics. And as soon as that time came, I *made* you criminals. Now I can do whatever I want to you, and the public will applaud me for it."

Reznik grabbed Casey's chair and started dragging her towards the water. "But Heroics isn't the goal. The Legion is. And I need *you two* to tell me how to find them."

"What the hell are you doing?" Cass demanded.

"Oh, I'm sorry, did you want to go first? Admirable, protecting your sister like that, Mrs. Hamil. Unfortunately, I don't play by your rules. Besides, you said *you* don't have any answers. Maybe *she* has some."

"I don't," Casey said nervously. "I really don't."

Reznik stopped her chair at the edge of the tank of water. "I'm sorry, Mrs. Carter, but I really just don't believe you. If you tell me what I want, maybe we don't need to go any further."

"G-Go to hell."

The general laughed. "Oh, Mrs. Carter. Hell is for people who are in the wrong. And between the two of us, I can guarantee you that that applies much more to you than to me."

14

Claire watched as Kara fidgeted in her wheelchair, staring at her Heroics communication sunglasses. "Honey," she said quietly. "You're not going to get anywhere by staring."

"It's better than nothing," Kara snapped. "I feel so *useless.*"

"We *are* useless. If the soldiers find out who you are, they'll either arrest you or kill you. The only people who might have a chance of surviving those options are Zach, Logan, and Thomas, and that's only *if* the military hasn't planned for people who can control metal. This whole thing was planned, Kar. And none of us were prepared for it."

"Yeah, well, we should've been."

"You guys have never been all that great at planning," Claire said lightly.

"Look how well that's always gone for us," Kara muttered. She leaned back and rubbed her neck. "Where's James?"

"He went out to the streets for a bit. He's still worried about the others, so he wanted to see if he could find anyone."

"This city's too damn big. He'll never find anyone."

Claire gently ran her fingers through Kara's hair. "You were always the optimistic one."

"Hasn't done me much good lately, has it?"

"Maybe not," Claire admitted. "But you can't give up yet."

Kara gave a long, slow sigh. "I'm tired, Claire. I'm tired of losing people."

Claire couldn't find anything to say, so she just kissed Kara softly and rested her forehead against the side of her wife's head. They were still sitting like that a few minutes later when James came in, followed closely by Logan, Thomas, Rick, AJ, and Zach.

"They were in one of Kate' safe houses," James said.

"I knew those would come in handy eventually," Claire muttered.

"Are you all okay?" Kara asked anxiously as her wife stood up to get them drinks.

"We're fine, but we haven't heard anything about Mom or Aunt Cass in a week," Logan said. "They were planning to hand themselves over to Reznik."

Kara looked at Claire. "And you wonder why I'm stressed."

"Tell me about it," AJ said dryly. He took a seat across from Kara. "I've convinced myself that they're fine, but I'm starting to lose my confidence."

James ruffled Thomas's auburn hair. "Hey, buddy, why don't we go upstairs? You can get some rest or play with the basketball net that's on the back of my door."

"Okay!"

When the boys were gone, AJ glanced at Zach. "Sorry. I forgot myself."

"It's all right. He knows it's bad." Zach rested a hand on Logan's shoulder. "They both do."

"The question is, what are we going to *do*," Logan said. "Can't we just go *get* Mom and Aunt Cass?"

"How, kid?" Kara asked gently. "You and your dad are the only ones here who have powers and could possibly go do something like that. And two people can't go up against an entire military base."

"We could try," Logan growled.

"Absolutely not." Zach sat down next to AJ. "I'm not risking your life in a potentially pointless mission, and your mother would *kill* me if I even attempted it."

"We need someone better at tactics than we are," AJ muttered. "I really wish Garrison wasn't on vacation."

"He *would* go visit with family in Bolivia right when the military tries to kill us all," Zach complained in a joking tone. "Jackass, daring to *retire* like a human being far more intelligent than the rest of us."

"A lot of people we could've used are out of commission right now," Claire said. "Brooke's in the middle of a break. Garrison and his family are out of the picture, other than his oldest son, Ethan, who's on his honeymoon with new husband Johnny Aller. Finn only just got back from Riverdale, so she's probably at Casey's bar with Kaita because they 'aren't' sleeping together. Rob Munroe moved out of state last month. Andrew and his family left Friday night just before all of this started to grieve with his wife's parents..." She shook her head slowly. "Reznik couldn't have planned this at a worse time for us."

"That was probably the point," Kara muttered darkly.

"Well, Zach, as you're the most high-ranking person here—"

"Don't give me that crap, AJ."

"*As the most high-ranking person here,*" AJ continued with a smirk, "you should make the call for what we do next."

Zach ran a hand through his hair and sighed. "I don't know," he admitted. "I really don't know. I can tell the Legion to go underground. I can tell them to stay in the base. I can suggest that we all stay as far out of the way as possible, but I..." He bowed his head. "I can't trust my judgment when it comes to Casey. I need to get her back, but I know we can't do it without getting ourselves killed or captured. I don't know what to do, AJ."

"You don't really need to make that decision on your own, Zach. I was just teasing you." AJ leaned back in his chair as he adjusted his tie. "Let's take the time to talk this through. I might not like it any more than any of you do, but we don't really have a better option. Running off half-cocked is just going to get more people killed. We can't do that. Agreed?"

"Agreed," Claire and Kara said simultaneously.

Zach looked at his daughter. "Logan?"

The girl sighed. "I'm not happy about it, but I understand."

"That's all we can ask for, kiddo." Zach lightly messed up Logan's hair. "The only way we can help anyone is to survive long enough to do something."

Logan nodded, but out of the corner of her eye she saw Rick turn and slip away towards the door.

Logan caught up with him. "Where do you think you're going?"

Rick turned to face Logan, a guilty glint in his eyes. "I'm going to see if I can find my brother and my parents. I have an idea which section of safe houses they might be in."

"You shouldn't go alone. Let me go with you."

"No, Logan." Rick took a few steps towards her. "You need to stay here, in case your dad gets an opportunity to go after your mom."

"Richard..."

"I'll be fine. I know I don't have powers to protect me, but honestly, having powers right now would probably be *more* dangerous."

She gave a quiet sigh. "Just... keep yourself in one piece, okay? I'm not sure what I'd do with myself if I didn't have you to torment."

He laughed. "We're *not* dating, though?"

"No, Rich, we aren't," Logan said with a small smile.

"Oh, I know. If we were you'd hit me upside the head for even *thinking* of going out there by myself. Since we aren't, you just yelled at me instead."

"That's a fair distinction."

Rick took her face in his hands and kissed her softly. "I know you're going to find a way to get out there after your mother. I don't blame you. Obviously I'm doing the same thing. But if I have to be careful, you have to be careful, too. Got it?"

Logan laughed. "I got it, Richard."

"Good." He headed for the door, pausing with his hand on the handle. "We're going to get through this, right?"

"I don't know, Rich. I honestly don't."

He shot her an arrogant grin that seemed forced, as if he was trying to make her feel better. "We'll get through it."

As he left, Logan let out a long, ragged sigh. "I certainly hope so."

"We should start doing something," Isaac said as he paced back and forth in front of his parents. "I'm tired of waiting. It's been a week. We've given it enough time. That's enough."

Ray made a frustrated noise. "We've been over this a million times, Isaac. This isn't the same as the other enemies we've faced. These people could very well have legal standing to arrest us all. If we do anything against them, we could go to jail for the rest of our lives. We *can't* do anything. I doubt the others are taking the risk to go running off into something as uncertain as this situation, and we aren't going to just because you have delusions of grandeur."

"Some leader you are," Isaac muttered.

Olivia shook her head slowly. "Honey, you're going to get yourself killed if you keep acting like this."

"So? Isn't that what we're good for?" Isaac asked nastily.

Ray took a small step backwards, a stunned look on his face. "Son," he said softly, "I only hope that you never have to deal with the full reality of how wrong you are."

Casey could barely see as the chair she was in was dragged back to the spot right next to Cass's. Her glasses had long since fallen off of her face, but the blurred vision was a very low concern when compared to the burning sensation in her lungs.

"I might never drink water again," she croaked out as she tried to stop herself from shivering despite being soaking wet.

"I was thinking the same thing," Cass agreed in a scratchy voice. Casey could only make out the vague shape of her sister, but she knew that the other woman was just as drenched as she was. Reznik had been forcing them underwater repeatedly for at least a half-hour, but to his ever-growing frustration, it had gotten him nowhere.

Reznik helpfully put Casey's glasses back on her face and then grabbed her by the throat. "You're both *stubborn*, aren't you?" he growled.

"You could say that," Casey replied with a shrug. As he let her go and took a few steps away to think, she coughed loudly. "I knew I didn't like swimming."

Cass laughed. "You don't like *anything*, do you, sis?"

"I liked scotch, and look where that got me."

"At least you weren't breathing it."

"Felt like I was some days."

"*Enough!*" Reznik whirled around, taking his handgun off of his belt and aiming it directly at Casey's head. "Enough. I'm tired of both of you."

"Oh, is this where you kill us?" Cass asked. "Because I really don't think you tried hard enough to interrogate us."

"I see that I'm not going to get anywhere with you. I'm just not going to be successful there. I thought maybe I could, but it's just going to take far too long. And to be honest, I know exact what will speed this process up."

Casey raised an eyebrow. "Not bothering to talk to us at all?"

"No, although that's still an option." Reznik smiled slightly. "The thing is, I've been conducting interrogations all week. You weren't the only two who made yourselves vulnerable, be it on purpose or accidentally. And I'm curious as to whether one of my interviewees *in particular* could get the two of you to… open up, shall we say."

"What the hell are you talking about?" Cass demanded.

"Why don't we find out?" Reznik raised his radio to his mouth. "Prisoner #282739 to Room 8, please."

About five minutes later the door opened, and the two corporals who had brought in the water tank entered again, half-leading, half-dragging a young woman with brown hair. She was covered in blood and had clearly been beaten, badly enough that she could barely stand. A deep gash in her forehead was still steadily seeping blood, and her right eye was black. When she was forced to her knees in front of Reznik, she coughed blood onto the floor.

"No," Cass whispered. "Oh, no."

Reznik smiled pleasantly. "Hello again, Ms. Hamil."

"Didn't I tell you to go to hell?" Aubrey asked, mock confusion in her voice. Her voice was surprisingly strong given how severely injured she appeared.

"Yes," Reznik said, "but this isn't about interrogating *you*. Now be quiet." He turned to Cass and

Casey and clapped his hands together. "See? I told you that you two aren't the only people I've been hosting in my lovely little prison. Does that make you feel less special?"

"I'm going to kill you." Cass's voice was low and ice-cold. "I don't care what it takes. I'm going to kill you."

"If it's any consolation, your daughter has quite the spine. She never answered any of my questions." Reznik patted Aubrey on the head patronizingly. "Even for one of you Heroics people, that's impressive."

"I'm not a member of Heroics," Aubrey said. "I've been trying to tell you that for days, but you're too damn stupid to listen."

Reznik delivered a solid kick to Aubrey's lower ribs that caused her to double over in pain. "I believe I told you to be quiet."

"Touch my daughter again and I'll—"

"And you'll what?" Reznik interrupted. "You're tied to a chair. I could beat this kid to death right in front of you, and the only thing you'd be able to do is yell at me not to."

Cass strained against her bindings, looking both terrified and furious. Casey, worried, slowly said, "This doesn't have to spiral out of control. You don't have to do this."

"I do, actually. Neither of you is being very cooperative." Reznik grabbed Aubrey's hair and pulled her so that she was kneeling straight up again. He then aimed his handgun directly at her head.

"Don't," Cass said immediately, her voice hoarse. "Please, don't."

"There's no reason why I shouldn't. Unless you have information for me."

Cass didn't reply. She was too busy staring at Aubrey, helpless and close to panic.

"Don't tell him anything," Aubrey muttered through gritted teeth.

Reznik kicked her again, this time simply adjusting where his gun was pointing instead of righting her when she fell over in pain. "If they don't tell me, I'll kill you. And I doubt they would be able to live with that, so—"

"Thurgood Avenue."

"What?" Reznik turned to Casey.

She took in a slow, deep breath. "The Legion headquarters is at 1317 Thurgood Avenue. That's all I know."

"That wasn't so hard, now was it?" Reznik smirked. "Thank you so much for your assistance, Mrs. Carter."

"Go to hell."

"As friendly as your niece, I see."

"*Go. To. Hell.*"

Reznik shrugged and turned to leave. Before he got to the door, Cass said, "Please."

"Please what?"

Cass swallowed. "Please let me go check on my daughter."

The general considered her for a moment and shrugged again. "I don't see why not." He looked at one of the corporals. "Point a gun at the kid. If Hamil here so much as moves, shoot immediately."

"Yes, sir."

Reznik walked over to Cass, pulled out a knife, and cut the woman loose. He did the same for Casey on his way past, and then he and his corporals left the room. As soon as the door shut behind them, Cass was on her feet, bolting over to Aubrey and getting down on her knees next to her.

Aubrey was trying to get back up, struggling a bit from both her injuries and the rope that was binding her wrists together. Cass put her arms on her daughter's shoulders and gently pushed her back down. "No, baby, relax for a second." She brushed Aubrey's bloodstained hair off of her face and lightly kissed her forehead. "Just relax."

"Everything hurts, Mom," Aubrey admitted in a whisper, her defiant expression faltering now that Reznik was gone.

"I know, baby. It's okay. It's all right." Cass was shaking as she clumsily tried to untie Aubrey's wrists. "It's okay."

Casey joined them, putting a hand on Cass's shoulder. "Let me get that." She crouched down and calmly removed the rope. Then she gently touched Aubrey's arm. "How are you doing, kiddo?"

"Better than I would've if I had a bullet in my head. Thanks for that."

"I-I just froze," Cass stammered. "I d-didn't know what to say. I didn't even r-remember the a-answer to his question."

"Mom, it's okay."

"It's *not* okay. What if Casey hadn't been here? I would've... He would've..."

Casey grabbed Cass by the shoulders, turning her around to face her. "Hey. Stop. Panicking isn't going to help anybody, and you're just going to freak Aubrey out. *She's okay.* Maybe a little banged up—more than a little—but she's *alive*, and we're going to make sure she stays that way. It's okay. We're okay."

Cass shivered. "I'm not used to—"

"What? Being the useless one?" Casey teased gently.

"Being this afraid," Cass whispered.

Aubrey, who was anxiously tapping her fingers against her leg in sets of three, scoffed. "Get used to it. You've only managed to get through about twenty years of the three of us. You have a lot more to go through yet."

Cass gave a quiet laugh. "Good to see your sense of humor wasn't damaged."

"Pretty sure everything else was." Aubrey sat up slowly. "Ow. That rib's probably broken."

"You're an idiot, you know that?" Cass asked affectionately, resting a hand on Aubrey's cheek. "A brave, reckless idiot who should've just told these guys what they wanted to know."

"As if you would've told them anything."

"Mm. True."

"I think I'm getting thrown under the bus here," Casey complained.

"No, Case, I think we can all agree that there are some things we can't withstand." Cass's eyes darkened. "Including levels of physical pain. Reznik just hasn't pulled those out yet."

"I vote we figure a way out of here before that happens," Aubrey said nervously.

"I'm definitely with you there, baby," Cass murmured, gently stroking Aubrey's hair. "I'm definitely with you there."

"But first... we can't leave until we find out what he did with..." Aubrey trailed off, swallowing.

"With..." Horror lit in Cass's eyes. "Oh, hell. You weren't alone when he took you?"

Aubrey shook her head and her voice cracked. "He has Rowan, Mom. And I have no idea what they're doing to her."

15

"You'd be useful for sneaking into movies without paying," Alix said as she and Max walked through a fence directly onto the grounds of Reznik's military base.

"I haven't paid for a movie since I was fourteen."

"That's stealing, Wraith," Alix scolded with a grin.

"Your hero name is *Thief*."

"I'm insulted by your implication." Alix took her gun off of her belt and checked the magazine. She turned a small dial on the side of the gun and put it back in its holster.

Max narrowed his eyes, looking nervous. "Are you... using real bullets?"

"I have it turned to the 'real bullets' setting, yes. Stun bullets don't work that well on body armor, and I'd bet that these guys are going to have some of that. I can switch back before I shoot if I want to, but I'm prioritizing not dying over the risk of killing somebody."

"You would be okay with that?"

Alix's voice got soft. "I killed Alice Cage, Max. And I know I've killed other people before, too." She sighed. "I've accepted that. Can you?"

Max hesitated. "Yeah. I've just admitted to stealing movie tickets for twenty years so I guess I can't judge."

"Idiot," Alix laughed.

"So you've said." Max led Alix through a nearby brick wall, which happened to be the way into a supply building. "Well, this is convenient. At least if you had left your ring on it would've been a slight challenge."

Alix studied a rank full of military uniforms that lined the back wall. "Huh. Dressing like the enemy?"

"That's a federal offense, Thief."

"We're *well* past that point, Wraith."

"Good point." Max pulled a lieutenant's jacket off of its hanger and put it on over his black t-shirt. "I knew ditching the Legion jacket would be a good idea."

"You did that because you didn't want random people to shoot you on sight."

"Don't ruin my fun."

Alix replaced her navy leather jacket with a captain's jacket and started scanning the racks for combat pants that would fit her. "This is a terrible idea, but at least I'm fake-higher ranking than you."

"At least we have that," Max said dryly.

Max and Alix made their way through the complex extremely casually, rarely running into any soldiers and playing themselves off as military whenever they did.

"This is shockingly easy. Have these people never paid attention to who works here? Their observational skills *suck*," Max muttered.

"You're tempting fate way too much, Wraith."

They stopped in front of a map and studied it for a moment. "Too bad they haven't conveniently labeled the dungeons," Max commented.

Alix scoffed. "They didn't need to." She pointed at a large section of warehouse space on the far side of the map. "I noticed this area when we came in. It had dozens of wiring systems running into it. Enough electricity is being pumped into these buildings to power the whole city. For storage? Yeah, okay."

"Do I want to know what a prison would need with that much electricity?"

"Probably not." Alix frowned at the map for a moment. "I have an idea."

"Am I going to hate it?"

"Nah. Well, maybe... nah." She pointed at a building labeled Energy and Consumption. "Think you can cut the power to the fake warehouse while I go break in and look around?"

"Why do we need to split up?"

Alix shrugged. "Because I like terrible ideas today."

Max just stared at her.

"Also because we don't know for sure that you'll be able to keep the power off for an extended period of time, and this way we'll be able to work simultaneously instead of consecutively."

"That's more reasonable."

"Good." Alix glanced down at her watch. "Don't do anything until at least... let's say 15:25. That'll give us both plenty of time to get where we need to be. But if you need a bit more time, that's fine. It's really only important that I'm where I need to be at the exact right time."

"All right." Max rested his hands on her shoulders. "Try not to get yourself killed, huh?"

"Aw, but I'm so good at it."

Max grinned. "Somehow I'm not surprised."

Alix pulled him down and lightly kissed him on the cheek. "Try not to get yourself killed either, Oakley. I'm starting to like you."

"Only starting?"

"Don't push your luck."

Cass maneuvered Aubrey into the chair Casey had been tied to and crouched down in front of her. "How are you feeling?"

"Uh, sort of like how I imagine it feels to get hit by a bus." Aubrey squinted at her mother. "Why are you and Aunt Casey covered in water?"

"Well... Reznik sort of decided to test how long we could hold our breath. Repeatedly."

"Are you saying that he tried to *drown* you?" Aubrey asked incredulously.

Casey cleared her throat and coughed as she stole the chair that had been Cass's. "I think the technical term is 'dunking.' Maybe. That might've been that thing that was used during the witch trials."

Cass gave a weak laugh, but Aubrey's frown never left her face. "Mom?"

"Yeah, sweetheart?"

"Do you think he... I mean, he killed the Galaxy Boys after less than a week..."

Casey and Cass exchanged a glance. "Reznik killed the Galaxy Boys?"

Aubrey nodded stiffly. "He wanted to recruit them and they wouldn't go for it. So he killed them. He was threatening me with that, as if it would make me change my answers."

"*Recruit them?*" Casey shook her head slowly. "This guy doesn't know a damn thing about empowered people if he thinks it's that easy."

"I'm not sure he does think it's that easy," Cass muttered. "That's probably why he's going through all of this just for a damned address."

"Oh, I want much more than an *address*, Mrs. Hamil," Reznik said as he walked back into the room. "All empowered people are good for is being soldiers. That's all I want. But I need a healthier supply than what Heroics can give me. The Legion is much more... *substantial*. So I need *them*. The address will help me, but I need more. I need specifics. Security systems, powers of members who are frequently at the base, names of empowereds in leadership positions... you know, the important things."

Casey made a frustrated noise. "Why the hell would we know that? Let alone tell you?"

"Well, I—"

"What did you do with Rowan?" Aubrey interrupted, staring at Reznik with cold hatred.

The general frowned at her. "Who?"

"*The woman I was with when you arrested me, asshole.*"

"Quite a mouth on this one, isn't there? You might want to try disciplining your child, Mrs. Hamil."

Cass smiled humorlessly. "You don't want to know what *I* want to call you."

"Cute." Reznik rubbed his chin for a moment as he thought. "Oh, *right*. That one. The hero from the Legion. She's in the company of my second-in-command, Lieutenant Colonel Sarah Amirmoez."

"What are you doing to her?" Aubrey demanded.

"*I'm* doing nothing," Reznik replied innocently. "*Sarah*, on the other hand..."

Aubrey got to her feet far too quickly and had to be caught by Cass so she didn't collapse. "If you hurt her, I'll—"

"What is it with your family and empty threats?" Reznik shook his head slowly. "Besides, I just *told* you that *I'm* not doing a thing to that girl."

"What exactly does that mean?" Casey asked.

"Fine, you really want to know? I have audio from her cell from about half an hour ago." Reznik raised his radio. "Room 8, filter in audio history from Prisoner #76926."

About a minute later, sound started coming into the room from speakers on the ceiling. There was a faint noise that was similar to static or electricity in the background, but it was quickly muffled by two voices.

"*Where is the Legion base?*" a female voice asked.

"*All I'm gonna tell you is to go to hell,*" Rowan's voice responded. It sounded weak and full of pain, as if her interrogation was already well underway.

"*We've been through this before. This doesn't need to get any worse, kid.*"

"*I don't really give a damn you—*" The static noise got louder, and Rowan screamed.

Aubrey tried to lunge towards Reznik, but Cass easily stopped her. "It's okay," Cass whispered softly, holding her daughter tightly. "Shhh. It's gonna be okay."

Rowan's screams lasted for an unnecessarily long amount of time before the static sound faded back down to background noise and her voice broke off into exhausted gasps for breath. "*How many times... are we going to do this... before you give up?*"

"*Depends,*" the other woman said. "*How much longer do you think you can survive this?*"

The recording continued for five more minutes, most of which was just Rowan screaming. After about four minutes, she yelled, "*Stop! ...Please, god... Stop! Okay! I'll tell you... whatever you want just... please stop!*"

Aubrey stopped struggling against Cass. Tears had long been running down her cheeks, but her eyes seemed to get even more watery as she whispered, "I've never heard Rowan beg before."

"*Where is the Legion base?*"

"*It's at 1317... Thurgood Avenue.*"

"*Who is the Legion leader?*"

"*Some guy named... Kilowatt. I don't... know his real name.*"

"*Thank you for your cooperation,*" the interrogator's voice said.

"*That's really... all you want to... know?*" Rowan asked incredulously.

"*No, but I think you need some more incentive to continue being so helpful.*"

"*Wait, what are you doing? Please, please, I told you what you—*"

Rowan's voice broke off into cries of pain again, and the audio cut out. Aubrey stared at Reznik, stunned. "What are they doing? Rowan did what you wanted!"

Reznik chuckled. "I need to make sure all of my facts are correct. The only way to do that is to make sure that the person I'm getting information from gives me the same answers when they're put under even more stress. The only reason Mrs. Carter here is in the clear is because the Legion hero gave the same address."

266

"You don't need to keep hurting her," Casey said coldly. "There's no reason for this."

"Of course there is. You think I hired Sarah for her sunny personality? She finds interrogations like this *fun*. Be glad I conducted yours, and Sarah spent the past two days working on the girl. I—"

Reznik was interrupted when the lights flickered out. He frowned up at the ceiling and took out his radio. "What the hell is going on?"

"*I have no idea, sir. All power to the detention buildings has been cut.*"

"Damned heroes, probably. Think they can just waltz in and save their friends." Reznik shook his head. "Idiots. If you'll all excuse me, I need to go take care of a few problems. Do stay here, would you?" With a smirk, Reznik left the room.

Aubrey's legs gave out and Cass gently lowered her back into the chair. "They're going to kill her," she said hoarsely. "They might already have. That audio wasn't live."

"Hey, don't think like that." Cass brushed Aubrey's hair back softly. "People in this family attract people who can survive. I doubt Rowan is any different."

"I can't lose her, Mom," Aubrey croaked.

"You won't have to." Cass pulled Aubrey into as tight a hug as was possible given the younger woman's injuries. As she did, she looked over Aubrey's shoulder at Casey and saw her own fear reflected in her face.

Neither of them thought it was the truth.

16

Alix made her way through the prison structure, avoiding those soldiers she could and knocking out ones she couldn't. She didn't have time to try manipulating the nosy ones, and Reznik's people were shockingly easy to put down.

The power had gone out at the exact time Alix had suggested. She could only smirk as she mentally noted Max's punctuality and kicked in the back door of the supposed warehouse complex.

Now she was well through the structure, having already eliminated most of the rooms as possible places for any Heroics members to be stashed away. She knew it was a rather stupid mission, going headfirst into enemy territory on a bad feeling, but if she ignored it and it had been right, she would never forgive herself.

Alix came to a stop as she entered a long hallway lined with numbered doors. "Sketchy enough," she murmured under her breath.

As she walked down the hall, she noticed that a board next to each door had what seemed to be random numbers on them. The numbers on one door, number eight, caught her attention. This was the only door with three numbers listed next to it, and something about them was sticking out to her.

"But what is it?" she mumbled. "282739... 22739... 2277439..."

After a long moment, a thought clicked in Alix's head and she searched her memory for an image of a phone keypad. Despite a few wrong turns, she eventually realized exactly what the numbers were.

"Oh, no," Alix whispered. "Aubrey, Casey, and Cassidy. Son of a bitch."

"If there are any soldiers in there, you should know I'll kill you if you touch any of them."

Cass looked up at the intercom speaker on the wall near the door, startled. "Al?"

Casey scrambled over to the button and pressed it. "Alix? What the hell are you doing here?"

"Hazarding a guess that you and Cass were stupid enough to get yourselves arrested. Not sure why you had to drag poor Aubrey into it, though."

"*We're* stupid? *You're* the one who came out here like it was a good idea."

"Oh, I'm sure you're really upset. Should I open the door, or just stand out here all day?"

Casey laughed. "I vote for the door."

"Coming right up."

"Alix, I love you," Cass said with a heavy sigh.

"You could've put a bit more feeling into that, Cassidy."

"I also could've not said it at all, jackass."

Alix snorted loud enough that the intercom picked it up. *"Do you want me to leave you here?"*

"You wouldn't do that to Aubrey."

"Damn you for having children I like."

"Love you too, Alix!" Aubrey yelled as loudly as she could.

"You all right, kid? You sound hurt."

"I'll live. Probably."

There was a pause. *" I think I might come back after I've found and killed Reznik."*

"Later, Alix," Casey said. "We have bigger problems to deal with right now."

"Oh, fine. Ruin all my—" Alix broke off into a quick, startled cry of pain.

"Al? *Al!*" Cass looked scared, but she calmly held up a hand to stop Aubrey from standing up as the young woman stared in horror at the door. "Alix, I swear to everything you hold dear, if you're joking around with us, I will *kill* you!"

"It's not a joke, Mrs. Hamil," Reznik's voice said through the intercom.

Cass paled, and Casey just bowed her head. "General, please," Cass said, her voice cracked. "Please, don't hurt her."

"I don't know; it seems that we have a trespasser. And I need to interrogate all trespassers. How else will I know why they're here? What if they're a genuine threat?"

"General," Casey said softly, her head resting against the wall. "Please. She's just with us."

"I would buy that, Mrs. Carter, except apparently someone is walking through solid objects in order to turn our electrical systems off. The only reason our intercoms even work is because that particular system is connected to a separate power source. Your friend here is with someone. And I'm going to find out who. I'll be back with you all in a few minutes." Reznik gave a short laugh. "Oh, and the Legion girl has a short break from Sarah. My lieutenant colonel has more urgent matters to deal with. Like finding exactly who was sent to save you three."

The intercom cut out, and Casey turned to face Cass and Aubrey. "Walking through solid objects, huh?"

"They're together all the time now; are we really surprised?" Cass asked.

Aubrey shook her head slowly. "Brooke would be having a field day right now."

"You're not?"

"I won't until I..." Aubrey was fidgeting with her hands and not looking at her mother. "He says she's alive, but... Well, y'know."

Cass ran her fingers through Aubrey's hair gently. "Yeah, I know."

"Oh, hell. I just figured it out."

"Figured what out?" Cass asked.

Casey was pale. "The woman who was interrogating Rowan. Sarah. I recognized her voice, but I couldn't figure out why."

"You know her?"

"So do you. She was the woman who claimed Zach was dead during that mess with Alice Cage and Edward Caito. The one who forced Zach to kill Tag."

Cass gave a low whistle. "Oh, that's bad."

Aubrey frowned. "How bad?"

"Let's just say Max had better be damn good at hiding."

"Niall, do you have your laptop with you?"

He looked up at Kate from a chair in the kitchen, his brow furrowed. "Well, yeah, but I can't use it much, given the whole total lockdown thing."

"Do you have one of those mini generators?"

"I don't know. Why do you want my laptop?"

271

Kate sat down across from him. "Since I have nothing better to do, I want to know who the manager used to be for the warehouse where the Galaxy Boys were found. It occurred to me that if the kids picked the lock, whoever put those boys in there most likely had the key."

"Fair enough." Niall retrieved his laptop and set it up, connected to a small crank generator. "Good thing Cass had us download full WI files onto an offline system before this mess."

"She's a smart woman. What have you got?"

"That warehouse was closed last year... the manager was..." Niall hesitated. "Y'know, I'm not sure this list is actually updated. Maybe we should just—"

"Who was it, Niall?"

He gave a long, slow sigh. "Clarice Wagner."

Kate's green eyes went cold. "Clarice Wagner."

"Yeah."

"I told Cass and Casey not to give her a chance. I told her she didn't deserve one." Kate stood up, her hands in tight fists. "Stay here with everyone else. I'm going to go have a chat with my favorite ex-con."

"Kate," Niall said quickly, getting to his feet as well, "be rational about this. You don't know that Clarice had anything to do with this."

"The odds are astonishing. I won't do anything stupid, Niall. But I need to *do* something. And Clarice Wagner is something I can handle."

Once she had stormed out of the room, Niall gave a quiet scoff. "You sure about that?"

The front door opened, and Rick walked into the safe house. Niall jumped to his feet and hurried over to hug his son. "Are you okay?"

"I'm fine, Dad," Rick said, relieved. "You?"

"Better now. You Mom and Ciaran are here, but I had no idea where you were."

Rick hesitated. "How's Mom?"

Niall shifted uncomfortably. "She was fine until about ten seconds ago."

His son's eyes narrowed. "What's going on?"

Kate had intended to go to Clarice Wagner's home by herself, but she somehow ended up with Jacob and Rick as her backup. Ciaran and Niall had stayed at the safe house to keep an eye on Riley and Erin, but the younger boys had insisted on accompanying her.

"You guys really didn't need to come with me," Kate muttered as she walked up to Clarice's front door.

"She doesn't have powers. This is the *one time* I can be useful," Rick joked.

"Yeah, and Rick's not usually very useful, so he should have this chance."

"Shut up, Jacob." Rick played with the zipper of his sweatshirt. "Besides, Mom. You're not exactly Clarice's biggest fan. I want to make sure you're okay."

Kate glared at him. "You mean make sure I don't do something to her?"

Her son stared at her calmly. "I mean make sure that if you *do*, you're fully aware of what you're doing at the time."

"I always know what I'm doing," Kate muttered as she knocked loudly on the door.

Jacob glanced at Rick. "You're much braver than I am," he mumbled.

"Sort of makes you wonder why I'm afraid of Logan," Rick replied grumpily, folding his arms across his chest.

"Oh, no, that's not surprising in the slightest."

"What's that supposed to—" Rick was interrupted when Kate kicked down Clarice's front door. "Mom!" he hissed.

"What?" she asked innocently. "It was open."

"I'm from a family of criminals," Rick sighed as Kate walked into the house. "I'm going to end up in prison for the rest of my life before I even hit eighteen."

Jacob clapped Rick on the shoulder. "Look on the bright side, Richie. You won't have to go to college."

"I *like* school."

"You're a nerd."

"You have an IQ of 132!"

"Yeah, and I've gotten straight C's throughout my scholarly career. Smarts don't equal educational success, Richard. Just like educational success doesn't equal smarts." Jacob smirked. "You should know that, Mr. Straight A's."

Rick pushed Jacob irritably, but before they could start any sort of fight, Kate appeared in the doorway and snapped, *"Boys!"*

"Oh. Right. Sorry, Mom." Rick sheepishly followed his mother into the house, with Jacob close behind.

Clarice Wagner's home looked like the residence of someone preparing for the apocalypse. The windows were boarded up with wood that looked to be from destroyed furniture. The floor was littered with shattered lamps and decorations, and kitchen knives hung above the entryway like a trap for intruders.

"Watch the tripwire," Kate said, nodding at a thin line of thread that crossed the hallway near the knives.

"Huh." Jacob carefully stepped over the thread. "Not very friendly, is she?"

"I guess she knew we were coming," Rick commented.

Kate looked troubled. "Well, she knew *someone* was coming." She walked further into the house until she got into the kitchen, where a table was turned over. Brown hair could be seen over the edge of it.

"Please, I didn't say anything, I swear, I didn't say anything," a woman's voice begged.

"We aren't here to hurt you, Clarice," Kate said, her voice surprisingly gentle.

There was a pause, and the brown-haired woman behind the table slowly and stiffly stood up. Clarice's eyes were full of sheer panic. Her nose looked broken, as did all of the fingers of her right hand. She was keeping weight off of her left leg, which looked slightly twisted, as if something had been done to her knee. Her face and clothes were stained with dried blood, as if whatever had happened to her had immediately caused her to shut down and lock herself away without a single thought towards taking care of herself.

"Oliver," Clarice whispered hoarsely.

"What happened to you?"

"Th-They wanted the key to a warehouse... I don't know what for... Said they knew who I was and what I had done... That's why they picked the building I used to manage... Said this way they would only be hurting someone who deserved it..." Clarice swallowed. "Said they'd come back and do worse—then kill me—if I told anybody."

"*Who*, Clarice?"

"I don't *know*! Some soldier types!"

Kate nodded. "Let me guess. A general with black hair?"

"Y-Yeah. And a woman, I think she was Middle Eastern. She was the worst one, honestly."

"Must be one of his go-to problem-solvers," Kate muttered. She frowned at Clarice slightly. "Why didn't you contact one of us, Clarice? I know we don't like each other, but you've been on good terms with some of the others."

"I couldn't," Clarice rasped. She stumbled out from behind the table and grabbed Kate by the front of her jacket. "I couldn't. How could... Casey and Cass have done a *lot* for me, I... how was I supposed... to admit that I... I mean, I had no *choice* but to give them the key, you have to understand that, Oliver."

"I do understand," Kate said softly, leading Clarice to a nearby stack of books and forcing her to sit down. She glanced back at Rick. "Mara and Wyatt, 124 Brewer Street. Three blocks down." Rick nodded and hurried out of the house. Kate crouched down in front of Clarice. "You haven't learned, have you? Cass got you parole. She and Casey gave you a job. They gave you a chance to do something with your life instead of wasting it in prison for something that happened when you weren't even thirty. Do you really think they're the type of people who would take that away from you because someone hurt you into giving them what they want?"

Clarice gave a noncommittal shrug. "Maybe. Like the soldier types said. I deserve it."

Kate bowed her head, a guilty look in her eyes. "That was all a long time ago, Clarice. And I think you've paid for it already," she muttered.

"I'm sure you really believe that and aren't just saying it because I look like I got punched in the face," Clarice replied dryly.

"I'm pretty sure you *did* get punched in the face."

The older woman chuckled quietly. "That's not a denial, Oliver."

"You're right. It's not." Kate leaned back on her heels. "You wouldn't be buying my sympathy if I gave you one."

"True."

After a few minutes of silence, Rick returned with Wyatt Jones. The paramedic wasn't in uniform today, instead dressed in khakis and a maroon and orange college sweatshirt.

"Mara's at work. Hospitals have been busy trying to keep everything going in the power outage. Rick said you needed some help?" Wyatt asked. His eyes immediately went to Clarice and he bit his lip. "Ah. I see why." He quickly walked over and moved Kate out of the way so he could crouch down in front of Clarice. "How long have you been like this?"

"Not sure. Week or so I guess."

"And you didn't think a hospital was necessary?"

Clarice averted her gaze. "I-I was... too scared to go."

Wyatt glanced at Kate, who muttered, "Bad guy. Don't ask."

"Noted."

Kate turned to Rick and Jacob. "If Reznik killed the Galaxy Boys, I doubt he's playing nicely. I'm going to go find out what he's up to at that base of his."

The boys exchanged a look. "We're going with you, Mom."

"Absolutely not."

Jacob snorted. "If you don't let us come *with* you, we'll just go by ourselves."

"Rick, your father will be *furious* if I let you go."

"What's he going to do? You're already divorced, and I'm almost eighteen so it's not like he'd try to take away any of your custody rights. Plus, I mean, Ciaran has been going out and shooting criminals with arrows since he was fourteen. I really don't think Dad would have much ground to stand on in the 'keep Rick home' argument."

Kate sighed heavily. "Son, you may be the nice one, but you're definitely an Oliver." She rubbed the back of her neck. "Look, if you want to get out a bit, that's one thing, but I don't really think this is the mission to—"

"This is the *exact* mission I *have* to be on," Rick interrupted, his voice suddenly getting serious.

"Why's that?"

"Because these guys killed Uncle Justin, and they might have killed Seamus."

Kate paled. "That's..." She cleared her throat. "That's not..."

"What? That's not a good enough reason?"

His mother closed her eyes and sighed again. "All right," she whispered. "All right. But you both do *everything* I say, understood?"

"Understood," Rick and Jacob said simultaneously.

"Go wait outside."

The boys left the house, and Kate turned back to Wyatt and Clarice. "Interesting control you have there," Wyatt commented. His voice held no judgment, but there was still a questioning look in his eyes.

"I lost all parental control over the boys when I lost complete control over myself," Kate replied. "They usually respect me, because they're good sons, but... if they've stubbornly set their minds on something, I can't stop them. And Jacob is Cass's kid, so I have no hope of stopping him from doing anything, ever."

"You should have some more faith in yourself, Kate."

"Yeah, well, you don't have kids," Kate muttered rebelliously.

"I will soon enough," Wyatt said.

Kate punched his shoulder. "Mara never said anything about that!"

"That's because we were waiting for a good line to come in on," Wyatt joked.

"Ugh, that was terrible. I feel bad for your kid already." Kate glanced at Clarice. "She going to be okay?"

"I won't be sure until she gets to a hospital. It's not good that she left these injuries for so long. But I'll stay with her. Go ahead."

"Thanks, Wyatt."

As Kate turned to leave, she heard Clarice's hoarse voice say, "Kate. Thanks."

Kate paused. "I don't think you've used my first name in decades."

"Don't get used to it, Oliver."

With a smile, Kate nodded and walked out of Clarice's house.

Alix opened her eyes and groaned softly. Whatever had hit her in the head had been heavy and metallic, and possibly sharp. She wasn't sure, but she thought she could feel blood dripping down the back of her neck.

She would've checked whether the sensation was real or not, but there were more pressing matters preventing her. Her arms, legs, torso, and head were all strapped down to some sort of metal chair that was reclined just slightly, allowing her to see the top of the door in front of her but not the bottom. Before she could properly get her bearings, the man seated in a normal chair next to her stood up.

"Good, you're awake," Reznik said. "For a moment there I was worried Sarah had killed you."

"I don't die that easily," Alix grumbled. "Trust me; you aren't the first megalomaniac who's given it a shot."

"I don't want to *kill* you, Ms. Cage. I want you to *help* me."

"It's Tolvaj," Alix snapped. "And I think I'd rather you kill me."

Reznik took a deep breath. "Look, Ms.... *Tolvaj*, I'm really tired of playing with you people. I'm really tired of the attitude that all of you Heroics people apparently possess."

"You're the one who put an arrest warrant on me for the murder of a friend of mine," Alix growled.

"Because I need answers. From you. And I'm tired of the runaround."

"What's your point?"

"My point is that I'm only going to ask you once. How do I stop your friend who can walk through walls?"

Alix laughed. "Your interviewing techniques suck, General."

Reznik shook his head slowly. "I keep giving you people chances. You keep throwing them back in my face."

"It's called loyalty. Have you heard of it?"

"Of course. I'm loyal to this country. And I think I can do a much better job of running it. That's the point of all of this. If I can militarize vigilantes, I can show my worth. I can rise even further in the ranks, until the only next step is complete control of the military."

"You want to be *president*?"

Reznik chuckled. "No. I want the military to run this country. And I want to run the military."

"So you're planning a coup," Alix realized.

"In a sense. And I need your kind to make it happen. But for some reason, nobody's been volunteering their services. So instead, I've decided to *make* them serve me."

Alix swallowed. "You're why empowered people have been disappearing off the streets. You're the one who killed the Galaxy Boys."

"Of course." Reznik straightened his rank insignia pin on his uniform. "I would try to convert you to my cause, Ms. Tolvaj, but unfortunately, you're of no use to me aside from your information on your intangible friend. So this will be the last time we speak. I'm sorry you couldn't be a part of the best possible future for your country."

"Yeah, I'm sure I'll be missing a whole lot," Alix said sarcastically.

"You will." Reznik left the room.

A few minutes later, a woman walked in. She was tall and thin, with pale blue eyes and dark blonde hair. Alix recognized her but didn't know her name. She was an empowered thief who had been one of the first people captured by Ciaran when he became a member of Heroics. She had, back then, been an energetic, happy woman. Now she looked like she had been beaten so far into submission that she would never do anything on her own willpower again.

"The general wants information on the individual with the phasing power who is loose on our base," the woman said.

"Uh huh. I already told the general that I don't really care."

"It doesn't matter much. I can make you tell me."

"That so? I'll have you know that I can take a lot of pain, so it'll be interesting to see how you manage to accomplish that."

"Oh. I'm not going to try to get you to *say* anything." The woman walked over to Alix and stuck what felt like a rubber mouth guard in her mouth.

The piece made it impossible to speak, and Alix was in the process of wondering how it could possibly be useful during an interrogation when the woman rested the palm of her hand against Alix's forehead. A feeling like a strong migraine shot through Alix's head and her teeth clenched tightly, only stopping from slamming against each other because of the mouth guard.

Memories started to be pulled to the front of Alix's mind, cycling very quickly from the day she first joined Heroics forward. They suddenly slowed down to a more understandable speed when she got to memories of the last week: Playing cards against Max; arguing with him over the differences between Heroics and the Legion; their all-night discussion of what each of them was and wasn't comfortable with, which had ended with Alix kissing him on the forehead and Max stammering like an idiot as if she had told him she loved him.

"Interesting," the woman murmured. "Why are you thinking about him? Is he your partner in crime?"

Alix shook her head, but the migraine pain intensified. A slightly older memory played out in real-time in her mind:

"I think my ribs are broken."

"You're a terrible fighter."

"Am not. You just hit really hard."

"You're capable of letting my fist go right through you, *and it's* my *fault that you suck?"*

"It's the ring."

"Aw, hell, I forgot I was wearing that. I'm sorry."

"It's not really the immense pain that made it awful. That's real silver, isn't it?"

"Oh, right, the gold, silver, and platinum thing."

The memory disappeared with the pain as the woman's hand moved away from Alix's head. "Gold, silver, and platinum," the woman said. "So that's his weakness." Alix shook her head again, panic in her eyes.

The woman just stared at her. "Thank you for your cooperation."

While Alix sat, still trapped in the chair, the woman turned and left the room.

Zach leaned against a door frame and watched as Thomas slept on one of the beds in the safe house Claire and Kara had claimed. The boy had fallen asleep about half an hour ago after barely sleeping for the past week. As Zach silently watched his son, AJ appeared next to him.

"How are you holding up?" AJ asked quietly.

"I'm worried. But it helps that I know where all of my kids are."

"I wish I did."

Zach chuckled softly. "Yeah, but your kids are your kids. They can take care of themselves."

AJ smiled. "Yours can't?"

"Eh. Maybe. If it's a day when they're taking more after Casey than me. And Logan's smarter than both of us, so I suppose I can't actually judge."

"Logan's smarter than both of you, and *he*—" AJ pointed at Thomas "might not actually be your child, because I'm pretty sure he's more mature than anyone else in this family."

"I wouldn't be shocked." Zach patted AJ on the shoulder. "Everyone's going to be okay, brother. We have to believe that."

"We do. And I think I have a way to make sure this all ends sooner rather than later."

Zach raised an eyebrow. "I'm listening."

Kate walked up to the front gate of Reznik's military base. The lieutenant standing at the guard station held up a hand to stop her. "Excuse me, ma'am, can I help you?"

"Yes, hi, I'm a vigilante, and I'm here to surrender myself," Kate said brightly.

The lieutenant blinked, surprised. "Really?"

"Nope." Kate raised her crossbow and shot the lieutenant with a Taser arrow. Almost immediately, alarms started to sound throughout the base. Kate smirked. "Alarms in my honor. It's like I've joined the dark side." Whistling softly to herself as she pulled out a second crossbow, Kate headed through the gates and into the base.

17

"If those alarms aren't for Max, this is the worst-guarded military base in the world," Cass said dryly as she listened to the piercing screeching that was echoing from the hallway.

Casey shrugged. "My bet? Our idiot friends can't sit still for five minutes and they've all picked the same day to do something about the problem."

"We're really good for that."

"It's why we work so well as a team. We can make dumb decisions at the same time when we aren't even in the same room."

Aubrey stood up suddenly, and Cass grabbed her shoulder. "Whoa, kid, I'm really not sure you should be standing."

"Not sure?" Aubrey asked with a small smirk.

"Your father's the one with the medical degree. Although I'm the one who usually ends up injured, so my 'not sure' is pretty darn sure."

"I agree with you, but I've had a dumb idea of my own, and with these alarms going off it may be the best time to try it out."

"And what's that?"

Aubrey carefully made her way over to the door, which Casey was still leaning next to. "Aunt Casey, could you move over a bit? I want to get to the intercom."

Casey scoffed but shifted out of the way. "Hope your idea isn't to demand for someone to let us out, because Reznik doesn't seem the type."

"That's not the plan." Aubrey pulled her ring off of her finger and snapped it apart, making it fold open on a hinge.

"What the hell?" Cass muttered, getting to her feet and joining her sister and daughter.

"Have you never seen this?" Aubrey asked innocently. "Brooke and Jacob got it for me when I started college. They thought it was funny because they were the engineering types and I wasn't. Didn't stop me from wearing it, though."

"What is it?"

"A ring that can fold out into a screwdriver."

Cass and Casey both stared at her. "You're joking," Casey said.

"I'm really not."

"Reznik let you keep that?"

"I'm not sure he even noticed I was wearing it, even when I was spinning it around on my finger. He might've just not thought it was important. I certainly wasn't going to make it seem like it was. I acted like it was a completely unimportant piece of jewelry so that I could use it whenever the time was right."

"Honey," Cass said seriously, gently taking Aubrey's face in her hands. "If the voice in your head *ever* again tells you that you do not belong in this family, don't listen to it, because you're such a Hamil it's almost painful."

"She's actually more like my side of the family," Casey commented. "You, Brooke, and Jacob would've used that thing days ago and gotten yourselves killed."

"Shut up, Case."

"It's not exactly like I'm *lying*, Cass. You—"

While her mother and aunt bickered, Aubrey pulled away and went back to the intercom. She unscrewed the plate over the speaker and ripped the wires out of the wall. The argument stopped immediately.

"Aubrey... what...?"

"The door has a magnet lock," Aubrey said as she looked at Cass. "It needs power to stay closed and sealed, but it didn't open when the power went out. Why?"

There was a pause, then Casey started to laugh. "Oh, man. How did I miss that?"

"Thank you for making me feel dumb," Cass said dryly.

"The intercom still had power," Aubrey explained. "It was on a different grid. Probably the same grid. Disrupt that grid..."

Perfectly cued, the magnetic lock clinked off and the door slowly swung open. "Kid, you're a genius," Cass said.

"Yeah, well, I'm just glad it worked after all that buildup." Aubrey folded her ring back into a circle and put it back on, spinning it slowly.

"So am I." Casey pushed her glasses up on her nose and carefully glanced out into the empty hallway. "Why don't we see if we can find out who's making such a disturbance, shall we?"

Max heard the alarms go off throughout the base, but he wasn't sure whether they were over him or over something else that was going on. Most of the soldiers he saw were running towards the main gate, which made him think that he wasn't their biggest concern at the moment.

As he stepped into a nearby mechanical supply building, something heavy smacked him in the chest. He saw the object swing towards him again and he tried to let it phase through him, but it simply hit him once more. Max dodged out of the way and took a few steps backwards, trying to get a better look at his attacker.

The woman was dark-haired, dark-eyed, and wearing the silver leaf-shaped badge of a lieutenant colonel. She was holding what looked like a trophy, which struck Max as an odd weapon until he realized it was gold in color. A feeling of horror ran through him, but his voice was calm as he asked, "What, have you run out of bullets?"

"No," the woman replied. "It was just the only thing I could find that was gold, silver, or platinum and was any use as a weapon." She studied the trophy. "I got this for holding the record for number of people knocked out in the first five minutes of practice fights during training. There wasn't a record for that, but my CO was so impressed he made me an award."

"Your CO sounds a bit like Reznik."

"Probably because he was." The woman tossed the trophy in the air and caught it. "The general and I have been working together since I joined the army. It's been a spectacular arrangement. I get to work out my anger issues and be useful at the same time, and he gets complete loyalty."

"I'm not even going to take the time to tell you how horrifying that is. All I'm going to ask you is how exactly you know what I can't phase through."

"Your girlfriend told me."

"I don't have a girlfriend."

"Really? She seems quite fond of you, going by what my interrogator told me about how badly she didn't want to give us any information on you."

"What—" Max paled. "Alix."

"And the boy catches on. Congratulations." The soldier clapped sarcastically, the trophy tucked under her arm. "At this rate you'll figure out the evil plan when you're, say, fifty."

"Where is she? What have you done with her?"

"Please. You're going to have to try just a bit harder than that. Who do you think you're dealing with here?"

"A sociopath who likes hurting people?"

"No. Well, the second part is true. But I'm Lieutenant Colonel Sarah Amirmoez, little hero. I'll bet I've killed more people than you've ever saved, and I'm not going to answer a question I don't want to just because you think you can demand one." Sarah folded her arms across her chest, loosely holding the trophy behind her back. "*I* ask the questions. I don't answer them. If you don't believe me, just go ahead and talk to your little Legion friend."

Max's jaw tensed. "What Legion friend?"

"Oh, you don't know she's here? I thought you people cared more about your teammates than that."

"*What Legion friend?*"

"I think the Hamil girl called her... what was it... uh... Rowan?"

290

Max's hands tightened into fists. "Rowan? You've been..." He swallowed. "You've been interrogating Rowan?"

"I'm not sure *you* would call it 'interrogating' in the purest sense of the term, but—"

"What did you do to her?"

Sarah laughed. "Hero boy, we've had this conversation. I'm not telling you anything about your girlfriend *or* your little associate."

"Is that so?" Max asked coldly.

"Absolutely." She swung at him again.

The fight between them was quick, but to Sarah's surprise, other than a hard blow across his face, she had little success with her golden weapon. Max disarmed her, shoved her against a wall, grabbed a long wrench that was being stored nearby, and phased it through her chest. He held it there so that it wasn't hurting her, but with his hand tightly gripping her throat she couldn't move quickly enough away from him to avoid dying if she tried to fight back.

"I don't understand," Sarah growled. "I'm better than you."

"How old is that trophy, Lieutenant Colonel?"

"I don't know... twenty-seven years old?"

"And how long has it been since you've actually fought someone? Not just hurt someone. Actually fought someone."

"I-I... How long ago was the mess with Caito and Cage?"

"About twelve years."

Sarah's eyes widened, and she tried to stammer out a response, but Max just laughed. "You haven't actually had a real opponent in twelve years, have you? Sure, you've been torturing people, but nobody at this base is stupid enough to fight you, and Reznik couldn't afford to let you loose in Caotico. You're so far out of practice, and you don't even realize it. It's been like a week since I had to fight somebody, Lieutenant Colonel. I have the advantage."

"So what are you going to do?" Sarah demanded. "Kill me?"

Max's grip on the wrench in Sarah's chest tightened. "I'm going to ask you a question. You give me a straight answer, I'll take this thing out of your chest. You keep toying with me, and I'm letting it go. I'm not quite sure what it will do to you, but I'm willing to find out."

"First of all, I don't believe you. Second of all, I don't really care what you do."

"We'll see." Max positioned the wrench in the center of Sarah's chest. "Where are Alix and Rowan?"

"Hopefully, dead."

"That's not an answer."

"You're right," Sarah said cheerfully. "And I'm not going to give you one."

"I'm not *playing with you*, Lieutenant Colonel."

"Oh, I'm sure you aren't."

Max shook his head slowly. "You're not going to tell me, are you?"

"Now you're catching on. So what are you going to do, hero? I really don't think you're going to keep your word."

"See, that's the thing," Max said quietly. "I don't really like killing, but I don't like breaking promises, either." He lowered the wrench so that it was through a spot in Sarah's body that contained no vital organs, arteries, or bones, then let it go.

Sarah surprisingly didn't scream as the wrench resolidified inside of her. She gritted her teeth, her eyes watering as the pain clearly hit her, and put her hands on the handle of the wrench as if she was going to try to remove it.

"First of all," Max growled, "I wouldn't recommend that, even if it were possible. It's a *wrench*, not something that could be easily removed. Second of all, you're going to need to be a lot stronger than you could possibly be to get that thing out, because I also put it through the wall."

"What the hell for?" Sarah snarled.

"Because this way, you can't leave." Max took the radio from Sarah's belt and clipped it to his own. He also took her gun. "And this way, I know exactly where you are, so I don't need to worry about any more gold trophies being thrown at my face." He kicked the trophy further away from Sarah and walked directly out of the building.

Casey, Cass, and Aubrey cautiously made their way through the halls of the military base, but it didn't really seem to matter how careful they were. The building they were in seemed to be completely empty.

"What the hell is with this place? It's *definitely* the worst-staffed military complex I've ever seen," Cass muttered.

"And how many military complexes have you seen, sis?"

"Not many, but still."

They rounded a corner and almost walked directly into Rick. Casey, at the front of the group, grabbed him by the front of his shirt and slammed him into a wall, not immediately recognizing him. The moment she did, she let him go sheepishly.

"Sorry," she said. "Little jumpy."

"Little?" he grumbled, straightening his clothing. "You nearly took my head off."

"Yeah, well, nearly."

Rick rolled his eyes. "Thanks, Casey." He glanced at Aubrey and frowned. "Are you okay?"

"I'll live. What are you doing here?"

"Snooping. Mom's distracting the soldiers while Jacob and I split up and look around."

Cass took in a slow breath. "Okay, a few things about that concern me. Your mom brought two people with no active combat powers here?"

"We didn't really give her a choice."

"I'll buy that. My other concern is what exactly you mean by 'distracting.'"

Rick pointed at the ceiling. "You know those sirens?"

"Yeah."

"Those would be my mother and her crossbow."

Cass pinched the bridge of her nose and closed her eyes. "Somehow that doesn't surprise me."

"Wait," Casey said. "So you three aren't here with Alix and Max?"

"Alix and Max are here?"

Aubrey shook her head slowly. "This team is ridiculous."

"I take offense to that," Casey said mildly. "Have you found anybody else at all, Rick?"

He shook his head. "There are some cells in here that seem to be holding empowered criminals, but if you go anywhere near them they freak out and try to kill you. It looks like Reznik's been collecting them, brainwashing them, probably through another empowered criminal, and keeping them here like some sort of arsenal. A few were just being interrogated, and it looks like a few were tortured before just being killed outright."

"The brainwashing must be what he did to Lattimer," Cass muttered.

"My *boss?*" Aubrey sounded shocked.

"Ex-boss," Cass corrected. "Justin fired him." Her voice softened. "Lattimer's the one who pulled the trigger. I guess now we know why it was so easy for him to do it."

Casey nodded. "Reznik probably promised him revenge, brought him here without a fight, and brainwashed him so he couldn't back out at the last second."

"So Justin got killed because of me," Aubrey said in a dull voice, slowly starting to fidget with her ring. "If I hadn't told you about Lattimer—"

"*Don't,*" Cass interrupted. "Don't, sweetheart. This is *not* your fault. Got it?" She gripped Aubrey's shoulder tightly and glanced at Rick. "Do you know where Jacob is?"

"We have a planned meeting point."

"Then lead the way."

Alix was frustrated and tired of trying to get out of her bindings when footsteps came out of nowhere to her right. Max's stunned voice said, "Thief?"

His hands grabbed her arm and she was pulled out of the chair, phasing through the restraints as if they weren't even there. Max continued to hold her arm as she swayed slightly, trying to regain her balance.

"Thief, are you all right?"

Alix pulled the piece of rubber out of her mouth and irritably tossed it across the room. She then rested her hands on her knees and took in a deep breath. "Son of a bitch," she mumbled.

Max crouched down in front of her, concern in his brown eyes. "Alix?"

"I'm okay. I've been through a lot worse than what these idiots can do to me." She looked at the gash on his cheek and her eyes narrowed. "I just wish they hadn't been able to... They read my mind or my memories or something. That's how they know what you can't phase through."

"I was wondering about that," Max said in a mild voice. Alix angrily kicked over a nearby trashcan. "Hey, it's not your fault, Thief."

"I *know* that. But I don't like people I care about getting hurt because of me, whether it's my fault or not."

"People you care about, huh?" Max teased gently.

"Aw, shut up, Wraith."

"Not a chance."

Alix tilted Max's chin to get a better look at the cut on his face. "You're really okay?"

"Bit banged up, but it's not all that bad. You've done worse in those practice matches."

"It's not my fault you can't fight."

"You'd be surprised," he said mildly. He fidgeted as he put his hands in his pockets. "Should we get out of here?"

"In a sec."

"What are we waiting for?" Max asked curiously.

Alix took in a deep breath. "Understand that this does not change the current status of our relationship. Clear?"

"I... don't know what you're talking about... but okay?"

"I'm talking about this." Alix pulled him down by the collar of his military uniform and kissed him on the mouth.

18

A few seconds after Alix kissed him, Max heard the door open behind them. She gently but quickly shoved him away, grabbing his gun off of his belt and aiming it at the person walking into the room. She lowered it just as quickly.

"Jacob? What the *hell*?"

"I *thought* I heard your voice, Al," Jacob said. There was an amused look in his eyes, but he continued with, "Kate, Rick, and I are here. We thought we'd look around. Apparently we weren't the only ones who had the thought."

"Cass, Casey, and Aubrey are here, too."

"It's a party!" Jacob turned back towards the hallway he had come from. "Come on. Let's get out of here."

"Why are you in such a rush?" Alix asked.

"Uh, I don't want to get shot?"

"Good enough reason for me." Alix glanced at Max, who had heard the conversation but could only stare at them blankly. She rolled her eyes and lightly punched him in the shoulder. "You awake, Wraith?"

Max blinked rapidly and looked at her. "U-Uh, yeah. I... yeah." He cleared his throat. "Absolutely."

"Then follow the boy, would you?" With a smirk, Alix walked out of the room.

Jacob paused in the doorway, staring at Max through narrowed eyes. Max, who was moving the gun he had stolen from Sarah from his pocket to the holster on his waist, frowned. "Is there a... problem?"

"Depends. Are we going to have one?"

"I don't know what you're talking about."

"I'm watching you, Oakley," the boy growled. He turned and followed Alix.

Max sighed heavily and ran a hand through his hair. *"Oy vey iz mir."*

Reznik watched as a soldier who had been walking in front of him through the base was knocked down by a small arrow. He sighed and turned to face in the direction the arrow had come from. "Which one are you?" he asked loudly. "Targeter or Orion?"

Kate stepped out of the shadows of a nearby building, her crossbow aimed directly at Reznik's chest. "Targeter."

"Huh. I'll admit, I was sort of expecting the younger archer to be the one stupid enough to come here like this."

"Well, he's a lot less reckless than his mother is, so I'm not all that surprised that he hasn't shown up."

"What's the plan here, Targeter? You going to kill me?"

"I want to," Kate said, her voice tense. "I want to more than anything. You killed my brother."

"I don't remember killing anyone recently..."

"Justin Oliver," Kate snarled, taking a few aggressive steps towards Reznik. "You had him executed in front of his wife and daughter. You made them watch while one of your people gunned him down in the street!"

"Oh, right, Oliver." Reznik shrugged. "He was just a means to an end. I had nothing against him personally, although his lack of cooperation did annoy me. I don't like people who don't give me what I want."

Kate's hands were shaking as she took another step towards Reznik. "You know, I've been in this position before. Aiming an arrow at a person who was involved in killing one of my siblings. I let that person live. I'm not so sure I'm going to do it this time."

"That would be murder."

"That's rich coming from you."

"How did you even get in here? How were you not taken down before you got this far into the complex?"

Kate smirked. "Easy. Most of your soldiers are busy keeping up the blockade around Caotico and Fuego. There aren't that many people here, and I'd bet that most of them are sleeping quite soundly at the moment."

Reznik gritted his teeth. "I'm beginning to wish I had chosen a different city full of empowered people. They'd have to be less aggravating than you people."

"It's possible. But it's too late for that."

"You're going to kill me then? I'm disappointed."

"I—" Kate looked up as she heard the sound of an approaching helicopter. "What the hell is that?"

"That would be a helicopter, Targeter."

"Really not in the mood for the sass, General."

A screech of tires behind Kate signaled the arrival of Zach's SUV and he, Logan, and AJ got out of the vehicle. "I hope we haven't missed anything too interesting," Logan said brightly as she followed her father over to Kate's side.

"You sort of stopped me from killing this guy."

"Awesome. Why were you going to kill him?"

Kate sighed and lowered her crossbow. "Honestly, kid, I don't know. It wouldn't make any difference, would it?"

Zach rested a hand on Kate's shoulder. "Most likely? Not even a little bit."

"You have good timing, then."

"I've always prided myself on everything in my life being at the exact time it's supposed to be," Zach said.

Kate snorted. "Then why'd you marry your kid's mother when said kid was five?" she muttered under her breath.

Logan laughed, but Zach coughed loudly and said, "Why don't we stay on track, huh?"

"That's what I was thinking." AJ was walking towards Reznik, coming to a stop about a foot away from him. "Do you know who I am, General?"

"Yes. You're Cassidy Hamil's consort."

AJ smiled slightly. "I think 'husband' is a good enough term, but I'll accept it. Where's my wife? And Casey?"

"Somewhere." Reznik shrugged. "They were still in their cell last I saw them. They were with your daughter."

"What?" AJ growled.

"Oh, you hadn't noticed? What kind of father are you that you haven't even checked on all of your children?"

AJ took a small step towards Reznik, getting in his face. "What did you do to Aubrey?"

"Nothing." Reznik paused. "Well, that may be a lie."

Zach, looking concerned, started forward, but before he had taken more than two steps, AJ had punched Reznik in the jaw. Zach quickly grabbed his brother-in-law and dragged him away from Reznik as the furious man snarled, "*Let me go, Zach!*"

"You're going to break your hand," Zach said quietly.

"It would be worth it!"

"Stand down, Dr. Hamil," a voice said. A tall, dark-skinned woman in a business suit was walking towards the group, flanked by two men in black suits.

AJ immediately stopped struggling against Zach, and the older man let him go. "My apologies, ma'am," he said in a tightly controlled voice. "I, uh, had my reasons."

"I'm sure. It's okay. The general probably deserved it."

Reznik was fidgeting with the rank pin on his uniform. "P-President Kingston. To what do I owe this visit?"

"Mr. Carter here got in touch with me. He told me what was going on. I was already a bit concerned by the fact that a major city had gone completely offline, but when I found out exactly what you were doing in here? Well, I decided that I had to pay a personal visit."

"Th-That was your helicopter, then."

"Yes, it was." Tamara Kingston stared at Reznik with a hard gaze. "Now, General. Would you like to tell me what exactly is going on here?"

Cass rested a hand on Aubrey's back as they walked with Casey and Rick towards the exit of the building they had been imprisoned in. "How you holding up, kid?"

"I'm okay, but I..." Aubrey put her hands in her pockets and looked down at the floor. "I still don't know where Rowan is. And that scares the hell out of me, Mom."

"You really love her, don't you?"

Aubrey gave a sighing laugh. "Yeah, I do."

"Y'know, you could've told us about her. I know there are reasons why you didn't. But you could've, honey."

"My brain's funny like that. It doesn't really care whether I can do something. It tells me that I can't and I shouldn't even try."

Cass kissed the side of Aubrey's head. "That's okay. Just try to let us in a little when it gets bad, okay? We want to be a part of your life, Aub. That includes the parts that hurt. It also includes the part where you have a girlfriend."

"You're going to needle me about that for a while, aren't you?"

"Just a little."

"Well, look who got themselves broken out of prison," Alix's voice said. She was walking down the hallway towards them along with Max and Jacob.

"You're one to talk," Casey said as she hugged Alix tightly. "How did *you* get out?"

"Mr. Walks-Through-Walls wandered into my cell."

Jacob snorted. "Yeah, and then you made out with him."

Alix paled. "I-I... I did not... *make out with him.*"

303

"What exactly would you call it then?" Jacob challenged.

"We're not talking about this right now," Alix grumbled.

Max sighed. "Oh, thank hell."

"We're absolutely going to talk about it later," Cass said.

"Please don't." Alix noticed Aubrey and winced. "They really did work you over, didn't they, kid? You okay?"

"I think so. I— Jacob?"

The boy was staring at his sister, looking both horrified and stunned. He swallowed, tears in his eyes. "W-When you dropped that phone call, I wasn't sure if... I didn't know if... What did they do to you, Bree?"

"It was just a few beatings," Aubrey said offhandedly. "It looks worse than it is." She rested her hands on her brother's shoulders. "I'm okay, Jake." When Jacob tried to move forward, Aubrey tightened her grip. "Please don't hug me. I'm pretty sure it would hurt."

"Sorry," Jacob murmured.

"It's fine. You're fine."

"Somebody find a camera. Cass's kids are getting along."

"Shut up, Casey."

The radio on Max's belt suddenly started making noise and a voice came through it saying, "*This is President Tamara Kingston. I've taken control of this base. All soldiers are to surrender themselves at the airstrip within the next fifteen minutes or risk prosecution.*"

"Redwood is here?" Max whistled softly. "We're all in trouble now."

"Do you think she's with anybody else from either of our groups?" Casey asked.

Max shrugged. "I think if we head over to the airstrip we'll be able to find out."

"Then why don't we do that?" Casey glanced at Aubrey. "Maybe while we're there we can get one of these soldiers to ask a few questions about who they're still holding in this prison here, huh?"

"That would be nice," Aubrey said weakly.

"Good. Come on, then."

It took only a few minutes to get to the airstrip, and when the group got there, they found Kate, Rick, Logan, AJ, and Zach standing and watching soldiers gather in front of the president and her guards.

"Mom!" Logan sprinted towards Casey and practically tackled her in a hug.

"Hi there," Casey laughed.

"We were getting worried."

"Worried? About me? When have I ever done anything that deserved worry?"

"Most of your life?" Zach teased as he walked over to join them.

"Yeah, yeah. My most concerning decision was still marrying you."

"That's Cass's line."

"You were married to Cass?"

Zach shook his head slowly and kissed his wife. "You're lucky I missed you."

"Are you guys okay?" AJ asked as he hugged his son quickly and led him back over to Cass and Aubrey.

"We'll be okay," Cass replied.

"Are you sure? Reznik said—" AJ's breath caught in his throat when he saw Aubrey.

"Yeah, I know. We've been over it a few times already."

AJ pulled Aubrey forward and hugged her tightly. She gave a soft, strained laugh. "I think my ribs are broken, Dad."

"I'm sorry; I'm sorry." AJ stepped back and loosened his grip, putting one hand on her shoulder and one on her cheek. "God, you're way too much like your mother," he said in a voice of mixed affection and concern.

"Aw, come on, I'm not *that* reckless," Aubrey joked.

"I would defend myself, but I don't think I can," Cass sighed.

"Not particularly." AJ gently ran his thumb over a bruise under Aubrey's eye. "What did Reznik want with you?"

"I'll explain later. Right now I really need to figure out what these people did with Rowan."

"Rowan's here too? We couldn't find her but we didn't know if—"

"She's here. And they were..." Aubrey took in a deep breath. "T-T-They were torturing her, and I don't know if she's okay."

"Do you recognize any of these soldiers?"

Aubrey shrugged. "Those two corporals over there are the ones who brought me to Mom's cell."

"Give me a second." AJ walked over two corporals who were sitting on the ground a bit separated from the larger group. He crouched down in front of

306

them and started a conversation that none of the others could hear. After no more than a minute, AJ returned to his family. "I'll be back in a few minutes. Don't follow me."

"Dad? What's going on?"

"Just trust me, Aubrey. Please."

"Hey," Alix said softly. "I'm coming with you."

"I don't need—"

"AJ. I'm coming with you."

"... Okay." AJ rested a hand on Aubrey's shoulder and gave a tight smile. "I'll be right back. I promise." He turned and walked away, with Alix close behind him.

"What weren't you telling that kid?" Alix asked as she and AJ walked towards the building right next to the one Cass, Casey, and Aubrey had been imprisoned in. "Those corporals said something to you. Something bad. But you wouldn't tell Aubrey about it."

"Because I don't want her to know until I have more confirmation."

"You going to tell me?"

AJ's hands tightened into fists. "I'm not sure what sort of condition Rowan's going to be in. And I'm pretty sure she's going to need a hospital. I just didn't want Aubrey to see that before I had more specific information."

"What were they doing to her?"

"Electrocuting her."

"Explain something to me, General." Kingston folded her arms across her chest. "What exactly was the plan here? What were you trying to achieve? Because if you thought that killing all of the vigilantes in Caotico was going to win you points, you're pretty thoroughly mistaken."

"You don't get it," Reznik said nastily. "I've seen so many soldiers die, and there's no reason for it. We can use these people with powers. They can do so much more than a normal human soldier, and they can basically be considered cannon fodder. All they need is to be broken down so that they're willing to work for us. *That is what this country needs.* You don't understand that, so all I'm doing is taking the initiative that you refuse to take."

"General Reznik, people with powers are still people. They're my citizens just as much as people *without* powers. I'm not going to force them into military service just because you think it would be a good idea." Kingston looked at one of her guards and gave a slight nod. "I am, however, going to force you to stand to court martial for your actions here. You severely overstepped your authority, and I will not allow you to get away with it."

As Reznik was put into handcuffs by a guard, he said, "You have no idea what you're dooming your military to."

"It's got to be better than whatever it would be like to be under your command, General."

A guard led Reznik away, and Max walked over to Kingston. "Uh, ma'am, there's one other person you might want to talk to."

"Who's that?"

"A lieutenant colonel under his command. Sarah Amirmoez. I'm pretty sure she's been doing some truly awful things to people here."

"Do you know where she is?"

Max rubbed the back of his neck. "Pinned to a wall in need of medical attention?"

Kingston stared at him. "Dammit, Max."

"She really deserved it, okay?"

"Just... take Sanchez and go get her."

While Max and Kingston's second guard walked away, Kingston shook her head slowly. "I swear," she muttered. "I don't know whether vigilantism or politics are worse."

Aubrey paced back and forth, spinning her ring in sets of three around her finger. She stopped pacing when she saw her father walking back towards her, a grim look on his face. "Dad," she said hoarsely. "Dad, what is it?"

"She's alive, Aub," AJ said when he reached her. He put his hands on her shoulders. "But she's not in good shape. She's already on her way to the hospital. Alix has her."

"I-I-I... What... What did they do to her?"

"I'm not completely sure. But we're going to find out. We're going to head over to the hospital, and you're going to get checked out."

"N-N-No, Dad, I'm fine, I—"

"That wasn't a request, Aubrey," AJ interrupted. "You need tests. X-rays and MRIs. But while the doctors are making sure you're really okay, I'm going to be with Rowan, all right? I'm going to get all of the information I can get. I'm going to be there when she wakes up, and I'm going to do everything that I can for her so that you can take care of yourself without worrying that no one is taking care of her. Okay?"

Aubrey swallowed and nodded. "Okay, Daddy."

AJ kissed her forehead softly. "Good girl. Go ahead and get in Zach's SUV. We'll head over once I have a quick word with him."

Zach looked up as AJ walked over to him. "Hey. Did you find Rowan?"

"Yeah. She's not in great shape. I think she'll recover, but I doubt it'll be quick. Do you have your Legion database on you?"

"Uh, yeah, it's on my phone."

"Has it started working yet now that the president is taking over the city?"

Zach pulled his phone out and checked it. "Looks like I can get into the database, yeah."

"Can you, uh, look up Rowan's emergency contacts?"

"Sure." Zach typed in a few commands, then frowned. "Huh."

"What is it?"

"Her emergency contacts. The first one is Aubrey."

"Well, they *are* dating. I didn't know it was at 'put me as your emergency contact' levels, but I don't really find it all *that* odd."

"You might not say that about this." Zach turned his phone around so AJ could see it. "Her second contact is Janek van Houten."

AJ paused. "Isn't that her father?"

"Yep."

"Isn't he dead?"

"Yeah. He died long before Rowan joined the Legion." Zach shook his phone once for emphasis before putting it back in his pocket. "Long before this form would've been filled out."

"So the only people the Legion can contact for her in case of an emergency are her girlfriend and someone who's been dead for over a decade? Does she not have other family?"

"I honestly don't know. Clearly the Legion hasn't been bothering to check how useful the information on those contact forms is."

"Any idea who was listed as her primary contact before she started dating Aubrey?"

"It doesn't look like she had anyone listed other than Janek before Aubrey came into the picture." Zach shook his head slowly. "I'm getting a bad feeling, AJ."

"What kind of bad feeling?"

"The one where the team I now run completely overlooked the well-being of one of its members, apparently because it was too lazy to care." There was an angry glint in Zach's hazel eyes. "Because this is something that *somebody* should've looked into. Nobody on a team should have no one to turn to in a crisis."

AJ patted Zach on the shoulder. "Well, buddy, then it's a good thing you now have the power to change all of that. Good luck."

19

Rowan opened her eyes, but she wasn't completely sure she was awake. She felt groggy and heavy, and nothing was really making any sense to her. As she blinked up at the ceiling, trying to gain a sense of her surroundings, she saw movement out of the corner of her eye. She turned her head and saw AJ getting up out of a chair next to her bed.

"Hey there, kid," he said gently. "You're on painkillers, so you're probably feeling a bit loopy right now."

"Where am I?" Rowan asked, and she found herself surprised by how hoarse her voice sounded.

"Caotico General Hospital. We wrapped up the Reznik situation—we can talk more about that when you aren't drugged—and got you over here to recover."

"When was that?"

"Two days ago."

Rowan winced. "I must be pretty bad, huh?"

AJ smiled softly at her. "You had a lot of electricity shot through you. Yeah, you're pretty bad. But you're going to be okay."

"That's nice. Is Aubrey all right?"

"Yeah. Few broken ribs, bunch of bruises, concussion. They forced her to go home to rest, so I promised I'd stay here with you so that she would stop arguing with the doctors. And because I wanted to make sure you weren't alone."

"Nice of you, but you didn't have to do that."

AJ chuckled. "Save the loner act, van Houten. Nobody's buying it." He gently turned her head to get a look at the bandage covering a deep gash in her temple. She jerked slightly at the contact and he let her go. "Sorry."

"Don't be. And don't worry. That's a long-standing twitch that's not from the past week," Rowan said quietly.

He wanted to know, but he didn't want to ask. So instead, AJ said, "You did a pretty good job on yourself. Even got yourself a head injury. Those are a staple of this family, so you were bound to get one eventually."

"I... 'this family'?"

"What, you thought you didn't qualify? Kid, my daughter loves you. Like, wholehearted, never-cared-for-anyone-like-this-before *love*. You're as close to family as you can get without marrying someone or being Alix."

Rowan took in a shaky breath. "What's going to happen now?"

"I'm not sure. Reznik and Lieutenant Colonel Amirmoez are in military custody pending court martial for how all of this went down. The president is personally overseeing the cleanup operation to restore order throughout the city. Zach's trying to get the Legion together, and while I'm here, the rest of Heroics is trying to repair the damage Reznik did to our reputation."

"That didn't make total sense, I think because of the drugs, but it sounded good."

AJ gave a sharp laugh. "Good."

A troubled look formed on Rowan's face. "H-Has anyone... been by my house... lately?"

"Aubrey said something about needing to take care of something there, but she would only let Alix help her with whatever it was." AJ sat down on the edge of

Rowan's bed. "Speaking of your house, though... Zach and I took a look at your emergency contact information."

"O-Oh?"

"You don't have to explain it now, Rowan. Hell, you don't have to explain it ever. But if you can manage to try, I'd like to know why the only family member you have listed is your father, who, well, can't really be called if you're in trouble."

Rowan swallowed. "Can we talk about it later?"

"Absolutely. Like I said, we don't even need to talk about it at all. I just want to make sure you know the option is open."

There was a quick knock on the door frame and a doctor walked in. "Ms. van Houten," he said. "Good. You're awake."

"If that's what you were waiting for, you have great timing," Rowan replied.

The doctor didn't smile. "Now that you are, I'd like to talk to you about a few things. There are some things you need to know."

"I'll give you the room," AJ said softly as he stood.

"Wait; Mr. Hamil?"

"Yeah, kid?"

"C-Could... would you mind... staying?" Rowan looked scared, her dark blue eyes full of what was close to panic.

"Not at all, kid." AJ gave her a thin smile. "I can stay as long as you want me to."

Cass was in the process of getting changed into nightclothes when AJ came into their room, slamming the door shut behind him. She winced and asked, "What the hell happened to you?"

"It's not me that's the problem," AJ muttered as he sat down on the edge of the bed and rested his head in his hands.

"Oh, hell." Cass took a seat next to him. "It's Rowan, isn't it?"

"That kid didn't deserve this," AJ said softly. "I don't care that we barely know her. I know that she doesn't deserve this."

"What's going on?"

AJ was silent for a long moment as he took off his tie. He tossed it towards his closet, then said, "She can't be in the Legion anymore."

It took a while for the words to process in Cass's head, but once they did, they still didn't make any sense. "What do you mean? How could she not be able to be in the Legion?"

"Well," AJ said slowly, staring at the floor, "the electricity that Sarah repeatedly used on her damaged her heart. She's capable of living a normal life as long as she stays on medication, but the stress and strain of vigilante work would be way too much for her. If she continued being a hero, she would give herself a heart attack. She would die, Cass."

Cass closed her eyes and leaned against him. "God, poor kid. What's she going to do?"

"I don't know. She wouldn't talk to me about what she was going to do. She wouldn't really talk about it at all. I don't know if it just hasn't sunk in yet, or whether she's avoiding it as long as she can."

"Does Aubrey know?"

AJ shook his head. "Rowan wanted to tell her."

"That's probably for the best."

"Is Brooke back from Matthias's yet?"

"Yeah. She's highly upset that she was out of commission while all of this went down. It's not that there was anything she could've done, but I don't think she's okay with the fact that Aubrey got hurt and she wasn't there to stop it."

"She couldn't have stopped it," AJ said. He gave Cass a sideways glance. "You couldn't have either, in case you're worrying about that. Reznik took Aubrey before he even got to you. You refusing to cooperate had nothing to do with what he did to her, or to Rowan."

"I know." Cass rested her head on his shoulder. "Doesn't make me feel much better, though."

"I know what you mean. Our kids shouldn't have to deal with stuff like this. But they keep being put through it anyway, just because of what they were born into."

"Does that make us bad parents?"

AJ kissed Cass softly. "I don't think so. I think, given who we are, what *we* were born into, our kids never had a chance to avoid that. But for every bad thing that has happened to us, we've managed to do something good. And I don't think any of our kids would want to give that up for more peaceful lives."

"That should probably be more concerning than you're making it out to be."

"Maybe. But we can't regret our lives, Cass. If we do, the bad guys win. And neither of us has ever been very willing to let that happen."

"I can't believe you missed all the fun, Isaac," Logan said mockingly as she followed the older teen through the mansion. "It's not even like you were intentionally staying away to protect someone, like Ciaran was. You were *completely* out of the game."

"Keep talking, Carter, and I'll kill you," Isaac growled as he headed for the meeting room. "It's not *my* fault that my parents kept insisting that it was smarter to stay inside. It's not *my* fault that my father is such a loser leader."

"That's unnecessarily harsh, and you should feel bad," Rick said as he joined them, walking next to Logan.

"Don't even *think* about starting, Sullivan. You're completely defenseless. I could snap you like a twig."

Logan laughed sharply. "You honestly think you could even *try*? Before you even *raised your hand*, I would—"

"Can you guys shut up?" Brooke asked as she too fell into step next to them. "Isaac, your parents made the right call. Half of the Legion got themselves killed or captured by Reznik's people because they had the exact same thought you had. The only reason Heroics fared better was because most of the soldiers were off-base when our people went there."

"It wasn't just half the Legion, either," James said grimly, adding to the group along with Thomas. "Reznik's people killed around a quarter of the police force too, hoping he could frame the deaths on empowereds."

"It's a shame your mother didn't have the guts to kill him, Sullivan," Isaac muttered. "Jail's too good for him."

Rick tried to lunge for Isaac, but Logan easily pushed him back. "Don't you *dare* talk about my mother that way, you—"

"Hey!" Alix was standing in the doorway of the meeting room, watching them. "Work your issues out later, would you? We have things to talk about."

The meeting room was full of everyone involved in Heroics, family included. The only exceptions were Niall, who was with his brother; Erin and Riley, who were busy putting together the funeral Justin had been denied during Reznik's week-long occupation; and Aubrey, who had been instructed to stay in bed for a few days after leaving the hospital.

"So," Brooke said, leaning back in her chair, "is this where you're going to tell us all that you're shutting down Heroics, whether we like it or not?"

There was an outbreak of frantic muttering amongst the other kids, but Casey shook her head. "No. It's not."

"Why?" Brooke asked suspiciously.

"We talked about it," Casey said. "We decided that it would be a mistake to run away and hide. Not only would we never be able to stay in this city, but everyone would think that we were guilty of what Reznik was accusing us of. At this point, I think it's pretty clear that most know exactly who we are. To be honest, I'm pretty sure most people in the city knew who we were all the way back when we first stopped pretending that we didn't live in the mansion."

"So what happens now?" Ciaran asked curiously.

Ray cleared his throat. "We're going to keep patrolling. We're going to keep doing our jobs. While we're on the streets, Cass and Casey are going to work to fix the damage that was done to our reputation with the public, as well as the damage that was done to the reputation they had been regaining for WI."

"Basically what you're saying is that we just keep going like nothing happened," Isaac said, sounding annoyed. "That's pathetic. We should be doing more. Being proactive. Making sure Reznik pays for what he's done."

"He's going to," Casey insisted. "There was enough evidence at his base to put him in jail for life eight times over. There's no way he's getting away with this. Amirmoez is going to prison too, once she's out of the hospital."

"Jail's too good for Reznik. Kate should've killed him."

A heavy silence filled the room. "Isaac," Ray said slowly, "never—*never*—think that murdering someone is a better option than putting them in prison. It's one thing if someone gets the death penalty; it's another to decide that for ourselves. Our job isn't to be judge, jury, and executioner. It's to stop them so that the justice system can run its course."

"What if it doesn't do that, Dad? What if it fails?"

"Then we catch them again next time." Ray held up a hand as Isaac started to say something else. "And that's the end of this, Isaac. If we turn murderers now, the public will never trust us again."

Alix shifted uncomfortably in her seat. "Shall we move on? Zach had something he wanted to say."

"Ah, right." Zach stood up. "I've been discussing this with Ray, Cass, Casey, Kate, and AJ, as well as the higher ranking members of my team. We've come to a decision that..." He cleared his throat, looking nervous. "We've come to a decision. The Security Legion as you know it will no longer exist after this week."

"What are you talking about?" Logan asked, stunned.

"When Reznik took over this city, there was a total shutdown of communications. And even before then, there was an utter lack of unity in the hero community. The Legion and Heroics liked each other for the most part, but there were rivalries and undercurrents of dislike that put everyone in danger. To fix both of these problems, I proposed something that, well, sounded crazy at first, but gained fast support." Zach took in a deep breath. "The Legion and Heroics will operate as two separate yet equal hero groups within the city. They will divide patrol routes evenly, and act as if they are one team in terms of how these patrol routes function. The rivalries and bitterness stop. To this end, the teams will utilize one united communications system. This system will be monitored and maintained by a third team, built specifically for non-field duties, including medical needs, engineering, mission control operations, and weapon development. We're still working on a name for this team, but they will be responsible for both the Legion *and* Heroics. This way, there's no more confusion over which side has what information. There's no more arguing over whether something should be shared. There's no more hoarding of technology. We'll be a proper, fully functioning community of superheroes that can provide what's best for Caotico City and Fuego Village."

As Zach stopped talking, everyone who didn't already know of the plans started talking at once. After a few minutes, Alix yelled, "Okay, everyone shut up!" A few seconds later, the chatter died down. Alix looked at Zach, folding her arms across her chest. "Do you think this is the best way to keep people safe?"

"Yes, I do."

She turned one at a time to Cass, Casey, AJ, Ray, and Kate. "And do you all agree?" Once they each responded in the positive, Alix gave a nod. "Then we'll do it." She raised her hand as the others started talking again, and once more everyone stopped for her. "Look. We've been doing the same thing over and over again for years. And what have we really got to show for it? A few healed broken bones, a few extra friends and family members in their graves, and far too many nightmares. Nobody is really any safer. If we can do something to improve this city, for ourselves and for everyone else, why not give it a try?"

"What if it doesn't work?" Jacob asked.

"J," Alix said quietly, "if we spend our lives worrying about that, we'll never accomplish anything."

"Okay." Kara looked troubled, but she was nodding. "Okay. We should do this."

As most of the table began to murmur in agreement, Zach grinned. "Well all right then. I'll start getting everything started. I promise you this will work out, guys." He tapped Max on the shoulder. "I'm heading back to the Legion. You coming?"

"I think I'll follow in a few minutes. I have something I need to take care of."

"See you later, then." Zach left the room.

"Well then," Brooke said slowly. "I guess in a way we *are* getting rid of Heroics. Just not in the way I thought."

"Heroics will still exist, Brooke. It's always going to exist," AJ said.

"I know that, Dad." Brooke stood. "All I hope is that we're making the right call."

In the training room in the basement, Max found Alix shooting, emptying an entire handgun magazine into a target. He whistled softly. "I think he's dead."

Alix stuck the gun back in its holster. "I wish."

"You want to talk about it?"

She sighed. "Yes, but not right now."

"Fair enough." Max walked over and stood next to her. "Are you okay?"

"I'm better, knowing that Aubrey's going to be okay."

Max stuck his hands in his pockets. "Your well-being really is linked to theirs, isn't it?"

Alix shrugged. "I needed something to be loyal to. My brain needed something to get attached to, because it was falling apart at the seams. My friends seemed to be the best possible option."

"Better than alcohol, I guess."

She smiled. "True. The thing is, I've never really known what I was, Max. But over the past few years, it's really started to sink in that I'm their family. That's what I am. And that's made everything better for me. I knew *who* I was, but it was always a struggle for me, that thought of whether I was just a shadow of Cage or not.

The Hamils and the Carters gave me something to latch onto, something that made me feel human."

"If that's what you need, I'm glad you have it."

Alix took in a deep breath. "I like you, Max. And I know you like them. But I need to make sure you understand that they'll always come first. I know I don't *owe* them, but I can't put anyone above them, either."

"Even yourself?"

Alix hesitated. "I'm not sure I've ever willingly put myself above anyone else."

Max smiled slightly. "I'll make you a deal, Thief. I'll happily take third spot on your priority scale, as long as the Carters and Hamils are second."

"Who's first?"

"I thought that was fairly obvious. *You*."

She flushed. "I-I'm not sure I know how to do that."

Max kissed her on the forehead gently. "That's okay. You can learn."

Kate left the meeting last and found Erin sitting on the stairs, staring down at her wedding ring. "Hey there," Kate said as she sat down next to her.

"Kate," Erin whispered in a voice filled with pain, "I don't know what to do without him."

"Neither do I," Kate admitted softly.

Erin leaned against her, heavy with exhaustion and sorrow. "I can't even think about the... funeral... anymore. I just can't. And what's strange is, the only thing I really *can* think of is a memory, and not even a happy one."

"What do you mean?"

"All I keep remembering is the first time he showed interest in me. He was hitting on me in his usual jackass college-boy manner, and I kicked him in the shin. Hard. While wearing cleats."

Kate gave a weak laugh. "I remember that. Jay mocked him about it for weeks."

"It's funny in retrospect, but..." Erin shook her head, and her voice took on a shaky, cracked tone. "All those years I had him, and that's the only thing I can think of? Him being an asshole?"

"In fairness to you, that was pretty much Justin's default mode."

They both had strained laughs that faded away rather quickly into heavy silence. Then, quietly, Erin said, "I want him back, Kate. I just want him back."

Kate put an arm around Erin's shoulders and hugged the other woman tightly. "I know what you mean," she whispered.

20

Four days after Justin's funeral and two days after being released from the hospital, Rowan stepped through the front door of the Heroics mansion and was immediately met by Alix. "H-Hey," she stammered.

"Hi there," Alix said. "How are you feeling?"

"Not bad. Not great."

"Understandable. Cass and AJ are in the library. They asked to see you before you talked to Aubrey."

"That doesn't sound good."

"It depends. You'll have to talk to them to find out." Alix rested a hand on Rowan's shoulder. "Aubrey had me check on your mom while you were in the hospital. She wasn't in great shape after taking care of herself for a week, but she was okay. Is she still okay?"

"Y-Yeah. Thanks for helping."

"Not a problem. I told you I was more than willing to." Alix lowered her voice. "And because, given how Aubrey was talking, this might be a concern of yours? I'm not planning on telling anyone about your situation. Okay?"

"That would be appreciated," Rowan said weakly.

Alix smiled and released Rowan's shoulder. "You're a good kid, you know that?"

"I'm not always so sure."

"Be sure. Now go upstairs."

Rowan shut the library door behind her and leaned against it, folding her arms across her chest. She just stared at Cass and AJ for a moment before saying, "You wanted to see me?"

"Yes, Rowan, we did." Cass sat down on the arm of one of the chairs. "We need to talk to you about something."

"We asked Zach what he was planning on doing with you," AJ said. "He didn't know what we were talking about. Seems he was told that you were given a clean bill of health."

Rowan tensed. "That's because I'm not retiring, and I didn't want Kov giving me worthless assignments over the *possibility* that I could hurt myself."

"It's not just a *possibility*," AJ growled, looking concerned and just a touch angry. "And you won't just get *hurt*. This will *kill you* if you continue your vigilante work, Rowan."

"So?" Rowan muttered.

Cass shook her head slowly. "Have you told Aubrey yet? That you're planning on killing yourself?"

"*Don't bring her into this!*" Rowan snarled, straightening from the door.

"I don't have much of a choice," Cass said. "If I don't tell her, she'll never forgive me when you have a heart attack and die."

"That's not my problem. Aubrey can't know about this."

Cass raised an eyebrow. "And why is that?"

AJ smiled humorlessly. "Because she knows that Aubrey would never let her risk her own health just to catch a few criminals."

"Good. Then I should tell her just so that you don't do something stupid."

Rowan began to pace. "You can't tell her. She'll make me stop. I can't do that. It doesn't matter if I'm dead by twenty-five. I can't just quit."

"Why not?" AJ demanded.

"Because this is all I have!" Rowan yelled, stopping her pacing so that she could face Cass and AJ. *"This is all I have!"*

"What do you mean?" Cass asked quietly.

"The Legion is the only place where I can make enough money to…" Rowan swallowed, looking scared. "When I was a little kid, my mother and her entire family were attacked by random Czech citizens who thought all Romani people needed to be killed. They firebombed the house my family was in when my dad and I were out. My mother was the only person in that house who survived, but now she's a shattered, broken woman who can barely take care of herself without supervision. I'm *shocked* she survived the week Reznik had me. The only time my mother talks, it's deluded ramblings about how someone is going to come back and finish the job, or when she's telling me how goddamn useless I am, for whatever reason she's come up with that day."

Rowan leaned back against the door and slid down so that she was sitting on the floor, hugging her knees to her chest. "You already know my dad was killed when I was nine. I'm all my mom has left. Almost every single dime that I make goes to taking care of her. I'm lucky I graduated high school; there's no way I was ever going to go to college. I'm not qualified to have any job other than my work in the Legion or a job that won't pay enough to give my mom what she needs."

She rubbed at her eyes. "Aubrey only *just* found out about my mom. She doesn't know yet that I... that I have nothing. And I can't let her know, because she might try to help. Not patronizingly, but just because she cares too much. And I can't let her do that. I can't ask for help. I can't accept help. I-I just... can't. So she can't know about my heart. She can't make me quit the Legion. Because I need to be there, or I don't know what I'll do."

There was a long moment of silence before Cass walked over and knelt in front of her. "It's hard to get help when you're used to taking care of things for yourself for so long."

"Yeah," Rowan agreed hoarsely.

"The thing is, kid, you aren't by yourself anymore. You're not alone. And if you think for one second that we'd let you die for the sake of money, you're crazy. What do you think my trillion-dollar company is for?"

"I don't need charity," Rowan mumbled, though it sounded more like a reflex response than anything serious.

Cass gave a quiet laugh and jerked her thumb in the general direction of the elevator. "Kid, I pay the idiots on this team to do literally nothing. You really think I can't figure out how to pay you to do something? Especially when your only other option is an almost guaranteed heart attack? Please. That's not charity. That's me not being a jackass."

Rowan nodded once before looking down. "I'm scared," she admitted.

Cass smiled softly. "I know, kid. But if I know anything about you at all, it's that you're pretty damn tough. If anyone can get through this, you can."

"What do I tell Aubrey?" Rowan whispered.

"Just tell her the truth," AJ said gently. "You can do that."

"I don't want her to worry about me."

AJ chuckled quietly. "Rowan, I'm pretty sure she's going to be worried about you no matter what. That's kind of what she does best."

"You have ten minutes."

Ray nodded to the guard that let him into the interview room as he sat down across from Reznik. The general was giving him a look full of hatred. For a full minute, they just stared at each other in total silence. Reznik was the first to break the standoff.

"The leader of the pack. What an honor."

"I don't understand you."

Reznik scoffed. "I'm not surprised. You hero types are so self-serving that you never notice when something is actually *good* for society if it's not specifically good for *you*."

"See, *that's* what I'm having a problem understanding." Ray leaned forward, pressing his hand against the table between them. "You want the military to be in control. You want to be in control. But I don't understand how that would be good for anyone other than you, and I don't understand why you're so determined to use people with powers if you hate us. Even *if* we're useful as soldiers, the game you were playing with us was pointless."

"Pointless? No. There will always be people with powers. It's a waste of effort to try to eradicate all of you. But if you come up with a way to completely and

329

effectively control you all? *That's* progress. John Wechsler and Alice Cage were fools. A mind control device that controls only the body and can only work on basic instructions is useless. If you terrorize someone into submission and then torture them until you are their master, *that* is when you truly have control."

A sickened look formed in Ray's eyes. "That's what you were trying to do to Rowan. What you tried to do to the Galaxy Boys."

"The girl and that group of street punks refused to break. The girl was going to get a bullet just like the punks got, but I needed to keep her alive until I knew I wouldn't need her as leverage against the middle Hamil."

"Why involve that Hamils at all? Why go after them and Alix?"

Reznik shrugged. "Two reasons. First of all, like I said before, the stupidity of the plan built by John Wechsler and Alice Cage personally offends me. So I decided to take my irritation out on their children. Second of all, they have no powers but they have a lot of knowledge. If I was going to get any leads on the Security Legion, it was going to come from them."

"Cass said you felt that you could go after the Legion whenever you wanted. Why not just put out arrest warrants for them?"

"Because they're *rats*. They would've just hidden in their little base until you Heroics jackasses saved them from the big, mean general. I needed to know how to find them when they were driven underground. I didn't expect you all to come after me so quickly, and I certainly didn't expect you to be able to call the *president*."

Ray leaned forward further. "One more question."

Reznik sneered at him. "Only one?"

"Yes. Why are you telling me all of this?"

The general shifted closer to Ray, smirking. "Because you're completely unimportant to me, little hero. You're just a dog that I wasn't able to get a muzzle on. But trust me. Somebody will, someday. This city is a hellhole. There's only so long that it will tolerate people trying to keep it from being even worse. There are people in this city much more dangerous than me, hero. When they come for you, you won't stand a chance. They'll start dropping bodies." His voice lowered to a threatening growl. "And I hope that the first one that falls in this new war is yours."

A shiver ran through Ray, but he kept his voice steady. "I'm sorry to deflate your delusions, Reznik, but you're the person who was putting Caotico at risk. With you out of the way, I'm pretty sure my life expectancy is a lot higher than it used to be."

He stood and headed for the door. Reznik's laugh stopped him short. "Fine then. Don't believe me. It'll make it all the better when you're all dead and I'm not."

Ray opened the door but paused to look back at him. "Even if that does happen? You'll still be right here, in prison. I think I can live the rest of my life contently knowing that." He shot Reznik a small smile and walked out, slamming the door behind him.

Aubrey put her palms against the edge of the desk in one of the meeting rooms of the mansion and leaned against it. She frowned slightly when she noticed Rowan in the doorway, staring at her with a blank look on her face. "What?"

"N-Nothing, just... got momentarily distracted by the button-down-with-sleeves-rolled-up thing."

"My shirt?" Aubrey glanced down, her frown deepening. "What about it?"

"You just look hot, is all."

Aubrey laughed loudly. "I have a black eye and a split lip and you still think I look hot? You're hopeless, van Houten."

"Well, we both knew that." Rowan sat down in a chair across from Aubrey and started slowly spinning it back and forth in a half-circle. "I need to tell you something."

Aubrey straightened and started playing with her ring. "Sure. What's up?"

"I-I... Uh... I..." Rowan cleared her throat. "I definitely thought this was going to be easier than it apparently is. Uhm."

"Rowan. Talk to me."

"I have to retire from the Legion."

Aubrey stared at her. "What? Why?"

"The electricity that they used on me at the base... it uh... damaged my heart." Rowan swallowed. "I'll live a perfectly normal life on medication as long as I don't... have the stress of vigilante work messing with my body. I could give myself a heart attack if I don't retire."

After a moment, Aubrey walked around the table and put her hands on Rowan's shoulders. "How are you taking that?"

"Not that great. But I think I can manage with some... with some help."

Aubrey smiled and kissed her softly. "Well, you came to the right place. Haven't you heard? Helping people is what we do best."

EPILOGUE

Henry Reznik paced back and forth in his cell, anger fueling his steps. "They don't understand," he muttered under his breath. "They don't *know*. They don't know that I was *right*."

"That's unlikely to change," a voice said from behind him.

Reznik whirled around on his heel and came face to face with a dark-skinned woman who was smiling pleasantly at him. "Who the hell are you?"

"I'm one of the people you wanted to control."

"A hero then?" Reznik scoffed. "What do you want with me?"

"Oh, I'm no hero." The woman phased her hand through Reznik's chest and closed her fingers around his heart until it stopped beating. "I'm the farthest thing from it."

She walked out of the prison through the walls, meeting three other people in the parking lot. Silently, they turned away from the building and walked to separate cars, driving off into the night without leaving any sign they had ever been there at all.

Family Trees

CARTER

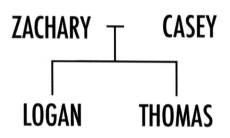

ZACHARY — CASEY

LOGAN   THOMAS

HAMIL

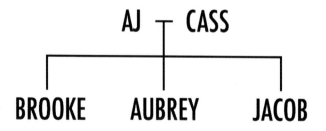

AJ — CASS

BROOKE   AUBREY   JACOB

OLIVER

JUSTIN ─┬─ ERIN REESE
        │
      RILEY

SAMPSON

RAY ─┬─ OLIVIA ABASCAL
     │
   ISAAC

SULLIVAN

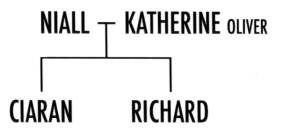

NIALL ┬ KATHERINE OLIVER

CIARAN   RICHARD

TYSON/HALL

CLAIRE TYSON ┬ KARA HALL

JAMES

WECHSLER

DIANA VAN DER AART ⊤ **JOHN** ⊤ **BROOKE** CASSIDY
("STEPHANIE CABOT")

ROBIN **TESS**
("CASEY", SEE "CARTER")   ("CASS", SEE "HAMIL")

About The Author

Alex Kost lives in southern New Jersey with her parents and their dog. She has a degree in film & television, which isn't extremely helpful for writing books.

You can contact her at alexkost.tumblr.com.